Two sisters, Anna and Arnthrúdur, seek to understand themselves, each other, their lives and their relationships with their lovers – with Valgeir, semi-detached from his wife, and with Z, the journalist named for the flash of lightning that attended her birth. Set in Reykjavík in the winter of 1997, the novel has snow as a central metaphor for love, for its beauty, its terror and its ability to overwhelm and suffocate. Approaching death casts issues of independence and commitment into sharp focus as, guided by poems, letters and memories, the women's contemplation achieves a blistering and loving honesty.

# SHAD THAMES BOOKS

Also in this series:

For details of Mare's Nest books, please see pages 265–70.

Z – a love story

Published in 1997
in the Shad Thames series
by Mare's Nest Publishing
49 Norland Square London W11 4PZ

*Z – a love story*
Vigdís Grímsdóttir

Cover image by Jethro, Squid Inc.
Original cover design by Börkur Arnarson
Typeset by Agnesi Text Hadleigh Suffolk
Printed and bound by Antony Rowe Ltd Chippenham Wiltshire

ISBN 1 899197 40 0

*Z ástarsaga* was originally published in Iceland by Idunn, Reykjavík, 1996. This translation is published by agreement with Idunn, to whom the publishers are grateful.

This book is published with the financial assistance of the Arts Council of England.

This publication has been facilitated by the generous participation of the Icelandic Embassy, London.

Mare's Nest Publishing is pleased to acknowledge the assistance of the Fund for the Translation of Icelandic Literature, Reykjavík.

# Z – a love story

## Vigdís Grímsdóttir

Translated from the Icelandic
by Anne Jeeves

MARE'S NEST

It's not possible to understand when people
become blue birds and vanish into the sunset

Hrafn Jökulsson

I have never described my journeys.

I have wanted to but it's as if I have always lacked the words with which to awaken my memory. Still, my story is about a journey, but then I am stubborn. I think too that most people want to take on the impossible and that they welcome a challenge.

And that's why I'm telling you the story.

I'm not writing it because I want my words to be carried away on all the winds that blow about me and that have blown about me and so that only the whistling of the words remains.

And you must know that I do trust you.

I trust you to listen.

# 1

*Anna: 'I was scared that I might never again be able to write or to love again.'*

My journey has begun.

But even though I am talking to you it's as if I myself am the only listener.

That's definitely how I feel.

'Be careful,' you whispered, when we said goodbye this evening.

Those were your final words.

Those were always your final words.

'Good night,' I said, as I put the receiver down and stared for a while at the shadows on the ceiling, at the familiar chandelier and the dried-up fly in its centre. I closed my eyes again and pretended to be asleep, although in fact nothing was further from me than sleep.

Now I'm walking alone down a white road.

I'm out of breath, my eyes are damp and full of grey-freckled mist, and yet I can see my footprints in the snow and the white countryside before me. How often I have been amazed when I walk along here at how the layer of snow hides the countryside with all its contours and every tiny irregularity, almost in the same way as I can imagine that time changes the landscape of memories, covering everything like a flimsy yet opaque veil. But of course I know there are mountains around the valley, and they too are hidden by snow. It may be true that man's every step is taken, I don't know, I can't think about that now, don't want to think about that now. I just want to keep on relentlessly and let no thoughts block my way. He who sees his goal sees no obstacle,

1

no frost, no fire, no land, and no memory either. He is driven onwards.

I am like him.

Everything around me is white.

And the lake by the side of the road is frozen solid.

'It's so shallow it's not surprising it freezes,' was what you said the first time we came here in winter.

*

In the summertime I often used to sit by that lake.

Whenever I had the chance.

I would fill up the blue wide-bellied watering-can that we had bought together and empty it over my head. The water would pour down my face and I'd gasp and shriek as it streamed down my breasts and over my stomach and then ran down my legs.

I used to play that game over and over again.

That was good.

That was wonderful.

In the springtime I used to cover myself with mud from the banks of the lake. I'd take a handful and plaster it over my neck and my collarbone, over my breasts, my stomach, my arms and my thighs and then smear it over my face and shoulders.

Spring mud is the best, it's smoothest and best.

I always believed that nature played an important role in my life.

I also believed that I had to believe that.

*

My shoes creak as they hit the snow.

Creak like your knees creak when you bend down.

At times you could be unbelievably stiff.

'I was just born with extremely thin knee-caps and don't you tease me about them,' you said when I mentioned the creaking.

I never mentioned it again but I laughed to myself whenever you creaked.

But do you know what, if you saw me now I'd remind you of the toy soldier in the old picture book who was setting out into the unknown. I've told you so often that when I was a little girl I used to think of journeys I made as my toy soldiers travel through the world, even though I had only three, never saw pictures of them and only read poems and a few adventures about them, which slipped out of my memory as often as I read them.

But this journey of mine has no toy-soldier uncertainty about it.

It has the one and only final certainty about it.

And the restlessness of soul that accompanies anything that is final.

There's no chance that I'll forget the restlessness.

In fact I can, without any second thoughts, liken my feelings to a blood-thirsty parasite which shamelessly sucks your hot blood and feeds off your conscience.

Without your blood and your conscience I would never have set off.

That's how you gave your approval to my going.

'Do it, if that's what you think is right,' you said.

But I know that you're not following me, even though I try to imagine that you are, that you're somewhere behind me struggling on in the darkness. I'm not one for romantic imaginings, I don't suddenly alter facts according to some whim and my hope doesn't rise up like a naked woman out of the reeds. If I think about suffering, for example, then it's only linked to the fear of having as little imagination as a fly, because I know that the certainty, the facts and the truth, all those three and that one, can't be escaped. And that's the reason why I also know that the yellow light that seems all of a sudden to be fluttering in the air in front of me like a candle flame is simply the extraordinary reflection of the fire within me.

There is a fire within me.

And it's that fire that's my real certainty.

Everything else is at a distance which is unreal.

I can feel how the flame lengthens and gives off sparks until it spreads out and lights up every nerve of my body, every muscle, every bone, every bloody bump and I'm all on fire in the darkness, but there are no flames. And just then all my consciousness and all my world wing their way to you as you sleep peacefully on your mattress next to the clothes you're going to put on in the morning when you visit me as you always do when you finish work.

At least that's how I like to think about you now.

I want to think about you being asleep – after all, it is the middle of the night.

Even so, I know you're awake and waiting.

You about you from you.

All of mine about you.

Yours about me.

*

I remember reading about the seven wonders of the world for you.

You enjoyed it so much when someone read for you in the evening and of course I had to spoil you, I wanted to do everything for you that you wanted.

I'm not sure whether I told you that but now you know.

You know everything now.

As usual you nodded off while I was reading and then jerked awake when I was halfway through the chapter about people who combust spontaneously all of a sudden and there's no warning beforehand. There was someone just doing some household chore, stirring a saucepan, boiling potatoes, frying an egg or baking when the phenomenon occurred. Suddenly they were in flames and a couple of minutes later there was some sort of browny-black stuff on the floor which looked like something between a skeleton and a log.

'That is really amazing,' you said.

'Um, I don't know.'

'But just think if you were on your way to bed and you combusted spontaneously, and that was that.'

'But after all this isn't a scientific journal. It isn't as if God had said it.'

'Still you ought to write about that. If I was a writer I would, I'd write about something that mattered, something that would make people think.'

'I've never said I'm a writer.'

I considered myself a poet.

You considered yourself a journalist.

You thought I was a reasonably good poet.

I thought you were a reasonably good journalist.

Behind everything we wrote was make-believe.

I hoped that make-believe lay in hiding, that it would creep up on me one day and put life into what I wrote. You had no dreams of your articles and letters coming to life with make-believe.

I wrote from desire and sometimes from stubbornness.

*

I want to care for you when you're awake.

I want it to be the morning after this night.

I want there to be a day, an evening, a night and another day after this night.

And that's why I imagine you tomorrow.

You're standing by my bed and you look happy.

You know I can't stand mournful looks, can't stand any pandering to anguish and tragedy, and you show no sign of fear or grief when you're with me.

I can trust you.

You bend over towards me and ask whether I had any dreams during the night and I can smell that same nice smell from your hair that you said nobody but me could smell because nobody had ever loved you like I do. I make up a story about a strange dream because I know you don't want to hear that I stayed awake by the fire keeping an eye on the clock. Still from time to time I pushed the bell and got the girls to splash or spray water over me, and I smiled heroically at them when they wiped my forehead with the blue flannel that's on the floor. I know you're scared when you ask me what I dreamed about but because you ask I make a dream up for you about white doves flying

5

restlessly about the sky with letters in their beaks, swinging between the clouds and dropping the letters one by one. And the letters are white and fall to the earth like veils and land in a basket belonging to an old lady who hums as she picks them up one by one and reads them. You smile when I tell you it was a pity I couldn't read what the letters said. But when I've finished telling you about the dream you take my hand, sit down on the chair by my bed and lay some flowers, probably yellow roses, on the crumpled duvet.

I imagine you tomorrow even though tomorrow is an illusion.

I imagine you as I want to see you.

*

'Tomorrow never comes,' you sang once when you had been claiming that the most sensible thing one could promise onesself and probably the best thing one could do for one's own happiness was to live each day at a time. That all one has is the present. The past is an drained cup. The future just an illusion. That was while you were sure and certain about what you wanted and thought that there were no lions in your path. I didn't love you any less because you thought your clichés were brand-new truths that no one else had so much as dreamed of. My affection for you increased my feelings about how tone-deaf you were, the notes used to creep so far away from any normal melody that it almost made me want to go out and look for a composer talented enough to invent a new scale.

I always had so many ideas when I was near you.

You didn't know about many of them.

'I sing because I like singing and I sing only for you,' you said.

'I like hearing you sing,' I replied.

And then you laughed and said that the best thing about me was that I didn't know how to tell a lie, that there was no point my even trying to, that the few times I had tried to this deep wrinkle above my upper lip always appeared.

Of course that wasn't true but I let you believe it was.

I lied to you over and over again.

But it made me feel good that you thought you were right.
And I laughed.
'Perhaps you aren't most beautiful when you laugh,' you said.

*

It makes me laugh again when I think about that now, quietly at first then the laughter gets louder and turns into a scream.

It's my life scream.

It's aggressive and demanding and I'm on fire.

I'm burning from the inside and I drag myself along like a crippled old man. I stumble down the road with the brown leather case in one hand, full of letters from you, and in the other the bag stuffed with firewood to heat the cottage.

The cottage is on the far side of my next footstep.

It's all we have.

*

You called the cottage a hut when we first came here.

Sometimes I felt that you were ashamed of what a comfortable life you led, perhaps you were afraid that I didn't understand how well off you were and how much you could allow yourself. I don't know whether it was because you thought I would take advantage of you, or that I would laugh at you. Anyway you said once that at times it was like I was greedy and that often you didn't like my teasing you.

'Do you think I eat too much?' I asked.

'There, you see,' you replied and then added on that occasion, 'The hut belongs to my uncle. He never comes here and I can use it whenever I like. He's the richest of us all, the rest of the family don't have any money at all compared to him, only just enough for ourselves. But of course it's great having an uncle like that.'

'Do you often come here?' I asked.

'Sometimes.'

'And always for the same reason?'

7

'I've had lots of reasons for coming here.'

'Tell me whether you think I eat too much.'

You didn't reply.

You usually knew what was right, that was one of the things about you that was such fun because you really didn't want to be like that.

You didn't want to be sure about any damn thing.

'I want to be spontaneous and I think I am,' you said.

To that I didn't reply.

\*

You're not sitting by the window waiting for me now.

Now it's not the summer of 1994 either.

It's the winter of 1997 and it's cold.

You're not standing on the veranda clapping your arms together to keep warm.

I'll sit here alone tonight because our time is over.

\*

'Be careful,' my sister said when I told her about you.

That was a year after we first met.

My sister always had a plan in mind.

She was always worried about me and didn't try to conceal it.

'And what do you want me to be careful of now?'

'Be careful of yourself.'

'Don't worry. It's just an adventure and it makes me happy.'

'That's exactly why you need to be careful,' said she, the one who thought she knew all the secret paths of love,

all the despair of one who wishes and grasps at straws,

all the sorrow of one who waits and knows no patience,

all the distress of one who shrieks in the silence and hears

no answer,

and the loneliness.

My sister with the suffering in her eyes and the broad smile.

My sister who claims she knows how to love.

Maybe I should have listened to her then.

'You don't take any notice of people, that's what's the matter with you,' she said warmly, telling me once more to be careful.

'Just philosophical today?'

'No philosophy, Anna, just facts. Remember the day you came back from the doctor's and told me everything? Do you remember that?'

'Of course I remember.'

'Do you remember what I said then?'

'I can't remember word for word.'

'I said, "Anna, did the doctor say the lights were red?"'

'Oh yes, I remember that now.'

'And what did you say?'

'I said that he had said they were red.'

'And what else did you say?'

'Did I say anything else?'

'You said that it didn't matter that the doctor said the lights were red because you knew they were blue, you just knew it.'

'That's what I thought then.'

'What colour did they turn out to be?'

'Oh, Arnthrúdur, don't go on like this.'

'Yes, I will go on like this, because it's just like this adventure of yours, it's red.'

'You know I never think about the future.'

'But you have to think about the dangers.'

My sister who claimed she knew how to love. My sister who knew how to suffer.

Perhaps I ought to have listened to her then.

*

I'm standing by the door of the cottage, leaning against the doorpost. I find the key in my pocket and open the door. The door doesn't creak but the mat in the hall is frozen. Everything is just as we left it when we were here last, except that it's cold and there's frost on the

9

windowpanes and on the floor. Your books and eggs are on the shelves above the desk opposite the fireplace and under each egg there's a poem.

Every time I came here I gave you an egg and sometimes a poem.

'Are you giving me an egg?' you asked when I gave you the first egg. You said that every time from then on.

And I gave the same reply, there being no other reply to give.

'An egg of life.'

> *Later on I felt that the question and answer were about love*
>    *and that you had always said:*
> *'Do you love me so much?'*
> *And that I had always answered:*
> *'I do.'*

'So you have a sense of humour?' you asked as you put the egg on the shelf and mentioned that it was the first time you had seen blue and yellow blend together like that.

I didn't understand you and didn't want to know what you meant.

I wasn't always interested in your musings.

I should have been, but so many of them seemed absurd and unconnected with everything I thought myself.

'Are you surprised that I have a sense of humour?'

'I thought you were a romantic,' you said, opening the window. And then you added that you loved nothing better than the smell of grass in the summer wafting in through the window and blending with the woody smell of the cottage and the dampness in the air. I didn't answer then either, because I really wanted to know whether it was your intention that we should meet only here.

But I didn't like to ask you.

I also thought you would tell me, and you did.

'This'll be our cottage.'

'Does this uncle of yours know about me then?'

'Of course not, but he knows I don't want anyone to know I come out here.'

10

'And doesn't he think that's odd?'

'He's not the sort to ask.'

'But is he the sort to keep quiet?'

'Don't worry about it.'

'I'm worried about you. It's you who wants to keep silent.'

'I don't particularly want to, I just have to.'

'So you don't think it's possible to be a romantic and have a sense of humour?' I asked, to put an end to the conversation.

I was tired of this conversation.

And I felt sorry for you, even though I didn't say so.

'That may be the question,' you replied, and it always struck me as amusing how you managed to let it drop in passing that you were well versed in the world's literature.

*

I throw the case on the table, take the wood out of the bag and light the fire.

The logs are damp and it takes ages to get a spark. It surprises me that while I'm trying my hands don't feel cold. I smile as I recall you always saying you couldn't believe anyone could have such warm hands.

I wanted to write a poem about warm hands.

But however much I tried, I couldn't.

That's how I often was where poetry was concerned.

Stripped and powerless.

I didn't talk to you about that, but I did say, half jokingly, 'Are you sure that I am a person?'

Sometimes I wanted to say something vague and bizarre.

I knew that people thought I was simple, you did too, and usually I didn't care.

'Never been more sure about anything, my darling.'

I started, I hadn't expected that.

I never used those words myself.

They've always been strange to me.

'Why did you say "my darling"?'

'I said it because I like saying it,' you said, and I knew you were racking your brains over why I was in doubt over you being sure that I was a person. I could see it by the way you shook your head and screwed up your eyes when you replied. Of course I had got to know you fairly well by then.

That was a year after we first met.

And that's how I knew that you were also wondering whether you had ever given any serious thought to whether I was a person and if you had done so whether it had ever mattered to you.

But you were quick to come to a conclusion.

I mattered to you and you believed I was your darling.

You never said anything that you didn't believe but it was always easy for you to change your mind. Of course you were an opportunist, though you actually found that rather uncomfortable. But it might have been because of your job, maybe your job necessitated changes of mind, I don't know.

'It's a sign of weakness not to be able to admit to having been wrong,' you said, and you wanted me to reconsider where I stood on trusting you.

'You can trust me when I'm with you,' I said.

'That's not enough.'

'I make no demands on you and you shouldn't make any demands on me.'

'You'll change your mind,' you said, fingering the eggs as if you were calling on them and the pictures on them to witness the fact that you were right. You always fingered the eggs when you were talking to me about something that was important to you.

And it was always important to you to be sure about me all the time. Be sure where I was, what I was doing and who I was doing it with.

For me, on the other hand, it was enough to be sure about you when we were together.

'Do you never feel like I do?' you asked.

'No, never.'

'Doesn't that mean that you don't care about me?'

'I'm sure about you when you're with me.'

That's all you said then.

*

At last I manage to get the fire going.

I sit down on the floor and shake my head as I hear the familiar creaking in the rafters, feel the cold stream from my bottom up my back as the fire inside me fades out of my bones and muscles and contents itself with caressing the inside of my skin as if just to remind me of its existence.

I'm still granted some time.

I pull the case towards me, open it and contemplate your letters all tied into bundles by my hands.

Seventeen letters.

Seventeen is my favourite number, that independent number in the myriad of numbers, the number that no other number relates to, meaningless in itself but still so lovely. I've sorted the letters by date and decide to compare the addresses on the first and the last. The handwriting has changed – on the first it's slow, the letters neat and painstaking – on the last it's hasty, and the letters are long and ill-formed.

Your handwriting like you.

You have no letters from me.

It was a sort of unspoken agreement between us that you would write to me and if I needed to answer I would talk to you. I don't think I ever needed to answer any questions because you never asked me any direct questions in your letters.

'I'm keeping your letters,' I said.

'I asked you to throw them away as soon as you had read them, didn't I?'

'I know, but I decided to keep them.'

'What if someone finds them?'

'Nobody'll find them. I've made sure of that.'

'How?'

'Just trust me with them,' I said, hoping that you would ask me why I had kept them. But you did later, when we knew each other well enough to brave it into the empty space, into that defensive ring everyone creates around himself, where access is denied to everyone and everything except one's own thoughts.

'Why did you say you were keeping my letters?'

'I haven't said anything about that.'

'But why do you?'

'I don't really know.'

I didn't actually know then.

But now I do know.

I kept them so that I would be able to bring them here with me when everything was over. I kept them to be able to burn them, to watch them blaze on the fire and feel them merge with the fire within me.

I had to do it.

Your words will always be within me.

Like you.

Like I always told you.

And now balance prevails and I'm as hot without as I am within, only it's a different sort of heat, it's not just the heat of the fire and the pain which lies concealed and is waiting silently for its ultimate visiting time, but rather the heat of the years and all the hours we spent together here and everywhere.

And I open your first and shortest letter and read it slowly.

I'm going to enjoy the words and hear them resound inside here for the first time and little by little they'll acquire your voice so it'll be just like you were sitting here with me reading them.

Just like I always imagined you were doing.

Almost every time I opened a letter from you.

*

14

*Anna,*

*You'll be surprised of course, when you open this letter and see that it's from me, who you don't know very well, almost not at all, but I couldn't help myself. I don't know how to say this, but something happened when we met, I don't know what it was and I can't find any explanation for it however hard I try. I always have to have explanations for everything and this something won't leave me alone and demands some confirmation in reality. I know this must sound bizarre and even ridiculous, but I've been terribly restless since I met you and I can't keep my mind on anything because I'm always thinking about how you were that evening, how you looked at me and how you laughed. Naturally you don't have to honour my request but still I do ask you to meet me. Who knows? Maybe I'll be able to do you a favour sometime. I'd like to meet you at the same place at eight o'clock on Monday evening and I do hope you'll be able to come.*

*Z*

\*

I laugh to myself as I throw the letter on to the fire and see it curl, and remember how warm it was that June evening as I walked down Laugaveginn.

'Not got much on this evening,' said a guy who was leaning in a tired sort of way on the handrail outside the Blúsbarnum.

'I never have much on.'

'And of course on your way to a date?'

'I'm always on my way to a date.'

'Can I come along too?'

'That wouldn't be appreciated,' I said, and I waved to him as I turned away, in a hurry now because it was nearly eight o'clock.

I didn't think much about what the letter said but it was nice to have got it, and although I didn't often think about coincidences and how one thing leads to another I couldn't avoid that thought then. The letter had given me something to think about apart from the news I had received that morning, which had so utterly changed how I thought about myself and about time. So this date had a purpose even if it was only that.

'Always the same idiot,' I muttered to myself the minute I opened the door of the Café List, stepped inside and came face to face with you.

'Did you say something?' you asked as I sat down.

'I just asked whether you'd been waiting a long time.'

'I don't know, I haven't been keeping track of the time.'

A year later you told me you hadn't dared get there any later than seven just in case I happened to come early, if I came at all that was, and that you'd bought yourself a beer and hadn't been able to keep your eyes off the clock. When you told me that I knew you must often make a point of ekeing out any chance of excitement in your life, even though it really went against your nature.

'It's as if I always have to make things difficult for myself,' you said.

'Wean yourself off it.'

'I really don't think I could.'

'You can still try.'

*

It was a while later that I got the idea for my new volume of poetry.

My writing had dried up ages ago and I often worried about never being able to write another word, about never having any ideas. Sometimes I lay awake at night contemplating the feeling of emptiness that goes hand in hand with such thoughts. Then, one morning as I was lying in my bed by the window, with the phone on the bedside table because I was waiting for you to ring, the idea came to me.

You were supposed to be calling in for coffee like you always did on Thursday mornings.

I was thinking what fun it was to have that rhythm to one's

Thursdays, you always calling in at ten o'clock and me always waiting for you to ring to tell me that you were coming as usual so that we could make love.

That was different from the other days.

They weren't about you.

And I wondered whether it was perhaps true what people say, that you couldn't expect much from a week that begins on a Monday, and then I had the idea about the book.

The idea just dropped into my head.

I would write a series of poems about Mondays and the first poem would be about that Monday when everything changed. So I immediately took to thinking about a poem every time I got a letter from you. And although I didn't intend the poems to be about what you said in your letters or about you, I did decide that they should match them in number.

I kept my word.

There were seventeen poems, just like your seventeen letters.

And when you came round and we had tumbled on the floor and made love as if we would never get to do so again, I kissed you and said ceremoniously (as if I thought my idea would please you as much as it pleased me) –

'D'you know what, Z,' I said, with my lips still on your mouth, because I didn't want to move them until I had told you.

'No, what?' you replied as you tried to push me off you.

'I've had an idea for a new book.'

'I told you you would,' you said, rolling out from under me.

But you didn't ask what the idea was.

And I thought it was because you weren't interested.

A week later, however, you asked how the book was going, whether I'd written anything and if I had whether you could hear it or whether I was one of those writers who thought an idea would die if anyone saw it before it was finished.

I didn't think so.

'Ideas don't die, people die,' I said, adding that I would love to read for you since you were interested.

'I'm interested in everything you do,' you said and you made me feel ashamed of having doubted it.

'I've only written the introduction and one poem which isn't really a poem at all. It's more like a mixture of facts and then a text made up from them.

'One at a time is fine for me, read it.'

'Do you want me to read the introduction too?'

'Of course.'

'I'll read it all, then, without stopping in between.'

'Do that. Begin then.'

I can remember how my heart seemed to miss a beat as I began.

And I hoped you wouldn't see how my fingers were shaking.

I didn't want you to know that I was shy.

But I didn't have to worry about you noticing that.

*

*This book contains nothing but texts about my own life.*

*They all have one thing in common, that they came about because of events which influenced me on different Mondays. That's why I'm calling the collection* Monday Poems.

*I have chosen to call these texts poems because I can't find a better word to describe them. I must confess, however, that more often than not the word 'poem' isn't quite right.*

*I've often wondered what sparks off a text that calls itself a poem, what the writer must be thinking about before and while the poem comes into being. I've always imagined that if I knew that I would understand the poem better and enjoy it more fully. This is why I have included with every poem a few words to explain why I wanted to write it.*

*Anna Gudmundsdottir*

*This book is for Z, who has made me happy more often than anyone else.*

*On Monday, 8 June 1994, I received some news and a letter that changed my life. From now on it can neither be organized nor fixed or connected to the self-evident concept of endless days. All that was once immutable and manifest collapsed and I felt that the only thing that scared me was that I might never again be able to write or to love again.*

*Neither of these fears proved right.*

*My fear is usually groundless.*


*If a letter arrives for me*
*on that summer day of my life*
*when time suddenly stops*
*i am sure it must be from Gunnar and he's thanking me for*
*the gloves i sent him before he went walking on the glacier*

*but*
*the letter isn't from him*
*and of course it's strange that i should think of a man who never says thank you for anything except when we've made love and i tell him that he's the best and the biggest and the quickest and that no one in the whole world is as good as him and anyway how could i think of him such a long time after we parted, we who shared nothing except an interest in thirties and forties films and a desire to sleep with Greta Garbo, unless in fact that was the reason i thought of him that day when everything changed*

*and*
*i have to admit that even now i wish there was someone waiting at home for me with hot chocolate and anticipation in their eyes*

*but*
*the letter which arrives is from you with the peculiar name*

*and i only dimly remember you in the crowded coffee-shop*
*where you were standing looking at me all the time until i had*
*no choice but to walk over to you and introduce myself*

*and*
*if in the future a letter arrives for me on such a momentous*
    *day*
*if such a day ever dawns*
*i know for certain it will be from you*
*written because love still exists*
*and because i needn't have feared losing it*

*

'Well?' I said.

'Well, what?'

'What do you think?'

'You know I don't know anything about poetry like that.'

'But do you think it's OK?'

'It must be.'

'And can't you say anything?'

I was hoping you would say something about me dedicating the book to you.

I wanted you to say that you liked the book being for you.

That the words I had written about you made you happy.

But you didn't say anything and I should have known why.

'Perhaps you should have read it for that Gunnar rather than for me, he might have understood it better.'

'Didn't you understand the introduction? It's supposed to be a poem.'

'I understand it the way I understand it.'

'Maybe I'm not remembering correctly, Z, but I seem to recall you saying you were interested in everything I did?'

'Who is he, this Gunnar of yours?' you asked, standing up and starting to put your clothes on.

20

Your movements were quick and angry.

I watched your muscular body. It was tauter than usual, the calf muscles stretched, and the biceps and buttocks tensed.

You sniffed, cleared your throat and kicked your toes on the floor.

I laughed to myself, even though I was in no mood for laughter.

That was the first time I saw the jealousy in your body, before it had just lain in your words, in a comment now and then that more often than not I pretended I hadn't heard.

'Gunnar is just an idea, he doesn't really exist,' I said, smiling, and putting my arms around your stiff body I felt it relax immediately. 'He doesn't really exist, understand? He never did. I was trying to read some sort of a poem for you and I hoped you'd understand it.'

And then you started crying.

You never asked me anything else about the poem or the book.

And though I missed it I was also relieved.

But later on I gave you the poem.

I gave it to you the day I knew the book would never be written but I didn't tell you that. I never spoke to you about it again but I gave you the poems so you could put them under the eggs and smile at me.

I knew you liked the poems even though you didn't say so.

And, unlike me, you were most beautiful when you smiled.

*

Your letters are not the only thing that burns in this fire.

My poems burn as well.

The fire burns fiercely.

Our words must burn as well as I do.

# 2

*Arnthrúdur: 'I feel ashamed and for a while we're engulfed in a silence so heavy and so full of memories that I'm afraid it'll burst our eardrums.'*

Sleep hasn't conquered me tonight.

It has however crept over to me and touched me but has only stroked my consciousness. I must have been aware of it, felt that sleep was going to steal something from me, fought against it and felt at the same time the ticking of the clock like a quiet accompaniment to the restlessness. I have also sensed Valgeir's breathing, heavy, slow and rhythmic, and all the time it's as if I've been about to admit defeat, although I haven't actually done so. So it's been a difficult night for me and anyway I don't like that space between sleeping and wakefulness.

I don't usually have any trouble sleeping and when things are as they should be Valgeir has to give me more than one dig in the ribs.

But he doesn't have to now.

And as soon as I realize what the reason for my resistance is his voice becomes clear, almost sharp and sleep loses the battle completely.

'Wake up, it's the hospital! Arnthrúdur!'

'Are they phoning so late?' I ask, looking at the clock.

It's a quarter past three and, remembering the occasions when they've phoned me at this sort of time, my heart beats wildly as I grab the receiver, kick the duvet away and think, at lightning speed,

that the time has come,

that now there's no escape,
that now she won't make it,
that now her body'll let her down,
and my mind wanders halfway into new worlds.

I've always thought like that and even though I don't believe in other worlds, even though I'm sensible and down to earth, thoughts of new worlds go rushing through my head. But before I can say anything it feels like everything gets stifled inside me and my thoughts go round in the same circle. So that's why without thinking I'm going to do what I always do,

scream at Valgeir,
tell him to pass me my clothes and get the hell out of bed,
tell him not to be always so slow on the uptake,
whether it doesn't matter to him that it'll almost certainly
    happen now,
whether he doesn't care about her,
whether he's going to let my sister die without me,
whether he doesn't know that I have to hold her,
whether he doesn't remember what I promised our
    mother.

I had promised Mother to look after her.

But this time it's different.

I feel his hands on my chest and my thoughts don't become words and my words don't become screams, my heart slows down and all the panic fades away as I look into his calm grey eyes and hear him whisper kindly, 'Calm down, don't be afraid, it'll be all right.'

'Are you sure?'

'I'm sure.'

And just then I hear Anna's voice.

Her voice is always with me and always has been:

I'm your sister and I'm healthy.
I'm your sister and I have the will-power to be the longest-
    living old lady of them all.
I'm your sister and I'm going to beat this.

'Is Anna there?' says a voice on the telephone and for a moment I don't recognize it, even though I recognize most of them, deep or thin, scared or optimistic, hopeless or encouraging.

'What do you mean? I don't understand, what do you mean, "Is she here?"'

'Is she at your place?' The voice becomes clearer and I know who it is, feel how unsure of herself the girl is and so reply forcefully and directly.

I have to dispel all doubt immediately.

'Of course she's not here, what made you think she would be?'

'She wasn't in the ward just now when I did my round. I ran out to the front and saw that she hadn't been discharged, looked for her clothes and shoes, but everything had gone. But she is on this ward, there's no doubt about that and it says in the night report that at ten o'clock she had a temperature and was complaining of pain. I don't understand it at all and I can't get hold of the doctor on back-up duty. I've phoned Anna at home over and over again, but she doesn't answer there either.'

'I called in and saw her at second visiting time. She can't have gone far, she was in a bit of a daze,' I say, having assumed the calmness I find so essential.

I know how to show self-control when I have to.

I know how to control my feelings when it's necessary.

And I do so now.

'She isn't here!'

*

When nobody answers at the woman's house I remember Anna once telling me that she often unplugged the phone at night-time so she wouldn't be disturbed.

'Do so many people phone her at night?' I asked, and I was somehow surprised that a woman like her couldn't get any peace and quiet.

'Sometimes they do. There's a bloke who often phones and hassles her, especially at weekends when he's drunk, of course.'

'Is that so?' I said, rather uninterested in the personal habits of this woman who I've never wanted to get to know.

I found her reserved and rather eccentric.

She normally didn't say anything when they came to my place and even though Anna said that it was just shyness, that she wanted to get to know me and wasn't really so reticent, I can't hide the fact that I couldn't be bothered. It may have been because there was no sympathy between us, we were different in every way imaginable. I always try my best to be direct and honest with other people and I think I'm generally frank and natural, so I don't easily tolerate stand-offishness and coy glances. I couldn't understand either why she thought she ought to be shy with me, one of the few people who knew her dreadful secret.

That was in the days when nobody knew anything.

And she treated her love affair like a murder.

That was in the days when she felt ashamed.

'Maybe that's why she's shy with you,' said Anna, who often saw things from a different point of view from me.

'It's beyond me why the woman refuses to acknowledge her own feelings,' I replied. Anna laughed like she always did when she could hear I was annoyed.

'Don't you understand fear?' she asked, with her eyes beautiful.

Her eyes were so often beautiful when she was being sly.

'Not that fear. I don't understand being afraid of how you feel.'

'But if she can't rid herself of it, don't you think she should do as she likes?'

'Just as she likes,' I repeated after her.

I let it drop.

My sister could be charming when she led me on some detour in the direction of a truth that I thought was my own. And that was what she often did. And on this occasion she put her head on one side, closed her eyes, fingered her chin, sat down on the nearest stool and reminded me of my own definition of doing as one likes: *You should have the right to do what is best for you whenever you want, as long as you don't hurt people around you.* In other words she was reminding me of the motto of my

25

own life, which I had certainly never made any attempt to keep secret.

'It doesn't hurt me, it's just how she is,' she said.

'I don't want her to harm you.'

'She can't. I'm too fond of her for that to be possible,' she said. And I recall that when I looked at her sitting there swinging round in half-circles on the chair – I know now that it was a few months after she fell in love with the woman – I thought that the simple three-phrase philosophy she had adopted from childhood might have made her a happy woman but definitely a worse poet than she could have been and would have wanted to be:

*You love the person who shows you love,*
*who is a good friend,*
*and doesn't miss what you don't have.*

'But doesn't it ever annoy you how she creeps around the walls?'

'I've never noticed she does that, but if I understand you correctly, my dear sister, I think it harms only her.'

'I'll never understand relationships like this,' I replied. And I smiled broadly when Anna shook her head and flicked her eyes up to the ceiling, which she would do frequently when talking to me annoyed her. Then she asked me, for her sake, to remember the woman's name, saying that most people found it easy and that even though I found 'relationships like this' strange (which she quite understood) people in them had names just like other people and that her name was Z.

I must confess that even the name annoyed me. To me it seemed like a sign of both affectation and quirkiness.

Not to mention pretentious in the extreme to christen a child with a name that doesn't have any meaning.

'Actually she wasn't christened, just named,' Anna told me.

'But named after what, if I may make so bold as to ask?'

'After the lightning her father saw in the sky when she was born.'

'But she's still afraid.'

'But maybe that's why she's also daring,' she said, surprising me again with her understanding of life and other people. When I thought about it, there was so much that surprised me.

The meaning of words and sentences turned into their opposites.

And people often surprised me afterwards.

But I tried not to let it show.

*

Z.

The name isn't just eccentric and affected, it's also as lonely and empty and dead as the letter is. Those are my thoughts as I ring the doorbell and her dark voice answers my question in the negative. I had hoped after all that Anna would be at her place.

To tell the truth I had felt sure she would be there.

I feel uncomfortable and press Valgeír's hand.

'No, she's not here, but do come up. I'm on my own.'

She lives in Sólheimar, on the third floor of a large block. I don't answer when Valgeir puts his hands on my shoulders and says, 'Arnthrúdur, be tactful with her.'

'You don't have to remind me, I know how to behave.'

He doesn't have to worry.

And I make him feel so on the way up in the lift.

I tell him first without words.

I kiss his throat and stroke his hair.

I make him feel that he's the man who makes me strong,

the man I can't live without,

and I whisper that I like it when he calms me.

Valgeir the rock.

And he was steady when he came for good,

when at last he came to me.

I had cried bitterly that day,

defencelessly like Anna did when she was little and was

afraid of the dark and said she didn't understand it and

didn't know what was hiding in it.

'The darkness is soft,' I would tell her when she crept into my bed, cold and shivering.

'But what's inside it?' she would say.

27

And I had no answer for that.

I still haven't, even with Valgeir standing close beside me as I ring the doorbell twice. I always ring twice. Opening the door before the sound stops, she stands there silently in the doorway. She's wearing a Japanese dressing-gown, her hands are in her pockets, her face pale and drawn and her eyes red.

She's beautiful.

And I suddenly have the feeling that she's uncomfortably beautiful.

I can see that Valgeir likes the look of her.

I can see it by the turn of his face and the slight movements of his mouth.

I look her straight in the eye and try to push those thoughts away from me.

I shouldn't be thinking like that now.

'Come in,' she says in a half-whisper, as if there was somebody listening in, and I feel a slight surprise at never having been to visit her before.

Of course I had often been invited.

I might have felt better now if I had accepted.

'Come with me,' Anna often said during the last few months.

But I always put it off.

And now I'm here looking for her.

I can see that she doesn't quite know what to do.

She clasps her hands together.

Looks from one of us to the other and asks in a serious voice, 'Where is Anna? She wasn't feeling well when I left her. I phoned her later, at eleven o'clock, and she was going to go to sleep.'

She smooths out her dressing-gown as she's talking and I'm struck by the elegance of her movements, by her delicate hands and her slender fingers.

It comes as a pleasant surprise.

I notice that Valgeir is watching her.

'She isn't at the hospital. Do you have any idea where she could be?' he asks quietly. I add that together we have to find out who she's friendly with and where she could have gone.

'I can't imagine she's gone far,' she says.

'Do you have any friends in common?' I ask.

'She has lots of friends but there's nobody both of us are friendly with, nobody that we see together,' she says, looking down at her feet.

I needn't have asked her that.

I knew what the answer would be.

'We use the time we have to be together, just the two of us,' Anna had told me when I asked her the same question, but that was two years ago and I was a bit taken aback that nothing had changed.

But I hadn't asked her again.

It may be that I just assumed things had changed.

I don't know.

I haven't thought about it before now.

'All the bars are closed,' she says and I can sense how bewildered she is.

'Isn't there a bar down in Vogar that's open all night?' asks Valgeir.

'I don't know,' she replies, 'but then I wouldn't.'

'I've never heard of a bar down there,' I comment, staring at Valgeir.

I'm surprised.

I didn't know he knew so much about bars.

But I hide my astonishment.

I'll keep it for another time.

'Anna goes all over the place,' she says.

And when I study her long blond hair, her long slender neck and her feminine build I don't quite understand why she is like that.

She doesn't look like the women I've seen so often at Club 22.

I can feel myself blushing as these thoughts go through my head.

I wish I knew what Valgeir was thinking.

And in my mind's eye I can see Anna's laughing face.

'We'll find her,' says Valgeir and it's only when I hear his comforting words that I'm really aware of how worried she is.

Sometimes I refuse to see the obvious.

I have a trick of looking away.

'Don't pigeonhole people like that,' was what Anna replied the first time I asked her (actually I often asked and she always laughed) how it was possible that women like her and her friend, women who weren't butch and who had their whole future before them and could land any man they wanted, turned instead to each other.

'I'm not particularly ladylike,' she continued, 'if anything, more boyish really, but do you really think that it shows outwardly? Isn't love all about feelings, Arnthrúdur?'

'I understood you completely when you loved Gunnar,' I said.

'Then you ought to understand this, even though it's different.'

'So you *do* think it's different now?'

'Z is the love of my life, Gunnar was just an aperitif. But you understand your own love, so why do you think mine is different? Haven't I always understood you?' she asked, and then told me I shouldn't worry.

'But are you sure you're really happy in a sort of secret liaison like this?'

'I'm as happy as I can be and I don't think you understand the expression "secret liaison" in the same way as I do. Anyway, we all have a liaison of some sort, don't we?' And I felt that these words were aimed straight at me.

*

I recall that I stared fixedly at her as if I had lost the power of thought, as if my eyes had become riveted in her eyes, until suddenly I looked away and smiled. Of course, she was right, she had always understood me, there was no mistake about that, and I had also understood her,

until four years ago,

until things became what she called serious,

but still I tried to believe what she said herself,

that she was happy,

that it didn't bother her that she was having a relationship with a woman who was too afraid to face up to her own feelings.

'Perhaps you have that in common,' she said.

30

'Not at all, I'm not afraid of my feelings.'

'Then why are you afraid of hers when they're so like your own?'

'Is that what you mean?' I replied, feeling I was making excuses for myself.

I was used to making excuses for my opinions.

I didn't have an opinion unless I knew why.

I was used to weighing things up if I was interested in them.

*

There were just the two of us sisters and not much of a gap between us.

She was thirty and I was thirty-two.

And we had always been close.

'Let's make a pact,' said Anna when we were little.

'What sort of pact?' I asked.

'That we'll always stick together.'

'OK. Let's.'

'We'll both cut ourselves and make ourselves blood-sisters.'

'We don't have to do that, it's OK if we just say an oath.'

'Let's cut ourselves.'

And I gave in.

I was used to doing anything I could for her.

So we both cut our fingers, mixed the drops of blood, and licked the cuts.

That's how we sealed our everlasting love, our understanding and our mutual concern. But I always seemed to have the last word, maybe because I was that bit older or maybe because, as our mother used to say, she was a daydreamer, always having to try everything, test everything out, be everywhere and careful not to miss out on anything.

And she asked me to look after her when she moved away.

It was then that she asked me to take care of her.

'Look after your sister,' she said.

'I promise I will,' I replied.

Between our mother and me there was a friendship.

Between us there was trust.

31

She felt she had a reason for asking me, even though she'd never had any trouble with Anna, any more than she had with me. We were very ordinary, run-of-the-mill girls who nobody ever had particular reason to complain about. But our mother said she sensed something in Anna that she didn't fully understand. And when I suggested that maybe she had these groundless fears just because she was going away, she said that that could be so but she felt it was something more than that. Then she asked whether I thought she was a bad mother and whether she should be more worried than she was.

Our mother who always did her best.

Our mother who always thought about us first and then about herself.

Except that time.

'Of course not. You've been good to us so we will miss you, but we want you to go, we want you to be happy. Don't worry about Anna, she can look after herself, she's grown up now, and anyway I'll keep an eye on her,' I said.

And I fully believed what I was saying.

Anna was twenty-one then and well on her way in French and Literature.

I however was reading Law and it was going well.

We were living together in a nice flat on Hverfisgötunni, right opposite the hat shop. Before that we'd been well looked after at our mother's, until she met that man and moved to Norway with him a while later. Our father had disappeared out of our lives when I was four and neither of us remembered him. Mother said he had found another woman and made himself a new home.

She said that had been for the best.

They had both agreed about that.

They had never understood each other.

But she never spoke badly of him.

'Your father was a good man,' she always said when we asked about him, but for some reason we never felt the need to meet him or go in search of him and we never wanted to know more than she told us either. But her brother, a pleasant chap who had worked for most of his life near Mývatn in the north and who stayed with us when he came into town, said that Gudmundur had been damaged goods whichever way you looked at it.

'So I invited your father ptarmigan-shooting one day,' he grinned, 'and that's when it happened. And if you ever have any trouble with a boyfriend, girls, you just get in touch. I'll be right there and I'll invite him on a ptarmigan-shoot.'

When we lived together Anna and I often laughed about that and joked that now the time had come to call up Uncle and if there was no answer we should just apply for a gun licence ourselves.

'Shouldn't I just phone Uncle for you?' Anna sometimes asked me when panic about Valgeir was sending me over the edge.

Maybe I hadn't seen him or heard from him for a week and, even though he had often told me that I didn't need to worry about him, that he still loved me and would one day be with me for ever, I didn't trust him when he was with his wife and didn't come to see me.

That time was almost unbearable.

And I often thought that he was my greatest source of suffering.

I met him first in a pub at the beginning of June 1993.

Exactly one year before Anna met her.

'I want to see you again,' he said.

And so it happened . . .

*

'What is it that makes you so afraid?' Anna asked me.

'Perhaps he won't come back.'

'You always say that.'

'But perhaps it'll happen this time.'

'He said he'd come, didn't he?'

'I can't believe what he says.'

'Why not?'

'I don't know what he's like when he's with her.'

'Hasn't he told you that he doesn't feel good about it?'

'Of course he has, he couldn't very well say anything else.'

33

'Has he ever told you a lie?'

'No.'

'Then believe what he says.'

'I saw him once coming out of the ice-cream shop in Hjardar Laganum with two ice-creams, and he was laughing. He leapt into his car and it looked to me as if he was feeling just fine.'

'What were you doing there?'

'I happened to be driving past their house just as they came out, so I decided to follow them.'

'Do you think people never laugh when they feel bad about something?'

'Of course they do, but there was something about that laughter, it was so good-spirited, happy almost.'

'If I were you I'd stop thinking like that, stop spying on him, stop driving past his house and his office and try going out instead, with me maybe or with someone else, and then be happy when you meet him and enjoy the time you spend together.'

'And stop having any expectations?'

'Not at all, have your expectations all right, but stop discussing them with him and enjoy life.'

'I've tried, but I can't.'

'He loves you, I know he does,' she said. And I laughed to myself when, of all the conversations we had had about this, I thought about that one.

And Valgeir came, like he said he would.

But the fear didn't leave me.

It was as if it loomed over me whenever we weren't near each other and now, even though we've been living together for nearly three years, I have to steel myself to take my eyes off him.

I don't want to be like this.

I don't want to feel this frenzy inside me.

I want to be able to go my own way securely, to look at the sun or the sky and see the sun or the sky, perhaps even both when things are good. But it doesn't happen. The sun is dull and I don't care about the sky, Valgeir's face hovers over everything.

The same questions still trouble me.

What's he doing?

Who's he with?

I've often gone to ridiculous lengths to get an answer.

I've had a crowbar under the driver's seat, just in case.

'You must stop phoning me so much at the office,' he said one evening when he came home. 'You must trust me, I deserve your trust. I've never deceived you.'

I knew he was telling the truth.

I made everything into a joke and pretended not to care.

But I knew that he knew that I was pretending.

We had had this conversation before.

'I don't know why it is, but I always have to hear your voice.'

'I'm not seeing Hanna, believe me, and I don't want to. You're the one I want to be with, that's why I left her. Can't you understand that?'

I understood.

But I didn't feel it.

I understood.

But I didn't believe it.

I didn't know whether he missed her.

I didn't dare ask.

He never talked about it.

*

'Valgeir, what bar were you talking about down in Vogar?'

I can't help myself.

I ask him in a teasing tone when she goes into the bedroom to put some clothes on. I'm glad she's getting dressed. I found it disturbing while we were sitting here, phoning everyone we could think of. Some people we woke up, others had just come back from a bar, but nobody had seen Anna or knew anything about where she was.

I'm sure she won't disturb me so much when she's dressed.

We sit waiting for the police, there's nothing else we can do.

35

I know I should talk about something else but I can't.

I have to know for certain about the bar.

'What bar?' he asked, absentmindedly.

'You mentioned that there might be a bar . . .

'Yes, there was once, I seem to remember, but so what? She isn't in a bar that doesn't exist, is she?' he replies, making me feel ashamed of asking such a trivial question. I know this is neither the place nor the moment but I can't control my thoughts and I have to know at once, so that it doesn't consume and pursue me.

'Have you been there, Valgeir?'

'No, and for God's sake stop it now!'

And I remember what Anna said but, even so, I can't calm down.

'Don't mess things up by being jealous.'

'I'm no more jealous than anyone else is.'

'You're incredibly jealous, just like Z is, even though you don't understand women like her.'

'It's not the same.'

'Isn't it?'

'Valgeir, are you sure you haven't been to that bar?'

'Arnthrúdur, we can talk about this later. It can't matter now, not when we don't know anything about Anna. How can you think about such a little thing at a time like this? It doesn't make sense.'

'I can't help it, perhaps it takes my mind off it,' I say, as she comes in, fully dressed, and sits down on the sofa.

I look at her and see that she is still beautiful.

But it provokes me less.

Valgeir takes her hand and strokes it.

I become uneasy.

Why does he have to stroke her like that?

Why does he have to touch her at all?

I can't see that there's any call for it.

I look at her and see that her eyes are wet.

And I feel ashamed of the thoughts that I am at last managing to keep at bay. He's right, thoughts like this are out of place. Actually, I'm out of place myself, sometimes I'm not quite right in the mind, thinking the worst about everything, full up to the brim of such consuming bloody suspicion.

I manage to banish these unpleasant thoughts and nobody says anything and for a while we're engulfed in a silence so heavy and so full of memories that I'm afraid it'll burst our eardrums.

I'm relieved when she breaks the silence.

When she speaks I can feel her sorrow and her helplessness.

She provokes me less and less.

'It's so strange,' she says. 'I'm no lover of poetry but if I wrote her a letter she always gave me a poem a while later. I'm going to publish them,' she goes on, and it seems to both of us that she's talking to herself rather than to us, 'and the book's going to be called *Monday Poems*. I never told her that I learned the poems by heart, never told her because I don't think she really cared what I thought about them. Of course I have them written down, they're all where they should be, not here, but I learned them because then I felt she was closer to me. I wanted her to be here more often, but she was used to it like it was. When I wanted to change things and was in a position to do so, I don't think she wanted to, she was used to gadding about here there and everywhere and then I thought it was a good idea to learn the poems, while I was alone. Of course it may seem childish, but then that's how it is,' and as she speaks I look at her and feel a oneness with her. Not just because I know she has a tendency to be transformed by jealousy, but also because she reminds me of Anna when she talks, there's a hint of that sincerity in her voice that it's difficult to explain in words but which creeps into my voice as well when I've been with her for a long time. It creeps up on you like a ray of light and lodges itself in you after she's rushed off. I know I'm bordering on the sentimental but I can't help it.

And I can feel that her fear is no less than my fear.

And now she doesn't provoke me any more.

All of a sudden I want to put my arms around her, but I hold back.

At times fear makes a shambles of reason but then common sense protects you.

So I take her other hand.

And if I had suspected Valgeir my suspicions disappear now as I feel that his reassurances are heartfelt, just as mine are.

The three of us sit on the sofa holding hands.

It seems like a play by Chekhov and I'm just thinking about the plot when the doorbell rings and she jumps up.

She's light on her feet.

She's obviously expecting good news.

*

'And you are?' asks the policeman when Valgeir and I have both given him our names and explained exactly who we are, all of which takes an unnecessarily long time. But we don't make a fuss about that. We know that the report and the paperwork are a part of the process that the servant of the law can do nothing about.

And that making a fuss and being rude is a waste of time.

So we wait patiently, still holding hands.

All jealousy is gone from me.

And I can concentrate for longer on the present.

We're here to give each other support and to look for a solution.

'I'm her friend,' she says quietly, and suddenly I understand the significance of her choice of word. She could have chosen to use a different word, a word like lover. Under these circumstances I would scarcely have called Valgeir my friend.

But I don't give it any more thought.

These thoughts annoy me.

'What's your name?'

'Z.'

'Written like the letter?'

'Yes.'

'Age?'

'Thirty-one.'

'No, date of birth.'

'Second November 1966.'

'Occupation?'

38

'Journalist.'

'And where do you live?'

'Here, 28 Sólheimar.'

'When was the last time you saw Anna Gudmundsdóttir?'

'This evening. I went to visit her at eight o'clock and spoke to her on the phone at eleven o'clock.'

'How was she then?'

'Not well. She was in a lot of pain, but she had had an injection so it was getting better and her temperature was going down.'

'I know, they told me that at the hospital. I meant did you find her at all confused?'

'No, I didn't.'

'Then there's nothing in particular that she said to you, nothing special that could put us on the right track?'

'No, she was like she always is when she's tired.'

'And you can't think of anywhere she might have gone?'

'Nowhere other than places we've been talking about here, that they've told you about. We've phoned everywhere we can think of.'

'And you say that she still drove a car, even though she was on drugs. If she's taken the car it's hard to say where we should start looking, but if you're sure there's nothing else and the others can't think of anything, then we'll put our usual search plan into operation after we've put out an announcement for her on the radio and television. You'll get in touch with us, of course, if you hear anything. It's a strange story, but there's no reason for you to give up hope yet,' he says kindly as he leaves. Then as he's closing the door he calls out to us, 'Will you all be here, or are you two going home?'

We look at each other.

It reminds me of the play again, but it's probably by someone else, yes, of course it's by Arthur Miller with Marilyn Monroe in the lead role, yes it was made for television, unless it was Elizabeth Taylor who played the young woman, it was probably her, at least I remember she had dark hair. And as these thoughts go through my head it seems to me that Valgeir and I are rather set in our ways, rather old.

That we're responsible and assured while she's young and defenceless.

That we're on a stage.

That this is some sort of play.

I touch Valgeir's knee as he replies to the policeman's question.

'We'll be here,' he says without hesitation.

She smiles at him.

He knew what she wanted.

Valgeir always knows what women want and at the moment that seems fine to me.

\*

'Weren't you talking about Anna's poems?' asks Valgeir when the three of us are alone again.

'Yes, but I was just thinking aloud.'

'I'm curious.'

'Like I said, I don't know anything about poems but I like these ones,' she said, 'perhaps because she gave them to me, perhaps I am just so selfish. I don't think I understand them particularly well, but I understand them in my own way and then there are notes with each poem which help. I like having the notes, but naturally I don't know what other people think.'

She's more modest than I thought.

I thought she was a snob.

'She's never mentioned this book to me,' I say, wondering all of a sudden how this can be, maybe I haven't shown enough interest in her poetry.

The reason, of course, lies with me.

At least I have to admit to myself that I have always found her poetry shoddy and pretentious,

something still that she has to experiment with,

something I hope she'll grow out of.

But now I remember that she once said, 'You don't take any notice of me.'

'Do I have to do that too?' I asked.

'I'd like it if you did.'

40

'There are so many people in this poetry business, Anna.'

'Nobody like me.'

'Is that so?'

'It's true, there's always room for more. No two poets are the same.'

'Is that what you mean?'

'Do you think my books are bad?'

'Why do you ask?'

'I'm curious.'

'I preferred the first one. I don't think I understood the second one, but it's awkward for me to pass judgement.'

'Why?'

'It's obvious, I'm your sister.'

Mother likes her books.

*I can't explain it, but there's something about Anna's poems that makes one light-hearted. Not jolly, I don't mean that, but light-hearted. Perhaps it's the way she chooses her words and how everything blends together. I think she writes poetry best*, she wrote in a letter to me not long ago.

I curse myself silently for not having told Anna.

I'll tell her later.

'She never told me about the book either,' says Valgeir.

'It was obvious that she didn't want to talk about it,' she says thoughtfully, adding that it was no surprise she only talked to her once or twice about the poems, since poems aren't her cup of tea.

'*Monday Poems*, did you say?' I ask.

'Yes, I think I have seventeen poems now, yes, it's seventeen.'

'And you know all of them?' asks Valgeir.

'I did it for fun. I got the idea from a story Anna read once and told me about, the idea of learning the poems. It was nice to feel close to her like that, and of course it's good training for your memory.'

'Will you recite one of them?' asks Valgeir, with no trace of doubt in his voice. He believes she does know the poems by heart. I'm a bit doubtful but join in nevertheless. I want to do my bit to shorten the waiting.

'I don't feel I have her consent to do so,' she says.

'Do you feel you need her consent?' I ask, surprised.

'Yes, I don't feel that I can recite her poems without her knowing.'

'But didn't she give them to you?'

'Recite just one for us,' says Valgeir.

'I'm sure we'll feel better afterwards,' I add.

I encourage her and give her strength.

She can trust what I'm saying, and she does.

'I'll recite the poem then and the notes that go with it,' she says.

We nod in agreement and both of us are aware that she's nervous at first, that her fingers are trembling and her mouth quivering.

'I'll chose the one that comes first to mind,' she says.

\*

*On Monday, 1 May 1995, I wasn't feeling particularly well.*

*My girlfriend from across the road had sat with me for a while and had been telling me about her relationship with her lover. She was unhappy. There are few people I've met recently who get as much joy out of giving as she does, and it doesn't matter whether the presents are real ones or not. Mother always used to say, 'The wages of the world are ingratitude,' and since those days I've often wondered to myself why people like my friend never reap as they sow. I don't know the answer, and, of course, if I did I would have solved part of that mystery of life which nobody can solve. Sometimes the thought has crossed my mind that the tension accompanying grief can be positive because it shows you new pathways that you're not used to taking.*

*Why not enjoy the pain?*

*I wanted my friend to think about that and I encouraged her to do so.*

> *Walk to the frozen lake*
> *the flat surface shines*
> *see the deep hole in the ice*
> *on the bottom blue shoes*

*bend down*
*and drink*
*feel the ice turn to fire*
*feel it burn your tongue*

*never look back*

*don't miss the green green land*
*the bright bright roads*
*the soft soft nights*
*the wide wide days*

*slip your fingers into the hole*
*feel the churning mud at the bottom*
*take the blue shoes*

*they burn your feet*

*and the fire shoots along your body*
*from your tongue to your toes*

*enjoy the flames*

*and dance*

\*

'I suddenly lost the thread and my mind wandered. You'll have to say it again for us,' I say. 'Somehow I fell to thinking about Anna's neighbour, because if I remember rightly she told me that the people opposite her were old, quite old. I don't recall either that there was anybody there she called her girlfriend. But there may have been, even though she didn't tell me about her. She didn't tell me everything. And I suppose old people have lovers too, I'm not complaining about that, but I couldn't help smiling even so,' I go on, laughing.

She stares at me in amazement.

Valgeir is also amazed.

They don't know what's making me smile.

They don't know Anna's stories about the people opposite.

'What's so amusing?' she asks.

'Tell us, Arnthrúdur, why not? Z'll recite the poem again when you've finished, won't you?' asks Valgeir.

'Yes, I will,' she replies.

I can hear impatience in his voice.

I can hear sarcasm, too.

But I pretend I can't hear anything.

It'll be good for them as well as me to get their minds on to something else.

*

'Yes, I'll tell you if you want, and then hopefully you'll understand why my mind wandered. You see, Anna had already been living at Laugalækur for quite a few months by the time I got round to visiting her. I had put off going to see her for longer than I should have.'

'Get yourself together and come over, you can't be that busy,' she said, and I did as I was told. I didn't want it to look like what she was implying (although she never actually said anything, but then she never did make direct accusations). But I understood without her having to say anything.

And she was never slow to call round to me when I wanted to see her.

She was always considerate.

And so it was that we were sitting talking in her kitchen.

'How do you like it here?'

She looked quizzically at me.

She often looked at me quizzically when I asked her something.

'It's a quiet neighbourhood, the worst thing is that the only children you see here are just visiting, but the trees and gardens are nice, and I like it here. I'm getting to know the other people in the house, and in the house opposite. The people opposite are rather odd, all living alone in such big flats. Sometimes I think they must spend ages wandering around inside with themselves and their memories.'

'What's so odd about these people?'

'That's just my manner of speaking. Maybe people everywhere are a bit odd when you get to know them, special in some way, everyone a world unto himself, weird and strange,' she replied, making me fear that she was going to lose herself in these ruminations and forget what she was trying to tell me.

She sometimes did that.

But I knew the signs and stepped in to prevent it.

'Yes, but tell me about the people across the road.'

'There's nobody living on the ground floor. The flat belongs to some woman who lives abroad most of the time. I met her actually just after I moved in and introduced myself. She told me she preferred to have the flat empty when she isn't in Iceland, and then she pops over twice a year for a fortnight or so. She said she has a decent bed to sleep in, clean underwear and a change of clothes in the wardrobe, plenty of towels and bed linen, everything she needs in the kitchen, and chairs, a table and a comfortable sofa in the living room. Just about everything she could need while she's here.'

'Do you just come here for fun?' I asked her.

'You could say that,' she replied.

'Do you have family in Reykjavík?' I asked.

'No, I don't know anyone in Reykjavík now,' she said. 'I just come over to be in the flat. I'm fond of it, I've had it for so long. I give it a thorough going-over, spring-clean and tidy it, and polish everything. You know, my dear, one has to make sure one keeps flats in good condition, otherwise they become run down. Mine's in fine condition, but then I've always taken care of it and had respect for it. One has to water one's plants. One has to tend one's garden. That's what I've always said.' As she spoke I couldn't help but notice the strong undertone in what she said and the sorrow in her voice.

'Have you owned the flat for so long?' I asked.

'For twelve years I've been coming here twice a year, for twelve years I've been taking care of what it's my duty to take care of in Iceland, and I've done it gladly and I'm going to go on doing so, at least as long as I don't need help getting between countries,' she said with a smile. Then she invited me in for pancakes and white wine, which I'd never had before, not together. And everything in her flat was exactly as she had described. I drank the wine and ate the pancakes while she watched me with a smile on her face. She didn't say anything and neither did I because I felt I wasn't supposed to. And when I had finished eating I got to my feet and thanked her and she said that she looked forward to my next visit. That she would definitely invite me in again because it was invaluable to her to have met me, such a lovely person.

I gave her a hug when I was leaving and she felt hard to the touch.

She drew in her breath deeply as she finished the story.

'And who lives on the first floor?'

'A man of about the same age, about sixty. A really sweet chap with the bushiest eyebrows I have ever set eyes on. He runs a small whole-sale business and told me that he's lived alone for the past few years but that he does have children who call in occasionally. He said he actually doesn't much enjoy seeing his children because they take after their mother and her relatives. They're demanding and full of themselves, constantly bickering and finding fault, and incessantly meddling in the life he has made for himself. As for himself, he said he had never interfered in their lives and affairs, believing as he did that everyone was entitled to peace. He loves peace and quiet. Actually I've never seen his kids and I have wondered whether they don't exist mainly in his head and whether he can make a clear distinction between his dreams and reality. But whatever the truth is I enjoy being near him. We often have a drink together, and it gives him such pleasure to bring out his favourite copper glasses when I call in. And then he becomes quite talkative, gets out a pack of cards and tells my fortune, reads tea-leaves, tosses matches on the table and tells the future from how they land, brings out a box of soil and tells my fortune from my footprints.

'This is the way I do it,' he laughs.

'What can you see?' I ask, knowing he almost always says the same thing.

'I see various things.'

'Don't keep them to yourself.'

'I see that you'll live here for the rest of your life.'

'And do you see anything else?'

'I don't think that's so unimportant but in fact I can see something else, and I'm going to ask you to buy a lottery ticket and to do so immediately, and bring it over here to me and have a drink, and while you're swigging it down I'll lay my hands on the ticket and then there'll be no way that you won't win a lot of money.'

Of course, I've done that more often than I can remember and have always said, 'Didn't win this time.'

And he always answers, 'That's strange, but you will next time. Never miss a chance, Anna dear. I have an odd gift which more often than not reveals itself in women winning with tickets that I've laid my hands on.'

After that he usually asks me to leave but to come again soon.

He says he has lots to do.

I accept his invitation.

'So who's on the second floor?'

'A woman of about fifty, I should think, lives there. She lives alone too and looks rather eccentric. She wears weird clothes, like she's often in a dark overcoat with her grey hair hidden under a multicoloured headscarf. But she always says hello when we meet and she chats about the weather and whether it's going to change tomorrow or the next day. She always asks me whether I'm interested in religion because she says it's of paramount importance that people enjoy thinking about religion. She asks me the same questions every time I meet her but I know she doesn't expect me to answer. So I just nod my head. Although she lives by herself she has a son who comes to see her once or twice a week, and then there's trouble. I'm always surprised by the noise. The son seems quiet and polite, but there's something he and his mother don't see eye to eye about. He hasn't been there for more than an hour when this terrible din starts up, shouting and screaming, and I know it's her who's making the noise because you never hear his voice. If you open the window you can hear she's always going on about the same things, about tables and socks, but you can never make out what the connection is because of the racket going on. Then after a while, half an hour or so, the son dashes down the steps, leaps into his car and speeds away. A few minutes later she walks slowly down the steps, quite unflustered in her dark coat and with her coloured headscarf, and comes back almost immediately with a large bottle of Coke.

'And from looking at her you'd assume everything's fine.'

'Haven't you ever wanted to ask her what's going on?' I asked.

'It's not in my character to be nosy and now I feel that I've betrayed the confidence of this neighbour of mine by talking about her like this. After all, who am I to talk about other people and be surprised at what they do?' she said and then stopped talking.

'Anna has second thoughts so often when she's talking about other people,' I say. 'Sometimes it gets on my nerves, but it didn't that time. I can't remember the conversation any more clearly than that and she didn't mention anything else about the house across the road. But you can understand now how I lost the thread of the poem you were reciting, Z, and I wonder now which of these three you think she had in mind in the introduction to the poem, when she talked about her girlfriend across the road?' I say, with irony in my voice.

'It doesn't matter,' Valgeir says, and he asks her to recite the poem again.

And though he sounds a bit nervy,
    and though he looks a bit surprised,
        still I feel that we're more relaxed as she recites the poem
           a second time.

My story has mattered.

My interruptions aren't always worthless.

# 3

*Anna: 'You're not here with me now because I don't want you to be.'*

It was the night when I realized the book would never be published that I decided to give you the poems. Not because I knew the book wouldn't be printed and the poems would never see the light of day, but because I had grown fond of it.

I had become fond of this experiment of mine even though I realized that the most interesting thing about it was its name.

*Monday Poems.*

I had done as well as I could.

I couldn't do better even if I wanted.

Or even if I tried.

Putting my thoughts into words didn't come naturally to me, as it does to some. It was as if I couldn't get a grip on the language and never managed to put the right words together so they described what they were supposed to describe. I was forced to admit defeat and it was painfully obvious that compared to real poetry my poems were like Pat Boone sharing a stage with Pavarotti. It was the night that this suspicion of mine became a certainty and I had been sitting for a long time in a pub called the Vitabar. I used to go there if I wanted to have a drink by myself or talk to people or watch people who did not matter to me.

I did that more often after I met you.

And I was never disappointed.

I enjoyed the solitude and the information it brought me, even if the information had been bitter on that occasion.

49

When I got home there was a letter from you in the hall.

It was the fourth letter you had written me and I hadn't expected it.

It was the Christmas letter that I hadn't been expecting but had still been waiting for.

*

I see you in my mind's eye.

I see you leaping out of your car and quickly popping the letter through the letterbox.

It came of course on a Monday night.

It may not have been chance.

And I sat down at my desk and read the last letter of our first year, the letter you wrote on Boxing Day, 1994.

*

Now I'm holding it in my hand and looking forward to seeing it go up in flames alongside the poem. Suddenly I want to throw the eggs on the fire too. I know that instead of melting they'll turn black and remind me of the sky outside and the night inside me.

I give in to this longing.

As I throw the first three eggs into the fireplace a mixture of blue, white, yellow, red and green hues blends together and the eggs become colourless and ugly.

Colourless, ugly eggs of life.

I recall my feelings when I opened the letter on Boxing Day.

I couldn't feel the butterfly fluttering any more. It was good to feel the pain slowly lessen and finally disappear.

I recall my anticipation and joy.

Everything is as it was at that moment.

I'm alone as I read the letter once more.

*

*Beloved Anna,*

*The day before Christmas Eve has never been my favourite day but last Thursday certainly was. The time I spent with you was charmed and, to tell the truth, I don't know how I managed to conjure it up. It was difficult. I have never realized until the last few months how complicated a lie can be and how difficult it is to keep it up so that there's no break in the pattern. A lie is like a delicate silk rug with a pattern so intricate that the slightest mistake jumps out at you as soon as you see it. I'm terrified that someone will find out about me and at times I think that if that happens I won't be able to live, won't be able to look anyone in the face. In my most extreme fantasies I imagine the police knocking on my door and arresting me for treachery and deceit, and Hrafn standing in the witness box in the courtroom just like in an American film, pointing at me and saying, 'There she is, the woman who said she loved me. There she is. Take a good look at her, that's not a woman, that's inhumanity personified.'*

*But even though I'm scared it's like nothing can stop me any more, like it almost comforts me to think that Hrafn despises me, along with everyone else of course.*

*So it really wasn't sufficient for me to meet you in the morning as we usually do. I had to see you again. Just the thought that it would be a whole week until I saw you again made me feel like a torpedo was shooting up through my heart, so I told him I had to work late, that I had an interview to finish and still had to go to three places in connection with that and that he would have to finish off whatever still had to be done at home and I phoned you. Naturally I was petrified that he wouldn't believe me, even though there was no reason for it. Like you've so often tried to make me see, he doesn't know anything, but because I was scared I left messages everywhere to say I was coming. I'll sort that out tomorrow. My nerves were a bit on edge but I*

51

*hope it didn't affect you that evening. I didn't want you to be worried, so I thought it would be a good idea to go to the Loftleidir Hotel for a cocktail. Obviously I chose that bar because I didn't expect to meet anyone I knew there, and it's so out of the way and all that. But I really messed things up. You remember the lad who said hello to me, he's the photographer for the paper, and I could see what he was thinking from the sarcastic look he gave me. That's why I pulled out a piece of paper and pen, so he would think I was interviewing you. Then I felt so ashamed of not being able to let you know. I was so afraid you would think I was slighting you or that I felt ashamed of being with you. But you know that's not true. I love being with you and I wish I could be with you all the time, but I want us to meet where we can be alone. And where my heart isn't racing and my conscience nagging me. That's why from now on I want us to meet at your place, and to keep trips to other places for a bit later.*

*I know you understand.*

*Making love in the car afterwards was good, maybe better than it ever has been. I get such an extraordinary feeling when I think about us making love, such a special feeling. Each time we do it is the best. It was best of all in the car there and I've been thinking about it all Christmas. Thinking about it has been an escape from my life with Hrafn, although that isn't in fact any worse than it has been for the past five years. No worse except that it feels like just a half-life since I met you. It's just that my feelings have changed. And they can't be seen. Nothing else has changed. He hasn't changed at all. What we do together hasn't changed. We do everything in the same way as we always have done.*

*For example, when I got home that evening of the 23rd we had a cup of coffee together. He had finished wrapping up the Christmas presents. We drank our coffee slowly. This is always a good moment for us, and he didn't know that your smell was on my fingers (maybe that made the moment even better).*

*I really don't know what's become of me. I enjoyed talking to him about the article I hadn't done and lifting my fingers to my face to smell your aroma. At the same time I thought I was being disgusting.*

*So we drank our coffee and chatted about work and decorated the Christmas tree. I fell to thinking whether we would ever decorate a tree together, but I managed to ward off those thoughts. He put the lights on the tree and I did the decorations. Then we looked at the tree and kissed each other and said how pretty it was. I was aware of how fond I was of him and I told him so.*

*'I know,' he said, and then we went to bed.*

*Perhaps I shouldn't be telling you this, but you understand everything: we made passionate love that night. I thought I was on fire and about to burn up but I think it was also because I could smell your aroma on my skin. I imagined that he was you and that was no problem. Afterwards he said it had been lovely like he always does, and we went to sleep. Hrafn is a wonderful lover. He's considerate and sensitive. Our life together has always been good.*

*That night I dreamt that we were walking hand in hand naked along a white beach. It made me laugh when I woke up because the dream was just like a Danish Skagen painting, except that we had no clothes on. The beach was just the same. I so want us to be naked together on a beach. Just us two and a clear, starry sky.*

*Christmas Day was like it always is. We went to my parents, and my brothers were there with their wives and children. They cracked the same joke they always do when we're all together: 'When are you going to have a baby, Z? Are you going to devote yourself to the paper for ever?'*

*And Hrafn replied as he always does, 'I'm her baby, you ought to know that by now.'*

*The first time he said that I wasn't aware of the barb in his words.*

*And his pleading look didn't tire me like it used to.*

*I sat there and pretended to be following what was going on while I thought about you, about your breasts and how good it is to touch them, about your body and how excited you get when I touch you. My thoughts took me so far from the dinner table that my mother had to say something about it not being necessary to be quite so distracted on Christmas Eve.*

*'She's so dreamy, our Z is,' said Hrafn, stroking my hair, and I could feel he was hoping that I was dreaming about our baby. At times knowing him so well and us being so close upsets me.*

*I could never hurt him.*

*I don't ever want to hurt him.*

*We exchanged presents when we got home that night and then went to sleep, but before he closed his eyes he put his arms around me and said, 'If there's ever anything wrong, remember that you can always trust me.'*

*'I'm fine.'*

*'But remember even so,' he said, and I knew he was saying that because he needed to tell me he loved me and because I was so distant and didn't want to make love.*

*'I can't when I've eaten so much,' I said, putting my head on his shoulder.*

*I tried to go to sleep, but I couldn't.*

*I lay awake all night, thinking about you. Where you were, who you were with, whether there was a man sleeping by your side, whether you missed me, and I felt I couldn't wait until next Thursday.*

*It's Monday today.*

*And I miss you.*

*Z*

\*

I recall my happiness when I opened your letter.

I recall too how that happiness faded the further I read.

And I was puzzled why you should have written me a letter like that. I'm not any more.

I know now that your letters reflected that clean conscience of yours that it was so hard for you to break through.

I didn't know then that you had to clean up inside yourself.

I thought you were cold and lacking in judgement and that you would have done better to leave some things unsaid.

But I still read the letter again and again.

I understand it all now.

Your conscience captivated me at the same time as I felt it rise up against me.

It enchanted me like a black-and-white Russian film and threatened me because I could never understand it.

I can't do anything about the fact that when I look into the fire I see you and Hrafn making love and I can't help thinking that the years we were together you might have been much happier with him. Maybe you'll go back to him and make love the day before Christmas Eve, and forget me.

I hope you don't.

I hope so for your sake.

But I hope you'll forget the poem I wrote after getting your fourth letter.

'Always a poem,' you said when I gave it to you.

I can remember that the weather was rather like it is now, the snow startlingly bright, ice cracking here and there in the silence and tremendously cold. We were sitting with layers of clothes on by the fire, rubbing our fingers. We'd just lit the fire and we'd had to leave the car down by the road and walk up here.

Just like now.

Except that now it's colder, and you're not here.

'For every letter that you write me you get a poem,' I said.

'Neat.'

'So it's up to you how many poems there'll be.'

'I see,' you just said, as if you were afraid I would tell you more about what I wrote.

You needn't have been afraid.

I watched you read the poem.

You were beautiful in the firelight.

*

*On Monday, 1 February 1995, I met a woman in the Bíóbar. She was alone, getting on in years, and looked rather down, like people who sit drinking alone on Mondays usually do, with the remains of the weekend in their hair, their eyes red and a delicate tremble in their hands. I sat down beside her and asked if she wanted a beer. She said yes and a cheerful look spread immediately across her sad face. She told me about herself and tears kept coming to her eyes. For years she had loved her husband, always been faithful to him, just as he was to her, until one day he met another woman. A few months later he had gone and abandoned her. Their two children had left home too. She was in such terrible despair as she asked if I thought she would always be on her own. I told her she would be alone as long as she wanted to be and I felt I had lit a spark of hope in her breast.*

*I believe that you decide more for yourself in life than you realize.*

> *There's a huge river between us*
> *red, strange, and the current strong*
>
> *Yesterday i walked to the riverbank*
> *stood on a ledge and looked down*
> *i saw a bridge and thought i was dreaming*
>
> *rubbed my eyes*
> *but the bridge was still there*

*and suddenly i saw a clear line in the middle of the bridge*
*cleaving the red colour of the river*
*your face and mine were reflected in the line*
*between them stones of many colours*
*which we turned over one by one*
*telling each other what lay beneath*

*some things we couldn't understand*
*some things we didn't want to understand*
*some things separated us*

*so we ran away*
*and grew apart from each other*

*all at once i heard a whistling in the air*
*i looked up and saw that the clouds had gathered together*
*in the middle of the sky above the bridge and had built a tower*

*i couldn't see the top of the tower*
*you lay on the riverbank and looked up too*
*we saw yellow lights stream from the windows in the tower*
*and it was as if blindness had afflicted us*
*these lights were not for our eyes*

*we looked away*
*there were black cairns around us*
*mountains we couldn't climb*
*and tortuous old valleys with yellowing gravestones*
*we stood by the gravestones*
*and listened to the roaring torrent*
*'i can't see you because of the writing on the gravestones,' you said*
*'i can't see you either,' i replied*
*'Let's get out of here,' you said*

*but when we got up to the road*
*we still couldn't see each other*
*and it was then that we knew*
*we'd have to say goodbye*

*yesterday i walked to the river*
*and remembered having stood there*

*watching you turn a stone over*

*you smiled as you handed it to me*

*i still have it*

*and every time i touch it*
*i recall your love when it was best*

*your words when they were best*

*and your everything when it was best*

*i won't keep any other stone*

*There's a huge river between us*
*red, strange, and the current strong*

\*

The eggs have turned black and two of them shine in the fire.
   I throw our words over them.
   The fire swallows letter and poem.
   You must always be happy.
   You must always smile when you think of me.
   I stand up and walk several times around the room.
   I remember when we first came here.

You were romantic and beautiful and I was looking forward to getting to know you better, to being with you for two days in the sunshine and the warmth, to pouring water over myself and smoothing mud over you. I had decided to do it in the sunshine whenever we had the chance. And while you were unpacking the basket we always brought here in the summer I asked whether you minded if I went down to the lake.

'Of course I don't mind. You do what you like. I'll see to everything here.'

So I walked down to the lake and it reminded me of the lake in the children's story about Dimmalimm. There were reeds in some places around the edge, and it was still only June, and the ducks swimming in the middle of the lake didn't change direction when they saw me.

I took off my stockings and dress.

I took everything off and sat down by the lake.

I could feel the heat of the sun on my back, so I sprinkled water from the watering-can over myself until I started shivering and then I poured mud from the lakeside over my body. I smeared it over my face and neck, then stood up and decided to walk around the lake.

I heard your voice when you called me to come.

I didn't answer because I wanted you to come down to the lake.

And you did, and stood and waited while I walked round the lake.

'What have you done to yourself?' you asked.

'I've hidden myself in the earth,' I replied, going up to you and putting my arms around you and smiling as I felt you shiver. I put my hands under your jersey and felt your breasts with my muddy fingers, slipped my fingers down your trousers and touched the hair there and your breathing became faster. You took your clothes off and we lay down side by side on the grass and you began to lick my stomach, the mud tasted nice, all of us tasted nice.

'Haven't you ever made love with a woman before?' I asked.

'Can you sense that?'

'I didn't sense it, I knew.'

'Does it matter?'

'Not a bit.'

'Have you?'

'Yes.'

'But I thought you'd only slept with men. Haven't you slept with men?'

'Yes, but I gave it up a while ago.'

'I see.'

'Is Hrafn away?'

'Yes.'

'And is he going to be away while we're here?'

'Yes.'

'Do you never go with him?'

'I don't normally have time because of work,' you said then, but later on you told me you used always to go away with him until you met me. Until you began to feel such agonizing desire in your body when you thought about me. And so we lay there and nodded off. At least the sun had moved when I opened my eyes again and your breathing was regular. But you jumped up and said you were cold.

You were shy.

I can remember how beautifully shy you were.

I can remember how agitated and nervous you got when anything unexpected happened, and how much fun I got out of teasing you then. Those were the only times you didn't complain about my teasing you.

'She's only shy with you,' I said to Valgeir who had come over one day, as he sometimes did. I remember that day just over two years ago particularly well. It was the first and only time he came on a Thursday morning.

He knew I wanted to have those mornings on my own with you.

We were in bed when he came.

'I can understand that she's shy but I had to talk to you,' he said.

'I'll put the bedroom door to and then I can talk to you out here,' I said to him and to you I said that it was only Valgeir and that you needn't worry that my brother-in-law was going to rush straight off to the papers with the news of your supposed adultery. He was as silent as the grave. Then I kissed you, handed you a book by Somerset Maugham about some second-rate authors and told you it was

60

interesting, that you should have a look at it, and that I wouldn't be a minute.

But you were still anxious.

'Did he see I had nothing on?' you asked.

'No, actually he asked whether that fur coat you're wearing buttoned up to the neck and the fur hat on your head were from Feldinum,' I said, closing the door behind me.

I knew you'd get over it.

'Arnthrúdur's in a terrible state,' said Valgeir when I sat down in the kitchen with him.

'Now, this morning? Didn't she go to work?'

'No, she didn't go to work because I didn't come home until six. I was at a friend's house. There's a group of us from school who always meet up in September. We've been doing it for years, it's just a bit of fun, and we always stay for hours. But she couldn't sleep, said she had wandered around the flat because I didn't phone, then had got up about two and driven past this friend's house and hadn't seen my car or any lights in the windows. But it's so simple. I was with the guys downstairs watching television, and had parked my car in the next street because I couldn't find any other space. Then she'd got out of the car and looked through the windows and naturally hadn't seen anyone. And that was that. I can't make her see sense. She just cries.'

'Were you there?' I asked.

I had to ask him and I knew I would be able to believe what he said.

We were friends and trusted each other.

'You know I never lie, but please, for me, go and talk to her and pretend you just called in because you saw her car outside. I have to go and teach, but I can't stand the thought of her sitting there alone, making a mountain out of a molehill.'

'Go home and be nice to her, skip one class, the world won't come to an end. I'll be round in an hour, I can't get away any sooner, you know why,' I said, and he did as I suggested.

My sister who was full of mistrust.

My sister who didn't love herself.

61

'What do you think jealousy is?' I asked you as I lay down beside you again after he had gone. You were engrossed in the book and it was nice to see you reading. I thought you didn't read enough but I admired how well you remembered what you did read.

'I had my fill of novels at university,' you told me once.

'What's jealousy?' you answered. 'I suppose it's the most passionate expression of love.' You were more familiar with this expression of love than anyone I had ever been out with.

You were intimately acquainted with jealousy.

'And why do you think people become jealous?'

'Anna, my dear, you don't have to make fun of me.'

'I'm not, I mean it.'

'And am I supposed to answer and mean it?'

'Yes.'

'People become jealous because they lack trust.'

'Who don't they trust?' I asked, and you looked at me with those big eyes of yours and it hurt to see the pain and the desire for escape in them. It hurt to watch you feeling guilty but knowing you couldn't do anything about it. Sometimes I thought that you knew that it wasn't your pitiless self that controlled you but rather some mysterious power that had taken over your emotions.

'Do you remember, Z, the first time we went to the cottage?' I said, gently because I wanted to take the pain away. 'We made love by the lake, then went in and had coffee. Do you remember what we talked about?'

'No, wasn't it something to do with me and Hrafn?'

'Yes, and about jealousy and you said you were never jealous. Were you lying to me then?'

'No, I wasn't lying. I wasn't jealous then.'

*

It makes me smile to think about your first attack of jealousy and the sadness that followed and how I tried to comfort you after you'd broken the black statue my sister Arnthrúdur gave me, cut up the

62

painting my mother gave me when I was little and broken the mirror in the hall.

You were stark raving mad.

I remember looking at you and my legs felt paralysed.

I remember looking at you and praying that God would shift time.

I remember you running away from me crying and me getting a letter from you in the evening.

That was in March 1995 and I gave you the poems in August.

I throw them over two other eggs which glow on the fire.

They crackle and I'm hot.

Your voice is with me.

*

*My own Anna,*

*I want to ask you to forgive me. I can't keep myself under control, sometimes it's like I don't know what I'm doing, everything goes black and then there's an explosion. You didn't deserve anything of that, not what I said and even less so what I did. You must forgive me. It happened because you weren't at home that night and I didn't know where you were. I sneaked off to phone you as soon as Hrafn was asleep, just to hear your voice, not to say anything in particular. But you didn't answer. For the first time it felt like I was in a cage, I couldn't sleep, so I stayed awake all night and phoned now and then. I know it's because of me that we have this arrangement, because of me that we meet so seldom, because of my domestic circumstances and of course you can have all the freedom you want, go where you want and all that, but this is the first time I haven't been able to get hold of you, and I didn't know how to cope with it. I didn't know how to lick my feelings into shape. I imagined you with some man, your hands touching his body, your tongue in his mouth and you laughing and gasping in his arms.*

*I know I shouldn't think like this, that thoughts like these lie somewhere in between insolence and craziness, but this is what has become of me, this is what insecurity has done to me. That insecurity I always bring upon myself. I don't want to change anything, I know that well enough, I feel I can't change anything, I feel I don't have a good enough reason to leave Hrafn. I love him in my own way, the sense of security he gives me, and the memories we share and all the time together. I respect him as well, and he's my friend. But it's still you that I long for all the time and always more and more. I don't know how it will end. I was upset all night, smoked like a chimney until Hrafn came out and asked me what the matter was. I couldn't answer but just to say something, I said that I'd had an argument at work. That I just had to get it out of my system, there was nothing else I could do, but that he didn't have to worry. I despise myself when I lie to him and I despise myself when he believes me, which he did then just like he always does. So he went back to bed and said I should come in a few minutes, that there was no point sitting there smoking endlessly, it wouldn't change anything. But I couldn't do as he asked because I had to go on phoning you.*

*But you didn't answer.*

*Anna, you didn't answer all night!*

*And you didn't answer me either when I asked where you had been. You pretended you hadn't heard me ask. Of course you don't have to answer me, you're under no obligation to think about me, I can't make such a demand. But however things turn out I promise that that will never happen again. That you can count on.*

*Your Z*

*

Your promises repeated in a different way and in the same way.

They were always blown away by the wind.

Blown away until less than two years ago.

When I told you I was ill.

I couldn't keep it a secret any longer, I didn't want to tell you, I thought I knew how you would react but I couldn't keep you scared endlessly. It hurt when I looked into your eyes and saw the suffering reflected in them, that unfounded suffering springing from other people's love, hands, caresses and passion.

You didn't know that I had no more to give than what I gave you.

I had no more even if I had wanted to.

\*

And I have no more to give than what I give you now.

I read the poem slowly.

The wind ought to whistle through the rafters but it doesn't.

The snow ought to tip down but it doesn't.

My eyes ought to be full of tears but they're not.

But I hope you can hear me over there where you're sitting waiting for the night to come to an end. I know it will come to an end and in the end everything will continue as usual and new days will sneak up on you. One after the other they'll sneak up on you and surprise you until eventually you choose a new path for your life and our walk will be a memory.

I take a pill and by the time I've read the poem it's started to take effect.

I'm calm and there's quietness all around.

\*

*On Monday, 7 August 1995, I met an old man in Selfoss. We were both eating ice-cream in the Café Skáli when he spoke to me and asked if I thought autumn was on its way. I said I didn't think so. He said that was obviously because I was so*

*young, because he could see the autumn everywhere. He said*
*that the previous week he had also felt that terrible fear that*
*must grip everyone who has to say goodbye to his family and*
*go off on the journey whose end nobody has managed to deter-*
*mine, if it was a journey at all, if it wasn't just desolation and*
*emptiness. And now he had to face that the moment had come*
*to say goodbye and he wanted to cry.*

*I told him to cry, and he did.*


> *When the lights grow dim*
> *and dusk lies over our memories*
> *i'll remember you, old friend*
> *where you stand in the newly mown field*
> *the sea lapping before you*
> *the sun directly above*
> *and the sky dotted with clouds*
>
> *when the lights grow dim*
> *autumn reaches its resting place*
>
> *perhaps we'll meet*
> *berry-picking*


*

My pills have a strange effect, not always the same.

I found that out early on.

I find it best to take them in the evening, or perhaps I should say that I've found that for the last few months. The dose has been increased and recently I've been having injections too so I sleep a lot of the time. I don't always like having to sleep a lot.

I'm a night owl and I like hooting best in the evening.

But even the birds of the night know their visiting time.

'Morphine will lengthen the time you have, Anna,' the doctor said more than a year ago after he had made the decision to stop treatment.

The treatment had stopped working and had made things so difficult for me.

I knew that's what he would decide.

'Do you mean it'll postpone things?' I asked, wanting him to talk plainly and openly.

It suited me to talk frankly about things.

I found it better even though I was wildly angry with the truth.

'I mean it'll give you more time and better time, it'll kill the pain, at least for the time being. I can't guarantee you a postponement.'

'I was only asking, I want to know for certain,' I said, but I found him rather cold. I hadn't meant to be snide. I didn't find it funny at all but maybe I sensed a coldness which didn't exist.

I was exceptionally sensitive that day.

I knew it was the beginning of the end.

'Take the pills when you feel pain, don't make yourself suffer unnecessarily.'

I thanked him and left.

I wanted to scream but I didn't.

I was scared but I didn't want to be.

And then my time began running out.

To begin with the pills just made me feel happy, except for the first twenty minutes when I felt sick, but after that they took effect and it felt good. I felt positive when the pain disappeared, felt I could cope with the whole world, felt at least that I wasn't ill, that I didn't have to pretend to be well, because I was well and it was great. But what I didn't realize, until it actually happened, was that people found me difficult to take.

I should have known.

People always form some opinion and they're also quick to come to conclusions.

It was about midday on a Tuesday, in the middle of December 1996, and I decided to drive down to town, park opposite the supermarket on Laugavegur and go for a bit of a walk. I hadn't got far when I met three women I had known at school. They looked happy and

cheerful but speeded up visibly when they saw me. I didn't understand why because they didn't usually avoid me. I knew them well so,
thinking I might just have imagined it, I went up to them.

'Hello, girls, are you in a hurry?'

'You could say so,' one of them said.

'What's new?' I asked.

'Nothing special,' said another.

'What about you?' said the third.

'Just fine,' I replied.

'Doesn't look like it,' said the first one.

'It's only lunchtime, Anna,' said the second.

'You should go home,' said the third.

Astonished, I said goodbye and, as I walked back to my car, I heard
them muttering to each other. I really didn't understand what was
going on and didn't connect their reactions with my pills.

Sometimes I am awfully slow on the uptake.

I got in the car and drove home, and thought I must check whether
there was something wrong with my face, whether I looked different
in some way. As I walked along the street from the car, my friend from
the first floor ran over to me and took hold of my arms.

'Under the influence at lunchtime, dearie?'

'Under the influence?'

'You're not steady on your feet. Take my arm.'

'Give me your arm then, seeing as I'm so unsteady.'

And he helped me in and offered to sit with me for a while until I
felt better. Idiot that I am, I still hadn't cottoned on to the fact that I
was sometimes unsteady on my feet for a short time after I'd taken the
pills. I lost my sense of balance without realizing it myself, lost the
straight line if you like and walked crooked, careered off even in the
wrong direction. After that incident I was careful and didn't set foot
out of the house for an hour after taking my pills. It all fitted together
like a jigsaw.

'So there you are driving about blind drunk,' said my friend.
'Perhaps I could offer you a top-up, my lovely, I was just going to have
a drop myself.'

'Yes, do,' I said. He went off to fetch the bottle and by the time he came back I was sitting at the table smiling.

My smile has always worked well on most people, if not on you.

'You're quite different.'

'Like a newly minted coin.'

'You're sobering up very quickly.'

'I was pulling your leg.'

'Is that so? Women can always play tricks on me.'

And we sat drinking until after lunch.

And he told me about the women who had twisted him round their little fingers and pulled his leg and his arm and his finger and his thumb and his toe and his tooth. And the extraordinary thing was that he loved them all. He loved women so terribly.

'I do too,' I said.

At that he laughed till the cave walls shook, as he put it.

I laughed as well, and when I was leaving he gave me some new cream for my thighs – he had just become the Icelandic agent for it. I was to tell him what it was like in a week or so. He said he put great store by what I said and what my friends said. I was to massage my girlfriend with the cream too, it would do her good, her being so pale at the moment. So I phoned you and said I had a little something I wanted to give you, a little surprise, I was at home and were you in the mood to pop round.

'Always,' you said, and you came.

And that evening I massaged you with the cream and you stayed the night with me.

Even though it wasn't a Thursday.

You stayed with me because I wanted you to.

*

You're not here with me now.

You're not here with me now because I don't want you to be.

I throw the poem on to the fire and it disappears.

# 4

*Arnthrúdur: 'I'm going to try to concentrate and keep quiet.'*

We all feel better when she recites the poem a second time.

All the insecurity has left me.

All the jealousy hopefully nothing but a memory.

And it pleases me to watch Valgeir and see how he is watching her.

Actually it always pleases me to watch him when I feel secure. And I am secure about him here.

I contemplate him and see how he swallows the tale about the woman who gave more than she received and I can feel his amazement at how well she recites the poem. My story about the people in the house doesn't seem to put her off at all, since she never hesitates, never hits the wrong note. It's as if she becomes one with the words and disappears from view and in some bizarre way we become one with her and with what she stresses. She reminds me of Anna, not what she looks like because they're not alike, but her bearing, the sway of her hips and the movements of her hands while she's reciting the text and her voice.

It's like her voice changes too.

And without asking for it I hear Anna's voice coming through: 'I sway my hips when I stand still so that people don't see that I'm in pain. It's better if I move about even if it's just a sway sway sway. Believe me I'm sorry I didn't figure it out before I got ill that moving about like that can hide almost anything, a state of mind just as much as a pain.'

I don't think about that any more.

I want to talk to them about the poem.

I always want to talk about things I don't understand.

And this time I give in to it.

'I don't quite understand how you're supposed to take a poem which claims to have been written because of a certain incident, when you're acquainted with the circumstances and know better. You know there's no truth in it, that it's all a lie from beginning to end, and so what are the notes for?' I ask.

My observation isn't well received.

Neither of them seems to be interested in what I'm saying.

'Perhaps that's not what matters most, the thing about truth. Maybe what matters is how it all fits together, how it clicks into place and forms a whole. Not everyone knows Anna as well as you do, so what you call a lie other people don't see as being untrue because they have no idea about the real truth,' she says quietly.

I know that.

Does the woman think I'm a fool?

But truth is still truth regardless of what people know.

I don't reply, just stare wearily in front of me.

'Perhaps she moved this girlfriend of hers up a house or two,' says Valgeir, laughing quietly.

He evidently finds me amusing.

He obviously finds my remark stupid.

I hate it when he laughs at me and my ideas.

He laughs at me in order to agree with what she thinks.

'You're very compatible,' I say.

I can feel Valgeir deciding to change the subject.

I know he wants to make amends.

'And did you learn all her poems like that, Z?' he asks.

'Yes, like I said, it made me feel closer to her,' she answers.

'You said something about you having been ready to make a change but then she didn't want to change anything. Did you want to change everything when she told you about the illness?' he asks, adding that it wouldn't have been like Anna to agree to that. He said he hadn't met many people who were prouder than her and that at times he had felt her pride bordered on stubbornness.

71

'I knew nothing about her illness when I decided that I wanted to change my life and that I would have to do so. I had no idea about her illness. Naturally you can say that I should have seen various signs, but I just didn't. Anna was always happy and cheerful with me. But it was on New Year's Eve 1995 that I realized eventually that my life was going to have to change. And I let her know straight away. She didn't tell me about her illness until January the next year. When she was forced to. I could still have guessed that something was wrong, like I just said, just from the poems but I never read them really properly until after she told me she didn't want to change things, after the news, or the situation, as she herself always called her illness. I felt all the time that she didn't want to talk to me about these poems, and, to tell the truth, I was sort of jealous of them. I resented them for some reason. They got on my nerves. She must have talked about them to other people whose opinion she respected more than mine. She must have sat somewhere with more sophisticated people than me and talked to them about poetry like I talked to my colleagues about politics. It's my subject. Anna and I rarely talked about politics. I think I always regretted not taking part in her world, regretted what I didn't even want until it was too late,' she says, first rather hesitantly and slowly, then faster as she gets into her stride, and, although there's no whining edge to her voice, her unhappiness is evident.

I realize that this is no cry-baby but a woman of strong character.

She's sensitive and I can see that Valgeir is moved by her words. It's obvious from how he's looking at her, from the small movements around his mouth and from how dilated his pupils are becoming.

I want to know what he's thinking.

I'm beside myself sometimes if I don't know what he's thinking.

I can feel the jealousy flaring up again but I manage to stave it off.

I'm sure there's no reason for it.

She goes on talking but my mind is wandering. I try to keep it under control.

I try to think about what she's saying,
    try to think about Anna,
    about her illness,

about where she is and whether we'll have any news soon.

I want to stay here but I can't manage to.

I still can't control my thoughts, which are speeding over plains and mountains. Valgeir and I are at the centre of my thoughts and if Anna comes into them at all then it's not on her own account but on account of something she's told me about him for some reason.

I know that my egoism is boundless.

Anna would never behave like this.

She isn't an egoist.

She would never sit and think about herself if I was dreadfully ill and had gone missing.

She would think about me.

And, what's more, she always came when I needed her.

It happened so many times.

So many memorable times.

*

'I felt in my bones that you weren't all right,' she said as I opened the door, 'so I decided to drive past and when I saw the car outside I knew there was something up. Why are you at home today, are you ill or something?'

This was one Thursday lunchtime ages ago.

Valgeir told me afterwards that he had asked her to help.

He'd gone to her because he was at his wit's end.

'No, I may not be ill but I'm dead tired,' I replied nonchalantly, determined not to tell her anything. 'I didn't sleep a wink last night.'

I wanted to fight my own personal humiliation by myself.

I wanted to keep her out of the wretchedness.

'It's not like you to be so tired. Did you have a nightmare?' she asked cautiously, and I could see that she knew that if I had had a nightmare then Valgeir would have had some part in it.

Most of my dreams were about him.

In fact all of my dreams were about him.

'Arnthrúdur, you have to be able to work,' she said kindly.

But there was more significance in her words than I cared to hear.

She knew that I knew.

'It's an exception if I don't go to work.'

'I know, but it's not good for you to stay at home feeling bad. You lose your grip on yourself.'

I didn't want her to talk about me like a case history, so I replied and tried to be both supercilious and brusque.

'What do you mean?'

So she came straight to the point.

'Where was Valgeir last night?'

'What's he got to do with it?'

'Was he at home?'

'No, he went out with his friends.'

'And was that why you couldn't sleep?'

She knew the answer but she still asked.

She wanted me to think I was taking the initiative.

'Maybe, I don't know. I have trouble sleeping when he's not here, you know that, you know it as well as he does.'

And of course she took his side.

Anna always tried to make little of things in order to get things back in perspective.

'But he goes out so rarely that it shouldn't matter to you if it happens occasionally. You can count the times he's been out on his own since you started living together on the fingers of one hand. You mustn't stifle him altogether, he must have some room to breathe.'

I knew she understood me but felt that she had to say that.

'It's not my fault I couldn't sleep,' I said, and immediately felt ashamed of myself. I didn't want to discuss with her what I ought to be like, what I could change about myself, how I could improve myself, whether I should see a psychologist, just a few sessions, to tidy things up, she had found it helpful during her illness, it had done her good, surely it would benefit me.

I couldn't stand these suggestions.

I knew of far too many psychologists who confused people rather than helped them. The one that my secretary went to comes to mind.

To begin with, things went well. She took his advice, she was manic, poor girl, but the psychologist went and showed up drunk one day, acted strangely and pestered her, even behaved improperly. She could have gone to the police but she didn't. No, the people who claim to be able to helping others aren't always the right type to do so.

'I mean you should go to someone who comes recommended, not go and see that lunatic. Psychologists aren't all the same any more than other people are, are they?' Anna said.

I could see she had abandoned the subject for the time being. She put her head on one side and gave me a serious look and said, as if once and for all, 'Arnthrúdur, you need help. God knows but you need help.'

I can hear Z's and Valgeir's voices murmuring through my deliberations.

I stop thinking about that, brake, imagine I'm driving a car,

 that Anna is in the passenger seat,

 that she takes my hand and asks me to slow down.

She was often scared when I drove.

And I start to relax, put my foot gently on the brake until the imaginary car stops. I look at Anna, smile and there I am, in their conversation.

They're still discussing her poem.

And Valgeir is still amazed how sharp she is and how wonderful her memory is.

I don't recall him ever being amazed by how intelligent I am.

Or how quick I am to make decisions.

Perhaps he doesn't value me truly.

Perhaps he never will.

*

'Whether it's difficult to learn such a long passage? I don't know that it's so long, the poems differ in length, but I've had enough time. Actually I've had much too much time.'

Then she's silent and stares thoughtfully into space before continuing.

Neither of us says anything. We sit in silence and wait.

'And it was so strange that after I'd separated from Hrafn, my husband, or rather after he had moved out and I was on my own, it somehow transpired that the days I didn't see Anna I was completely alone.'

It's as if what she's saying comes as a surprise to her.

Her pupils dilate and she becomes agitated.

'Of course I was working as usual on the paper but I cut myself off from my friends and even stopped seeing my family, except my mother now and then when I felt I had to, and I didn't go out at all except on the few occasions I went out with Anna.'

It seems as if she's speaking about this for the first time.

As if she's never realized it before.

And you can tell from her voice that she's annoyed.

'Of course it was really fun to go out with Anna. But I was always thinking about the fact that she was ill, keeping an eye on her, making sure she didn't do too much or do something that would be bad for her. I was always afraid that she wouldn't look after herself well enough. But like I said I had such a lot of spare time for waiting and for myself. And in an attack of loneliness the idea of learning her poems came to me. In the old days I had always found it easy to learn poems, rhyming poems of course, and I've got a good memory for anything written down. I read slowly but I remember what I read. Anna used to say that I didn't read enough but in those days I just didn't have time. That was when I was married to Hrafn and going out with her at the same time. All my spare time went on them. I used to read a lot and I read a lot now. But she doesn't know. I don't want her to think I'm doing it for her. I don't want her to think I'm changing my ways for her, she wouldn't want that, she couldn't stand that, I don't think.

'"I don't want you to change anything about yourself, Z," she said the day she told me about her illness.

'No, I know it sounds as if I've dedicated my life to her and maybe that's the way it is, maybe everything will reverse itself, except that she would never dedicate herself to anything, she isn't like that, except maybe to these poems. Though I know she wasn't satisfied with them. I saw that sometimes from the expression on her face when she gave me them. I like some of them more than others. Some, I think, are pretty good, but I don't know, maybe I only think they're good because they belong to me. I'm a selfish person,' she says, taking a deep breath. She's been talking fast, quietly and fast, and I can see when she stops that she regrets having said so much. She obviously isn't used to it.

She looks apologetically between the two of us and says, 'Sorry if I've been going on a bit, I don't usually.'

'Can we get you to recite another poem?' I ask, without replying to her apology. There's no need to.

We have no need to forgive her.

That's not our business.

'Do, it'll make the waiting seem shorter,' says Valgeir. 'I'm sure they'll be in touch soon. I keep hoping inspiration will strike, but it hasn't yet. We'll just have to keep calm and kill time while we wait.'

'I'll recite the poem she gave me in September 1995. I didn't find it interesting then but now I like it because I understand it. I can see myself in it and I like that sort of text best. I'm a simple person and a simple reader.'

Looking at her I know she's not simple.

I can see that Valgeir is thinking the same.

*

*On Monday, 4 September 1995 I lost the friend I had lived with for a long time, whom I in fact once loved. I started out on a search for him to appease my sense of loss but I didn't find him because he had set off on the long journey more than a year previously. A sense of futility enveloped me and for the first time I found myself doubting whether there was any purpose in life.*

*If i had awoken and decided to write this poem*
*it would have been about an ordinary evening*
*yet misgiving would have lain concealed in it*
*like in your poem which is no longer*
*on the board above my table*

*if i had awoken*
*you would have been with me,*
*would have put your arms around me and whispered*
*that i needn't be afraid*
*you and love would always be there*

*but that didn't happen*
*i did open my eyes*
*and it was a bright morning*

*but i never awoke*

\*

'I remember at the time wanting to talk to Anna about that poem but not doing so. Rather it wasn't the poem that I wanted to talk about, I didn't understand it by itself, it was the context that I was curious about. I wanted to know who this man was who she loved, if he had existed at all, seeing as it's fiction and all that. But I didn't ask, I didn't want to be so prosaic, I was bad enough as it was,' she says thoughtfully.

I understand how she feels and I agree with her about the poem.

I don't understand thoughts of futility and I always try to keep them at bay.

'Poor Anna,' I say, though. 'That was a tough time for her.'

'Why didn't she talk to me about it? I don't understand that,' she says in an annoyed tone.

'She gave you the poem, Z,' replies Valgeir drily. Her remark obviously irritates him.

78

'You're right, how silly of me,' she says.

'Of course she didn't want to talk to you about what happened, at that time she didn't want to talk to you about anything unpleasant, she just wanted to have a beautiful time with you and to keep you away from any unpleasantness,' I tell her, remembering still the conversation we had after she learned of Thórdur's death.

*

'It's all so strange, Arnthrúdur,' she said, her voice shaking. 'It all seems so upside-down, so unfair and idiotic.'

'Perhaps that's not the right way to describe it,' I said, shocked because it was a long time since I had seen her so hopeless.

Her face was grey and there were black circles under her eyes.

'How should I describe it then? What do words matter in this sort of context, if there is any context at all, if anything matters anyway in this world?'

'You mustn't think like that.'

'I can't take this. I got this idea, to get in touch with Thórdur, and you know what I'm like when I get one of my sudden ideas, especially recently, I have to do something straight away. So I decided to look him up. I was sure he was in the country and I wanted so uncontrollably to see him and spend some time with him even though it's ages since we last met. I knew he always wanted to meet me, he used to say that, even when he was going out with someone else. Our relationship was so special. Anyway, I phone directory enquiries and find out where he's living and decide to send him a telegram, but it gets sent straight back with a message to the effect that there's nobody of that name living there. OK, so I pluck up my courage and ring his mother. That was tough, because she never liked me, said I was just using him, didn't know how he felt, only thought about myself, came and went as I pleased and never kept my word.

'She was pretty keen on passing judgement on other people and he was an only child.

'So much for that.

79

'She answers the phone and when I give my name and ask whether she can tell me where he is, say that I need to get hold of him, she replies in her dry manner, like she always did, except that now I can hear a sort of resignation in her voice:

'Anna, are you still phoning him?'

'I need very much to speak to him.'

'It's too late.'

'It's just this one particular matter I need to speak to him about,' I say, not suspecting anything, and anyway I was prepared for some ill-will on her part. I reckoned that she meant he was married or had moved abroad or something.

'He died last August,' she says, and puts the phone down.

'I sit there for a long time, staring into space, paralysed is the wrong word, bloodless rather. I can't move my fingers or my neck, my head is like a lump of steel on a stick and my feet are made of wax.

'For a while I'm so dazed that my mind is void of thoughts, then I come round and decide to go and visit her. I rush out and probably get out to Árbaer in record time. She opens the door and lets me in the moment I ring the bell as though she's been waiting for me, and I'm suddenly aware of how old she is. And my whole body feels her sorrow and I can't help it, I start crying right there in the hall. She puts her arms around me, that's something I thought I would never experience, and leads me over to the sofa, sits me down, pats my knee, goes into the kitchen, comes back with a cup of tea and sits down opposite me. Her voice is kind as she tells me she didn't know how fond I was of him. She says that I mustn't feel bad about it, at least about not knowing, because the funeral had been private, nobody had been there except the two of them and his sisters. He had taken his own life, one day he had just given up and nobody knew why, nobody at all, and that was maybe the worst thing, to know nothing and be left alone.

'It had such an effect on me, Arnthrúdur. All of a sudden I wanted to go to him and be with him. I was filled with regret that we had ever decided to break up.

'It was a good, trouble-free time that we had together.

'We agreed about most things and everything we had was beautiful and cheerful.'

'You were both only about twenty,' I said gently, 'and much too alike, both a bit crazy, more like brother and sister, like you said yourself.' I felt she had calmed down when she went off at a tangent, as she so often did in any circumstances.

'Brothers and sisters play best together. Everything else is just an approximation of that.'

'You should tell your girlfriend that, Anna.'

'Our time is spent on other things, it's too precious to be spent on sorrow,' she said, standing up to say goodbye.

When Anna wasn't feeling well she could never sit still.

She became restless and edgy and had to walk about.

*

'She just wanted you to have something beautiful together, Z,' I repeated. 'She didn't ever want to wreck the time you two had. But I can tell you, seeing as you want to know, that Thórdur was probably her first love. Actually I always thought they were more like friends, and she said herself there wasn't much passion between them, but she took it very badly that he took his own life. She even tried something similar, went down to the sea, out by the lighthouse I think, and was going to wade out, but she met some people there and managed to pull herself together.'

For Anna it's out of character not to face up to facts.

That's the only occasion I know of when she nearly cracked.

'I got a poem about that too, I can see that now, incredibly long and confusing. It took me a long time to learn it but a lot of it is really beautiful,' she says, knitting her brows. I think it's hard for her to accept that Anna had a secret from her and she finds it unjust that she alone decides what their relationship can stand.

That's what I can imagine but I don't know for certain.

I can see from the look on Valgeir's face that he's thinking the same.

81

We don't need to ask her to recite the poem.

She does so unbidden and, despite being visibly annoyed, her annoyance becomes indiscernible as she lets herself sink down into the world of Anna's poetry.

Everything falls away from her and there's suspense and reconciliation in her voice.

Valgeir looks at me and we both breathe a sigh of relief.

*

*On Monday, 26 October 1995, I was in mortal danger.*

*It was my own fault I got into danger, but fortunately I escaped unharmed along with my continuing life. When I contemplate how I was feeling that evening I have doubts as to whether I'm remembering right. Futility destroys every shred of common sense and clouds everything in fog. Indeed some people would term my experience madness. Perhaps they're right.*

*Perhaps the only true madness is made up of futility and the death-wish.*

*If it was evening i would be sitting by your side my friend*
*reading you a poem about love*

*in the background you'd see a picture of wild nature*
*terrific winds and crashing breakers*

*exactly*

*the breakers would lash on the pebbles*
*where i would be standing alone in outlandish thought*
*thinking about the bones the waves would wash ashore*
*i'm sure my head would be bowed too*

82

and because i had been considering so grimly
the purpose of my life
i would have made a hole in my coat pocket with my finger

and of course

somebody above me would be humming
that intricate song about eternity
as i would jerk my leg up
and the grey waves
would splash up my shin

doubtless
i would waste some adjectives on my legs
maybe my shins would be long
my thighs short and my toes blue
because i'd taken my socks off

and so
when i,
my mind full of grief,
would take one step
i would hear a whisper close by
'Can't you feel how cold my feet are?'

and i would jump
i'd jump out of my skin
which everyone jumps in
and start thinking about language
and the poems i perhaps still had to compose
and it would worry me deeply
that in the poem i wouldn't be able to jump
at this tragic moment
even if i had a shock
because it's such often-repeated nonsense

*so completely misused*
*that it loses its meaning when it happens to you*
*but then i'd be calm*
*on account of the poem*
*because poetry would be the last thing i would think about*
*while i was wading out*
*and the breakers crashing so fiercely on the stones*
*and old eternity grinning in the sky*

*no, i wouldn't think about poetry*

*instead i would begin to consider*
*whether i had done the right thing*
*all the time*
*but i would kick that thought out at once*
*i'd tell it to go and plague someone else*
*that it didn't belong in my head*
*i would quite realize*
*that i had just muddled along OK*
*otherwise i wouldn't be standing here*
*unable to swim a stroke but still taking one step*
*and feeling hellishly cold*

*amazing what thoughts go through your head on beaches*

*and then i would remember in the midst of all this misery*
*that if i was sitting by your side reading you a poem my friend*
*it would surely be a poem about love*

*and so i would take three steps back and then four more*
*and sit down on a stone and rub my foot*
*which would be purple just like Sigurlina's hands*
*wasn't it them that reminded us of preserved meat*
*or something pickled*
*and then i would put my woolly socks on*

*and when I had put them on*

*an old couple would probably come up to me*
*sit down by my side and ask what i was doing*
*i would say i had just been doing up my shoelaces*
*that i'd been paddling*
*then they'd say that was exactly*
*what they thought i'd been doing*
*and i would think them so shrewd about the world and me*
*who never understood each other*
*that i would ask them what poem they would read you this*
*evening*
*and of course they'd say they would choose a poem about love*
*that they had had read to them years ago*
*and i would ask what poem that had been*
*and they wouldn't be able to remember exactly*
*but it had been something about*
*spirits loving each other*
*and those words had appealed especially to them*
*on the spot i would leave it up to them*
*whether i shouldn't just read you this poem*
*and it would be a relief that they wouldn't know of anything*
*better*
*on the subject*
*at least i shouldn't try to improve on it*

*i had my shoes on now*
*and i must say i was determined to read this*
*poem for you but then suddenly i began to be afraid that*
*you knew*
*that it wasn't by me nor about us*
*and i waded out again*
*the waves were hot*
*now everything was ready*
*i took another step*

*if it was evening*
*i'd be sitting by your side reading you a poem my friend*

*and it would surely be about love*
*the breakers, the wind and eternity*
*rather formal*
*a little too sincere*
*and definitely in an*
*old-fashioned style*

*but i'm not by your side*
*and won't be until winter comes*

\*

'It's incredible how you can remember that,' I say, having nearly lost the thread of it twice. Still, time passed and it never passes so slowly as when one's waiting. But somewhere around the middle of the poem I suddenly fell to thinking about the cottage and thought it was strange that she hadn't spoken of it to us nor to the policeman.

There must be some reasonable explanation.

I thought I would mention it straight away.

'What about the cottage? You often go there, you haven't stopped, have you?' I ask in rather a loud voice. It doesn't escape me that she blushes.

As far as we're concerned she doesn't need to blush.

They needed somewhere to go and we understand that.

We always have done.

'She's not there, the road's blocked by snow,' she says. 'We tried to get there four days ago, before she went into hospital, but there was no way we could drive along the track. She's not there and, between you and me, I didn't want to mention the cottage to the policeman. It's all we've got. The only thing that's ours. The only thing we've got together. We don't want any outsiders there,' and she emphasizes every word she says.

It's important to her.

And we respect that.

'It's a lovely cottage,' says Valgeir.

'How do you know?' I ask. 'Have you been there?'

'I used to drive up there sometimes with Anna. We went the last time the road was open. It's beautiful around there, in the winter as well. You could almost say it's warm there even when it's cold, the countryside is so beautiful.'

I make up my mind not to say anything.

I make up my mind to suppress the thought.

What are they doing going off there together?

I lean back in the sofa, take a deep breath and listen.

I'm going to keep myself in check.

Without a doubt this visit is testing everyone's patience to the limit.

'I knew you sometimes went there together but I didn't know why,' she says. 'I never asked her, I didn't think she wanted to talk about it, there was so much she didn't want to talk about with me.' Her voice isn't accusatory but I can feel she lacks security.

Why does she know so little about where Anna went?

What sort of relationship do they have anyway?

'Anna likes driving about the place, or rather she likes sitting in the front and being driven about. She actually told me once that it was one of the things she enjoyed doing most. So I often invite her out for a drive on a Friday, because teaching is over early then, and she feels there's just enough time to drive up there. It only takes just under two hours to drive up into Svínadalur. I don't drive fast. We often stop on the way too, especially recently, and go for a walk and that's really the main reason why we go. She says I'm a good coach. As you know, the drugs have made her joints stiff. I know some good outdoor exercises for stiffness. But I haven't told anyone about these expeditions of ours, she asked me not to and said she didn't want anyone to know about her training, her attempts at becoming more supple. It could be that it hurt her pride, which she has rather a lot of. But whatever the reason, I promised her I would keep quiet. It didn't matter to me, I just enjoyed helping her.

'Just think, Valgeir,' she used to say sometimes, 'if there was a miracle and I could run like before, surprise Z one day by running over to her. I want it so much to happen, and that's why I want you to keep quiet about it.'

Valgeir's rather embarrassed as he relates this.

He speaks slowly and stops and starts again twice.

It's important to him that we both believe that he keeps his promises to people.

And he explains himself well.

I feel he has nothing to hide.

I know the slight movements of his body when there are white lies around.

'Did you go to the lake?' she asks, and she doesn't appear to doubt what he's saying.

'That was her favourite place. We often sat there for a few minutes, talking. It was there, there by the lake, that she told me about her dreams. Those strange dreams she used to dream after she had started on the drugs, but then of course she told you about them.'

'No, she didn't,' she said, resignedly.

'Do you remember whether she's written anything about dreams?'

'No, she hasn't, although a lot of her poems are rather dreamlike, but that's just Anna, everything about her is dreamlike.'

I can see that saying that makes her feel good.

She feels she's taking more of a part in her life.

She wants to ask about these dreams but she doesn't.

I ask for her, so that she'll feel better.

It calms me down too.

'What dreams were those?' I ask.

Valgeir looks thoughtfully at me.

I can see that he knows I don't mistrust him any longer.

He's confident as he says, 'It might have been different versions of the same dream. It was as if she was always half awake when she had the dreams and she laughed when she told me about them. She called them her serial dreams, her serial dope dreams, her serial novelette.

And she enjoyed them. She said they showed her the way forward.'

'Tell us about them,' she says, having got her courage back.

'I can't tell you like she did, but I'll do my best,' he replied, smiling at her.

He looks only at her, giving me not a glance.

I can see that through the slit between my eyelids.

But I'm going to try to concentrate and listen.

I'm going to try to concentrate and keep quiet.


'There's always a lake in Anna's dreams,' he says, 'that lake in a big wide meadow and she can't see anything except the lake in the middle of the meadow and she's with you, Z, somewhere on a long narrow road. You've been walking a long way when she sees the lake and asks you to go over to it with her. She asks you to walk with her over the meadow.

'The dreams always begin the same way: you're walking down this long road and she sees the lake and asks you to walk to it with her. And you do.

'And you're both standing by the lake, looking across the water and then something happens which splits the dreams up into several different dreams. It happens all of a sudden and at the same time the sky changes colour, was blue but becomes yellow.'


*The first time*

you see a swan in the centre of the lake, a white swan, enormously big and majestic. It sails like a ship back and forth and in a circle and it seems to you that it's showing off but both of you notice that it doesn't move from the centre.

Then an idea comes to her.

The idea is to talk to the swan, and she says, 'Come over here to us, you beautiful swan, come to us, we want to talk to you.'

And as she finishes speaking, the swan swims over to you, right up to the edge of the lake, and turns its tail towards you, so you know it's indicating that you should climb on its back. You climb on and the swan glides off with you over the lake, which is as smooth as a millpond and the two of you look down and see your reflections in the water and as you look you see the plants on the lake bed turn into long hands with beautiful long fingers which beckon you to come. You look at each other and suddenly you're naked there on the swan's back, you kiss and without saying anything you decide to jump into the water. As you do so the hands welcome you, they're gentle and kind and they stroke you.

And then she wakes up.


*The second time*

you're actually standing by the side of the lake, watching as the lake, which was as smooth as a millpond at first, starts to become rippled, the ripples change to waves and then to a rough sea. You're surprised because there's no wind by the lake and the air is so still that not a blade of grass moves. You stare out across the lake, holding hands and not saying anything, just contemplating the stormy waves, you lean close up to each other and don't feel scared. Then all at once you hear a song, an indistinct quiet and low song and it seems to you that it's coming out of the sky directly above the centre of the lake. You listen and you both know that you have never heard a song like it and you can pick out characteristics of Japanese, Russian and Western music mixed into it. The song increases in volume until it resounds over the whole lake with terrific noise and all of a sudden it's as if there's a whirlpool in the middle of the lake and you see the water disappearing into this central mouth, being sucked down and disappearing. As this happens the song stops. You look at each other and decide to walk over and as you step on the ground you feel heat from it. You walk to the centre and see a huge deep hole and you know you will have to go down it. You go down and to your amazement the hole widens and becomes larger and it's easy for you to walk along it. You haven't walked for long when you come to a green valley beneath a mountain, where there's a log cabin. You break into a run and soon you're standing before an open door. You go in and see two beds already made. You lie down and go to sleep. And then she wakes up.


*The third time*


there's a bench by the lakeside that you're sitting on and all around you there are lots of yellow benches with nobody sitting on them and at the side of each bench there's a small basket full of red roses, in front of each bench there's a small rug and in front of each rug there's a bottle of red wine and some apples. It surprises you that your bench is the only one that doesn't have roses, wine and apples, but you don't give it much thought, you just sit and look out over the lake where there are dozens of little grass boats rocking on the waves. Suddenly you hear a mumbling and grumbling, then sharp barking and as you look up you see a group of puppies running towards you. You realize that the puppies don't see you and you smile at each other as the puppies sit down on the rugs, one puppy on each rug. Then they start barking at each other and it sounds to you as if they're talking to each other. You both have the same idea at once, you stand up and walk amongst the puppies which stretch their paws out to you and you know you have to pick one of them up but it's difficult for you to choose. You walk back and forth until Anna suddenly chooses a puppy, saying she chose that one because it has such beautiful eyes. You take the puppy out of her hands and you both laugh when it licks your face. Then you notice that all the benches have disappeared and all the grass boats except for one lingering by the lakeside. In front of your bench there's a rug, wine and apples, and by the side of it there are roses. You sit down on the bench and when she wakes up the puppy has gone to sleep in your lap, you've drunk the wine together and eaten the apples, gone out in the grass boat and strewn the roses over the lake.

'I could go on talking about these dreams but I think I'll let that do,' Valgeir says, looking at her with his unbelievably beautiful eyes.

He could have looked at me just once.

But I don't let that bug me, not this time.

'Thank you for having told me that,' she says slowly.

She's happy.

He's made her happy.

He's made both of them happy.

But what price do I have to pay?

# 5

*Anna: 'I'll make a confession here by the fire.'*

And then I told you I was ill.

I put it off for as long as I possibly could. But when I saw you walking with one of the nurses on the ward (you hadn't told me that you'd been at school with her) I knew that the present situation couldn't continue.

You had your rights too and maybe I had disregarded them for too long.

But I was afraid of what your reactions would be.

I had no idea what you would do.

I had received a letter from you at the beginning of January, a long letter, and I had been concerned about what it said. For the first time I felt sorrier for you than I did for myself because everything in the letter was true, but what you hoped would follow in the wake of the truth was inevitably like a town built on sand.

It had to collapse some time.

*

I'm holding the letter now.

I wish I didn't have to burn it.

I wish we weren't in this situation either.

*

*1 January 1996*

*My beloved Anna,*

*I had to write to you tonight because tonight it's as if I've seen sense at last, as if a door which was firmly locked before and whose key was lost has opened. Of course I didn't look in my own pockets, I looked in everyone else's pockets instead but didn't find the right keys there, which was only understandable. There's a simple reason for this, as we have so often talked about, or as you have so often told me. The reason is in my own heart, in the fear there, the damned fear of not being the same as other people, the desire to be accepted and to find the right way and be happy during the long walk the same as other people are.*

*What's more I've never said a word when my brothers or the guys at work are complaining about people like us.*

*I haven't even said, 'What nonsense!' for fear of them guessing that I am what I am. So I've laughed along with them, bitten my tongue and laughed and even told stories myself.*

*Then I've gone home and wept.*

*And I've despised myself for being such a weakling.*

*It's not long since the following incident took place. It was just before Christmas, crazy at work, everyone on the paper was exhausted, the pressure had been unbelievable all week. Then the lunch break arrived. We had ordered beer and pizzas and were sitting and half lying around, feeling worn out.*

*Then one guy starts up, an OK chap with a good sense of humour, nothing wrong with him at all, married, has two sons, and he starts telling a story.*

*This is pretty well exactly what he, and the rest of us, said. You'll get the gist of it anyway, so you'll be able to see what I'm really like, though I know you'll doubtless laugh at me, if you don't prefer to stay silent. Interesting though how you've always managed to face yourself. No problem there.*

*OK, then I'll try not to get sidetracked.*

'I went clubbing at the weekend,' the man said, stretching at the same time. Nobody showed much interest, but I replied half-heartedly, as if my mind was on other things (which it was of course). As you know I always do my best to be polite.

'Where did you go?'

'Oh, just try and guess!' he grinned. He was different from how he usually is, really proud of himself. Usually he's quite unassuming, but then I don't really know him except as a colleague.

'Tell us where you went if you want to,' I said in a rather weary voice, and the others joined in.

'To the Risinu on Hverfisgata,' he said, and now he had everyone's attention. 'That was an interesting experience I can tell you, the place was crawling with gays and lezzies, like ants all over the place, and everyone pissed out of their minds. It's a really strange sight.'

I kept out of the conversation but I knew that my hands were shaking. I put my cigarette down just to make sure I didn't drop it, closed my eyes and leaned back as if I wasn't interested in the rest of the story.

'What was so strange?' another chap said. His tone of voice pleased me, that defensive tone you hear far too rarely, although there's often one person in the group who adopts it when this topic crops up.

But I still wasn't happy.

I felt this attitude should have come from me.

But I couldn't have uttered a sound even if I'd tried.

I detested myself.

'Seeing that, women with women, men with men, you know what I mean. I was like a fish out of water the whole time.'

'So what were you doing there?' asked the guy with the tone of voice.

'I just wandered in blind drunk with my friend. You could say I went in by mistake.'

'And of course you got out as soon as you could, or were the doors locked?'

'I would've got out a lot quicker if I could have, but I had some trouble at the bar. Some people are so bloody aggressive, they can't even take a joke. People like that are much more aggressive than ordinary people in ordinary clubs, you can't even compare the two. I wouldn't have believed it if I hadn't got mixed up in it myself. Maybe you don't believe that sort of thing until you get mixed up in it yourself. At least I would never have guessed before. But then I can be pretty bloody stupid and hellish slow at catching on.'

'So?'

'So there I am standing peaceably at the bar ordering a beer when this disgusting bloke comes up to me. His hair was all slicked-back, he had lipstick on and he was naked from the waist up. Then he somehow starts rubbing himself up against me. I move over a bit, he moves over, I move over a bit further, and so it goes on until I have to say something to get him to leave me alone because he's obviously making a pass at me.'

'And?'

'So I said, in a pretty loud voice, and not trying to sound particularly polite, I'll admit that, but I was really pissed off: "Leave me alone, you fucking queer!"'

'A split second later someone grabs hold of me and flings me away from the bar, and I hadn't even got my beer yet. He throws me up against the wall and asks what the fuck I'm doing there. Says I should cool off, and not say things like I had. So when I look at the guy who's holding me, I can swear I'm looking at a woman. It was a woman who had laid me flat, a big, muscular woman, right? By this time there's a crowd around us and, bugger me, I was shit-scared. Then just like that two girls grab hold of me under the arms and drag me over to the stairs. They were built like navvies, no joking. They hoist me down the stairs in this iron grip, without saying

96

a word, and tell me to piss off home and not show my face again until I've learnt better manners.

'"Where's your sense of humour?" I ask them. I probably sounded pretty angry.

'"Our sense of humour doesn't extend to you and your jokes," said another girl who followed the navvies down the stairs. She was good-looking, almost beautiful. And it sort of annoyed me that such an attractive girl was in a place like that. Then they kicked me out. So that was that, I thought it was just a big deal about nothing and bloody touchiness on their part,' he finished up. There was no comment.

I don't know whether everybody agreed with him, I don't think so, but nobody said a word. I wanted to say something, truly wanted to say something meaningful, but do you know what I said? My hands weren't shaking any more, and I said, 'Poor you, to get mixed up in that. Did you go straight home?'

But when I got home, I started crying.

I've tried to think about it as little as possible.

And as little as possible about us and the silence.

Then something happened at New Year which made me see everything in a different light, in a new light. It was just the same old light, but I hadn't been able to see it before.

I was standing by the window here. There's a nice view from here as you know, and the New Year's address was just coming to an end on the television and '1996' was coming up on the screen. Hrafn was standing behind me and he put his arms around me and I was thinking about you.

As 'Auld Lang Syne' began a rocket went off in front of me and hundreds of little red sparks exploded against the window pane. The sound was like the drumming in my head, like two saucepan lids being hit together, and I kissed Hrafn, put my arms around him and told him I needed to talk to him. And it was as if I was feverish and light-headed, as if the most difficult part was over, and I wanted to rush over to you, hug you and squeeze you and all that.

97

*And so we sat there all night and I told him everything. He was flabbergasted, of course, staring at me as if he'd never seen me before, and then he said something I'll never forget: 'Were you fooling me all the time?'*

*'What do you mean?'*

*'Did you never love me?'*

*'I still love you and I always will but I have to leave, you must understand that. I can't be without her and I can't live like this.'*

*'But you can be without me, you can live without me,' he said, his voice colder than cold echoing round the room. 'And don't put yourself out, I'll leave, I don't want to be near you a moment longer.'*

*He stood up, rather unstable on his feet, maybe he was a bit tipsy too, and he looked at me like, yes, I know it sounds unnatural, like a wounded animal, and said, 'It's not possible to humiliate a man more than you have done.'*

*And then he left and I was alone, with my thoughts racing in my head. They were hostile thoughts, painful, hard, soft, beautiful, and ugly. I lay down on the sofa in the living room, opened a bottle of vodka and drank till I fell asleep.*

*I didn't wake up until the phone rang at four o'clock the next day. It was Mother reminding me about dinner. I ummed and aahed and said I wouldn't be able to make it, that something had cropped up and I needed to be alone. I put the phone down, had another drink, which I really didn't want and I nearly threw up, fell asleep again, had a shower, and tried to phone you. There was no answer, you were probably out somewhere, so I unplugged the phone and started to write this letter.*

*I finished it at four in the morning and drove over to your place with it, but you weren't there.*

*I'm going to wait until I hear from you.*

*I'm calm and happy but ever so tired.*

*I'm going to lie here with the phone by my side until you call.*

*Call soon.*
*Love you,*

                                                                    Z

                              *

It's hard to throw this letter on the fire but I manage it.

Your letter about freedom arrived too late and it burns well.

Your letter about freedom arrived too late but you weren't to know that.

                              *

'Where've you been?' you said when I phoned you at work a week later. I had to be on my own for a week and reflect on how I should tell you. Then I decided to write the poem and give you it when you came.

I knew you would come as soon as I called.

'Hibernating, I've been hibernating and thinking.'

'What sort of hibernating, woman? I've been waiting and waiting. How can you make me wait like that?'

'I'll tell you when I see you.'

'Didn't you get my letter?'

'Yes, I got your letter. That's why I needed to think but now I need to see you soon and talk to you. We have to talk.'

'We can meet this evening.'

'No, let's meet on Thursday.'

'Why not this evening?'

'I've got various things I have to see to. Let's make it Thursday.'

'I must see you straight away, I can't wait, you know I can't wait. Now everything's fine, everything's different and I can't wait.'

'You'll have to wait. I can't see you until Thursday.'

'Meet me, just for a few minutes.'

'I can't, Z.'

'Why not, is there somebody with you?'

'I'm alone.'

'What do you have to do?'

'I promised I'd help Arnthrúdur paint her flat.'

'Is she decorating now? It's a strange time of year.'

'They're doing the whole place up. Valgeir doesn't start teaching for a while.'

'Let's meet on Thursday, then,' you said, and I was relieved to hear that you sounded calm, as calm as you can be.

I was no stranger to how impatient you were and knew that you'd rarely been worse.

You wanted to tell me about your dreams.

Which could come true at last.

Your dreams about the two of us.

Who had all the future together.

Everything together.

We could travel together.

Read together.

Wake up together.

Fall asleep together.

Drink together.

Socialize together.

Be together.

And be together.

And be together.

But it was exactly these dreams I didn't want to hear about, which I knew could never come true, knew would melt and turn to dust on the waves like mermaids in fairy-tales.

They were just fairy-tale dreams and make-believe.

But you didn't know anything.

You didn't know that the words,

    always,

    for ever,

    for ever and ever,

    eternally and evermore

were no longer words that graced my vocabulary. That's why I never responded in kind when you said, 'I'll always love you.'

I never said the word 'always' to you.

You can never say I lied to you.

You can say I hid things from you.

You can say I deceived you.

You can say I'm cheap.

You can say I don't tell the truth.

But you can never say I lied to you, but of course you never did. I was afraid of that, afraid you would say something like this but I should have known you better. I should have known what you're like.

'Steady as a rock through thick and thin,' you often said.

'I know,' I used to reply.

But of course I didn't know.

*

'Don't talk about the letter yet,' I said when you arrived. You put your arms around me and hugged me close and I knew from the red flecks in your cheeks, the quivering of your upper lip and the trembling throughout your body that you were upset.

I could see that you hadn't slept much.

'How did the painting go?'

'Fine, a bloody hassle of course,' I said. 'We had to empty the flat first and carry everything down to the basement and then spread dust-sheets everywhere, you're not allowed to get a drop of paint anywhere in my dear sister's flat. Fortunately she'd taken some time off work, so we got the whole thing done in three days. It was fun, people are so unrestrained when they're painting, so tired and scruffy and un-restrained. And we had music on all the time, of course.' As I finished I realized how unusually animated I was.

'Is something wrong?' you asked cautiously.

You sensed I was different from usual.

You sensed my anxiety.

You sensed that I wasn't well.

'No, I'm just a bit dirty but even though I've been painting all this time I have been thinking about you. It's not that. Here's a poem, add it to the collection.'

'Just quickly now,' you said, skimming over the text.

You didn't make any comment about it, but you read more slowly than usual.

*

*Monday, 8 January 1996, is one of the coldest days I can remember.*

*The icicles hanging down from my windows were so thick they reminded me of the broadest spears in any Hollywood epic, and it was so cold when I took the rubbish out that it felt as if my tongue had stuck to the roof of my mouth. So it was no surprise that Dr Zhivago was uppermost in my thoughts all day, and the scene where he struggles on towards Julie Christie over the endless desert of snow kept coming to mind.*

*There's probably nothing worse than unbearable cold.*

> *White snow in your eyes, my friend,*
> *and your hands white in the summer*
> *white are the nightingales on the casket lid*
> *white the dream on its base*
>
> *but the bird of spring flying over the hill*
> *has blue wings*

*

You read the poem twice, then folded the piece of paper into four like you always did and put it away in your bag. Soon it would go to its rightful place, under the eggs.

And here it is now, in my hands.

And the flames are swallowing it up along with the letter.

The greedy flames swallow and swallow and remind me of the fire in your eyes when I asked you not to touch me like that yet, because there was something I had to tell you first.

'Aren't you happy?' you asked. 'Somehow you seem so sad, aren't you happy that it's all finished, it's all over and done with, and we can be together and . . .'

I interrupted you.

'What did Hrafn say?'

'He rushed out, like I told you in the letter. He was agitated and angry as could be expected, but then he phoned me at work yesterday and we met at Horninu and he said he would rather be friends with me than nothing. He didn't want to know anything about you. He said he couldn't work up any interest in someone who had ruined his life.'

'He doesn't need to know anything about me.'

'Friendship scarcely means that I never get to talk about myself.'

'Did you say that to him?'

'Yes, I did, and I know things'll change between us. He needs time and, of course, I know it's been a shock for him. I wouldn't have liked to be in his shoes.'

'And what's it going to be like at work? How do you feel there?'

'I see no reason to broadcast it at work. I don't see that my private life is any more their business today than it was yesterday, but I couldn't really care less.'

'Are you sure it was the right thing to do to make Hrafn leave?'

'What do you mean?'

'I mean whether you can really do without him?'

'I can't do without you.'

'But you haven't asked me what I want?'

'I just asked you whether you were happy.'

'I'm not happy, Z,' I said. 'I'm not happy that you didn't ask me if I wanted things to change. I have my life just like you do and I always have done, both with you and without you. I like my life, I wander off here and there, and I'm used to it now and I don't want things to change.'

All of a sudden I got the desire to turn the game around on itself.

103

Not to tell you the true situation.

Not to want to comfort you.

I saw how startled you were and how you sort of curled up and looked heavy around the eyes. I asked whether you remembered the poem I had given you in September last year. No, you didn't remember it, you didn't remember the exact dates of my poems, you said rather arrogantly. Then I asked you if you remembered that above the poem I had said a few words about the yearning to travel. That you remembered so I added that someone who yearned to travel would never stay put in the same place for long.

You ought to know that feeling.

You said you hadn't taken the poem so seriously, just somehow thought it was fiction which it wasn't up to you to take literally.

'It was supposed to be fiction but the seed inside it is true,' I said. 'I do yearn to travel and I am restless. I'll tell you more about it later.' And I kissed you.

I kissed you for a long time,

    our tongues entwined together,

    entwined and entwined and I felt secure,

    I wanted to forget myself and I did forget myself.

I forget myself in the same way now with the poem in my hand.

My poem about the yearning to travel.

And the second letter you wrote me.

That was the letter that sparked off the poem.

A lot has changed since then but the yearning to travel has never left me.

Perhaps that's largely the reason why I'm sitting here now.

*

*Monday, 12 September 1994, I woke up with a desperate yearning to travel.*

    *It often happens. I had some coffee and toast to see whether the yearning would wear off. But my wish was not fulfilled and as the morning went on I became restless. I phoned the* coach station and booked myself a return trip to the airport terminal in Keflavík. My plan was to imagine I was going abroad. I even packed a few things in order to complete the picture. The journey to Keflavík went well. It was raining on the way and I watched how the raindrops licked the window and made the countryside awesome and more beautiful than it is.

I was off on an adventure with my friend, Bluff.


Always going away
with a heavy case i storm out into the wild
where the road ends and the sky begins

always going away
with a bag on my back and a thin stick
i dart among the clouds looking for the moon

always going away
with wine in a basket and bread in my pocket
i capture new moments in the sun

*

*19 August 1994*

Darling Anna,
For me the time we've had together has been wonderful. Sorry for sounding so sentimental but 'wonderful' expresses my feelings best. I would like to be with you much more and forget the obligations I have. But that's life, and perhaps that's 'just fine' anyway, as you're always saying. I find your attitude to life great, almost exciting. At least I've never met anyone who makes so few demands on other people. I've also never got to know someone so well in such a short space of time and we haven't even seen each other so very often and made only two trips to the cottage. Each trip better than the other one.

*There's a bit of a break at work now and I wanted to talk to you. I phoned a few times but you didn't answer. One day I'm going to give you an answering machine so that if you're not home at least I can hear your voice if I feel like it. Recently I've often felt that I have to talk to you. But perhaps it's odder that since I met you I feel hot more often than I used to and I sweat more. Hrafn has also told me I look better.*

*If only he knew why.*

*But I must bear in mind that I can't be too careful. Look before you leap and all that, and Hrafn is no idiot.*

*Talking of whom, since I mentioned him, Hrafn's going to New York at the weekend and I'm going to go with him. He'll certainly suspect something is up if I don't take up the chance of a trip to New York.*

*It'll be nice there anyway even if I do miss you.*

*I know it would have been great to go off to the cottage, but it's rather cold there now. Otherwise I would obviously have tried to fix up for us to go there.*

*I sometimes fall to thinking about how Hrafn's job is almost tailormade for us, what with him always going off on trips and us being able to be together then. Sometimes I feel so pleased about it that I feel like phoning the director of Icelandair and thanking him for sending my husband abroad so often. I never felt like that before I met you.*

*I used to miss Hrafn and life without him felt empty. Often I found myself doing something just to kill time until he came home. But life has had a lot of surprises in store for me in so many ways and recently it's like I even see differently when I look around, see different things than I used to.*

*I never had such crazy ideas before either.*

*Perhaps I think it's crazy to fall for someone like this.*

*But it's like everything is waking up inside me.*

*Spring on its way, or whatever.*

*Perhaps you think it's strange that I'm writing you a*

106

*letter, that I don't just tell you all of this when we're together. But that's just the sort of person I am and writing to you makes me feel closer to you.*

*Some things are so hard to say.*

*But we can always talk about what I say in my letters later if we like, if we want to.*

*I'm always going to write to you.*

*I hope you always read my letters.*

*I hope you don't ever throw them away unread.*

*You know, I don't think you can imagine how often I think of you and about you. Sometimes I think that thinking about you and the tension inside me are interlinked and will never break. Twisted together like rope.*

*You must know how I think but perhaps you do already. I've often found it strange what you know about me without my having told you.*

*But that's just you.*

*I'm going to think of you in New York.*

*I imagine you in the coffee-shop on Fourth Avenue where the Chinese couple with the rose-patterned aprons work. I can't fathom why they keep pointing with their thumbs to the table by the stairs. Suddenly I realize why. It's because you're sitting there with your back to me and you don't know I'm here. I whisper to Hrafn that I won't be a minute, walk past your table and touch your shoulder. You're wearing a blue dress and you look up and smile. What a beautiful smile you have. There's a curtain across the stairs and the couple point to them and we sit down on the steps. I'll never forget your neck there on the stairs of the restaurant on Fourth Avenue. There's a vein in your neck which I suck at and I almost forget that Hrafn is sitting waiting for me.*

*I'm going to think of you in New York.*

107

*I imagine you in the striped bar opposite The New C. Hrafn and I are drinking pina colada, actually waiting for the fourth round. He's tipsy and is talking about us having to move to a new flat. I'm thinking about how lovely your skin is but pretend to show interest in what type of parquet we should have in the living room. Your skin is all beautiful but your back is the most beautiful. When the waiter brings our drinks he pushes an envelope over to me. Hrafn doesn't see anything, I manage to open the envelope and pull out a letter from you. When I look up you're standing behind him. You beckon to me to come, I follow you out into the street and we make love quickly and frenetically in the alley next to The New C.*

*I'm going to think of you in New York.*

*I imagine you everywhere.*
    *You're the girl in the ticket office.*
    *You're the lead in the film we're going to see.*
    *You're the maid in the hotel.*
    *The girl in the lift.*
    *The stripper in the night-club.*
    *The artist's model at the art exhibition at the X.*
    *The biggest star on Broadway.*
    *I imagine you everywhere.*
    *And next to me in bed at night I touch your eyes, your throat, your breasts, all of you and let myself forget, and bite, sink my teeth into your throat, deeper and deeper, suck at your love with the blood, everything becomes you, and Hrafn, he becomes you as well.*
    *My imagination makes any journey without you a journey with you. Without my imagination I couldn't go anywhere.*
    *If I didn't have it, everything would be revealed.*
    *Loving regards,*

                                           *Z*

\*

I can remember that when I first read the letter I sat in silence for ages, staring into space, and thinking the same as I'm thinking now:

Z, oh Z, how simple everything is for you,
how fearless, free from shadows and exciting
and how I hope it'll go on like that,
how I wish for your feelings to remain unchanged,
for them to remain forever as free as the words in this
letter of yours.

But still I recall that something deep inside me didn't wish for this, that something that was the me I didn't want to have any say in my life, the me that made demands and was selfish and caught in the net of conventional feelings, the me who demanded her rights, wanted her due, wanted to control you and change you, and this me was thinking the same as I do now:

Z, oh Z, how demanding everything is for you,
how selfish, inconsiderate and exciting
and how I hope it'll change soon,
how I wish for your feelings to change,
for them to become as well formed as your handwriting in
this letter.

But I never spoke of these deliberations of mine.

I never spoke to you about my inner struggle.

I couldn't.

But the evening I got your letter, it was a Friday, I went to the Café List with the express intention of drinking myself into a stupor and forgetting about the letter. That was where we first met and I felt nearer to you there, there in the shadow of other people.

And when the waiter put yet another glass of beer down on the table and asked cautiously whether I was sure it was good for me to drink so much, I thought I saw you clearly among the crowd at the bar.

You were standing there as real as me, smiling at me.

And what else could I have done other than what I did do?

'Who's that blonde at the bar?' I asked the waiter.

'Which one?' he said.

'The one with the eyes.'

'They've all got eyes.'

'No, the woman with the big grey eyes who's looking at me, the one who keeps looking at me. You must know the one I mean.'

'I don't know what her name is, Anna. I have no idea what her name is,' he said, in a bored tone. It seemed to annoy him that I was taking up so much of his time.

I stood up and walked over to her.

I touched her shoulder and she became you.

I was somehow intoxicated with her.

And I imagined that you sat down by my side,

    and snapped your fingers against my cheek,

    and whispered that we should go out into the night,

    leave before the rain got heavier.

And I imagined that it was you I made love with that night.

But when I woke up I saw that it wasn't.

\*

Now it's the pattern of my life that I miss you all the time.

I never told you.

Quite the opposite.

All of me was so often quite the opposite.

Was.

\*

I throw the eggs on the fire.

And hope they'll turn black and melt, but they don't.

Your eggs of life don't melt like your letters and my poems.

The eggs go hard and black.

And when you find them –

Do me this favour, my dear.

Take them down to the lake and throw them far far out, hurl them out on to the water's surface, but keep one for yourself and one for the little girl you're going to have one day and a third one for the boy.

'I want to have a child,' you told me one day.

You had just come back from that trip to New York.

You looked well and you were happy.

'You should do.'

'Wouldn't you mind?'

'Of course I wouldn't mind, it'd be fun.'

'And would you want to babysit sometimes?'

'Certainly, but what do I matter in this?'

'You matter absolutely.'

'Oh yes, is that so?'

'Hrafn wants a child, but I've never wanted one until now. Don't you think it's strange that I should want so much to have a child right now?'

'No, I think it's quite normal.'

'When I've just met you?'

'Yes, because you've just met me,' I said, looking at you. You knew exactly what I meant, we didn't need to discuss it.

You wanted to disguise yourself better.

You wanted the good old helmet of invisibility.

You were that scared.

And we didn't need to discuss it.

*

But maybe we should have discussed it along with a lot else. Maybe we should have confided in each other more.

And maybe I should be more honest with myself now. I've got everything I need.

I'll make a confession now.

I'll make a confession to myself here by the fire because now I know everything better. That's the reason I also know why I'm getting cold.

It's not because the drugs are wearing off,

   not because the fire is burning low

   not because my life is running out,

but because I'm finding it difficult to accept what I did
wrong.

I'm finding it difficult to accept that if I had my time again I'd spend it differently.

I would give to you and allow you to do the same.

I wouldn't fight against it.

But my confession will stand like an iron pillar by this fire.

It was I who did wrong.

It was I who didn't want to take you into my confidence.

And I believed it was first and foremost for your sake.

So we could be free from worries for as long as possible.

I believed that for your sake you should tell me all your innermost thoughts, but that I should tell you only a little so that you wouldn't miss me when I was gone. Miss me like I knew you did anyway when I was apart from you. I didn't understand and maybe it was because I didn't want to understand that you would miss me more than you had to because I didn't confide in you.

That's why there was so much you didn't understand.

And some things you didn't understand because you had no grounds for understanding them.

You couldn't understand my present.

I wanted to have it to myself.

I closed it off to you.

Perhaps partly because you hurt me so often.

But it was mainly because I was a creature living in a hole in the earth.

And I dug that hole myself.

But you could understand and you were allowed to understand that part of my past that I deigned to inform you about. I wasn't niggardly about telling you about that if you asked me, because it was finished and nothing could change it. It was the finished part of me, coloured and faded chapters of me, complete with laughter and tears, all depending on what fitted each of them.

We could sit or lie for hours and tell each other stories from our childhood years, from our teenage years, from our high-school years and stories about ourselves when we were young and innocent.

112

You weren't niggardly either about the past.
You weren't niggardly about anything.

*

You: Have you always been like you are now?
  Me: What do you mean?
  You: You know exactly what I mean.
  Me: Judge for yourself from this story. I'll choose a short one.


*I*

always fancied my junior school teacher. All the time from
when I was seven until she left when I was eleven and just
beginning grade 7.

  She changed schools and we got a new teacher.

  I thought I'd never get over it.

  Never again to see her gorgeous face.

  Never again to hear her lovely voice.

  And I lay down in my room and cried and didn't
answer when Mother knocked on the door and told me to
come and eat. I lay there in the dark, shaking with
suppressed sobs and missing the woman who had taught
me how to read, write and do sums.


*I saw her in my mind's eye*

the day she walked into the classroom, said good morning
and blushed when one of the boys said she had a love-bite
on her neck. I hit him when we were walking home and
shoved stones down his trousers and he didn't know what
was going on because we had always been good friends.

  I knew I was prepared to kill my friends for her sake.

*I saw her in my mind's eye*

outside at break standing there stamping her feet in the
deep snow to keep them warm and I ran over to her and
offered to lend her my socks because I had two pairs on. I
remember how she laughed and said, 'No, my pet, it's
OK. Maybe another time.'

She called me 'my pet' without turning a hair and I
went hot all over and felt like I was the most important
person in the playground.

*I saw her in my mind's eye*

on the school trip to the Vestmann Islands when she was
counting us as we went on board the ferry. She was so
scared because one boy was missing. He was standing
behind her making faces and she was so relieved when he
jumped out in front of her. I thought she was the best
person in the world.

*I saw her in my mind's eye*

when she was teaching us geography and pointed at the
blackboard and said, 'Anna dear, can you remember where
Egilsstadir is on the map?' I got such a shock when she
said 'Anna dear' that I pointed to Ísafjördur by mistake.
And it was so good-natured of her to say that it could have
been there but it was in fact directly across on the other
side of the country. And she laughed and I knew she was
the sort of person who made the best of every situation,
the sort of person who would always stick up for me.

Perhaps she loved me as I loved her.

Perhaps she would die for me.

I saw her in my mind's eye everywhere in the darkened room and when I nodded off I thought she came to me and said that each time I missed her I should just turn the pages of my autograph book and then I would see how fond she had truly been of me.

And all my sleepiness was gone, I leapt up, found the book and looked up the page she had done when I was seven and had learned to read. She'd never do a page before that. And I pressed the book to me and knew that she would never have written, 'Be constant, loyal and true' to anyone but me because she loved me too. And in the corner, written with silver ink, it also said 'Remember me, I'll remember you.'

And then I went into the kitchen to get something to eat.

The autograph book lay open next to my bed for two weeks.

For two weeks I went to sleep with it on my chest.

And then I got used to my new teacher.


Of course I've always been like I am now. But what about you?

You: Judge for yourself from this story. I'll choose a short one.


*When*

I was seventeen, a hundred or so years ago, I was working in a hotel in Copenhagen. And, as often happens in memories, it was sunny all summer. Later on, when I was writing a dissertation about Icelanders in Copenhagen, I discovered that it had been a lousy summer and an unusually wet one.

But that's another story.

Anyway, I was working there in a hotel, in the rooms, cleaning, scrubbing, polishing and all that, but of course the real purpose was to get to grips with the language, otherwise my mother and father would never have let me go. They were very strict and made a big point of insisting that one had to do things for a deeper purpose than just for fun. And the amazing thing was that I did learn a lot of Danish but that may have been mainly because I had only been there for a week when I met Bengt and started going out with him. Time passed quickly when we were together, he was great and showed me all the best things about Copenhagen and it was always fun being with him.

But when I had been working at the hotel for less than a month a Norwegian girl called Berit, from Lillehammer, started work on the same floor as me. We worked the same shifts so we were together for at least eight hours a day. And because she was living with an old aunt and didn't like it there I offered to share my flat with her. I'd got a flat in a student residence that belonged to friends of my mother's who were in Iceland for three months.

As the summer went on I had less and less desire to be with Bengt, although he hadn't changed. I always wanted to be near her, go to pubs with her, lie in bed with her, laugh with her, share my thoughts and feelings with her, just be with her, but God knows it never dawned on me that I was in love with her. Then one day, it was at the end of August I seem to remember, we were cleaning the kitchen down the corridor and we'd finished everything except for defrosting the fridge.

She sat down and said she was tired, she'd been awake all night not feeling well. I didn't know about that because I'd been at Bengt's but I felt awfully sorry for her, so I told her to have a rest and that I would do the fridge.

I hadn't slept much either so I was on a bit of a high and to cheer her up and make her laugh I took a steel ice-cube tray out of the fridge and put my tongue against it. I got such a shock I tore it away again and, of course, the surface of my tongue stuck to it and blood poured out of my mouth.

She jumped up, grabbed a cloth, wiped up the blood, pulled me to her, put my head in her lap, stroked my hair, all without saying anything and then I noticed suddenly that she had a big scar on her knee and I started stroking it and after a while I had this strange feeling that I just wanted to stay like that and stroke her and kiss her legs and I felt hot and cold all over as I realized that I wanted to do much more than just that with her.

But nothing happened, I never found out what she felt and I hoped she hadn't sensed anything from me.

When we said goodbye (I've never seen her again) I thought my heart was literally going to break. On the other hand saying goodbye to Bengt was no problem and I never missed him.

But for a long time I felt this heaviness in my chest when I thought about her. She was pretty and when I saw you for the first time I had the same feeling and it's never left me.


What can you read from this?

Me: There's more to you than meets the eye.

You: Not any more.

And then we laughed and made love.

We always had the past together if we wanted.

*

The eggs go hard and black.

And when you find them –

Do me this favour, my dear.

Take them down to the lake and throw them far far out, hurl them out on to the water's surface, but keep one for yourself and one for the little girl you're going to have one day and a third one for the boy.

117

# 6

*Arnthrúdur: 'It makes me feel much better when I know what it is she's writing about.'*

Valgeir!
   I try but I can't push the thought away from me.
   But you needn't fear that I'll say anything,
      you can be sure I won't ask you anything,
      I don't wish for your weary looks and shoulder-shrugging,
      I don't expect you to understand, not now at least, but
         even though I keep quiet and will do so here I still
         want to know why I have to pay such a price.
   I want to know why you're sowing the seeds of doubt in my heart,
      and taking my peace of mind away,
      are you doing it on purpose,
      why do you always mention things for the first time to me
      when we're with other people, even with people we don't
         know at all,
      why can't you confide in me,
      Anna's my sister,
      she doesn't have to surprise me,
      she's never had to hide anything from me,
      why are you going around with her without my knowledge,
      and why has neither of you mentioned it,
      don't I matter at all to you, or all I've done for you,
      do you think I'm some stupid half-wit,
      not worth talking to,

what spare time have you had to go out for a drive here
    and there and what right do you have to keep them
    secret,
what right do you and Anna have at all to have secrets
    together?
I know you want to be kind to her because she's ill,
    and because you want to be kind to everyone,
    and because you want people to know you're kind,
    I understand you, that you can be sure of,
    but do you have to be kind to my sister at my expense,
    does she have something I don't,
    of course she has something to give I don't have,
    but do you really have to answer me as if it's nothing,
    as if there's nothing more natural than mentioning it now,
    couldn't you have chosen a better moment,
    why do you want a life I know nothing about?
I've been patient.
You can be thankful for that.
I can wait.
I agree that there's a time for everything, that there's another time
for everything.
I've listened calmly to you talking tonight:
    And I'll continue to be calm.
I'll show you that nothing makes me budge.
You'll see only coolness and composure in my face.
I can surprise you.
I have many variations up my sleeve that you don't know about.

*

'I had no idea about these trips of yours with Anna, I can assure you,'
I said. 'You two certainly managed to keep them from me.'
    I know he doesn't sense my feelings.
    I'm sure I've managed to conceal my fear.
    I can be a good actress when the need arises.

119

And I'm doing what I intended to do, I know I sound both interested and curious.

'I had to tell you now, and especially her,' he replies calmly as if there was nothing more natural,

nothing more natural than telling me nothing,

nothing more than he deigned to tell,

and then at the same time he talks about trust,

cries out for trust,

calls for trust,

even says he'll give up if I don't show him trust.

He should be in my shoes.

He should have sometime been in my shoes.

'And Anna didn't tell me anything,' I say.

I can't conceal the resentment in my voice.

'Like I told you both, she chose to keep quiet about it.'

'She had no need to surprise me if a miracle occurred. I can understand that she wanted to keep it secret from you, Z, but I would have thought she'd have liked to share it with me. I would have enjoyed going with you, walking, chatting, seeing the cottage and the lake, but she obviously had her reasons for keeping her movements secret from me.'

'She wanted to keep both of us at arm's length,' she says in reply.

She's likening us to each other with these words,

suggesting that we're on the same footing,

as if she has the same rights as me,

as if she feels the same as me,

still he'd made her happy with those dream stories. It

must have made her happy to know that she was the

focal point of Anna's dreams,

that everything focused on the two of them,

she needs to know too that he sacrificed a confidence to

make her happy,

to calm her down,

without thinking about me.

Really she ought to know that he's sacrificing my peace of mind by saying what he said instead of just staying quiet about it, since keeping it a secret was some point of honour for them.

She doesn't need to calm me down by drawing a likeness between us.

And he doesn't need to set himself up against me like some secretive animal.

He doesn't need to upset me, and anyway he won't succeed.

He won't get away with it.

I'm as calm as the calmest of weather.

'We all know what Anna is like,' he says.

'It's her privilege to be herself,' she says.

'And we have to accept that,' he says.

'Amazing,' I say, moving with a determined look to the telephone.

I pick up the receiver to let them know that I'm not going to continue this conversation, that I'm not going to start anything nasty, not be the cause of any unpleasantness. I pick up the receiver in a symbolic gesture to show them how one starts a new conversation, but when I get the dialling tone and Valgeir asks whether I'm phoning the police to see what's going on, I hang up and say, 'No, I suppose not, I suppose I'll be patient.'

And I sit down opposite them, look at them sitting on the sofa, smile at them and ask whether she has a hand mirror,

　　　because I want to put some lipstick on.

And there's no doubt about it,

　　　it has an effect, Valgeir looks more relaxed,

　　　he winks at me when she stands up to fetch the mirror
　　　　　and says, while she's out of the room, 'I wasn't trying
　　　　　to keep those car trips a secret, I just knew that Anna
　　　　　didn't want me to mention them, you know as well as I
　　　　　do what she's like. But I wanted to cheer Z up, and I
　　　　　think I did the right thing. She must be very worried,
　　　　　at least I know I'm feeling bloody awful, and so are
　　　　　you, so what about her?'

Valgeir the candid.

Valgeir the just.

As if I didn't know all that.

As if he needed to shove the facts down my throat.

As if it isn't all crystal clear to me.

'It doesn't matter at all,' I say, taking the mirror from her. I inspect my lips carefully, apply some lipstick and put my finger between my lips so as not to smudge my teeth.

'You're very alike,' she says, looking at me and smiling.

'Do you think so? Most people don't think so.'

'Not most of the time, but when you put lipstick on,' she says. 'Anna does that too, stands up all of a sudden and says she's going to do her lips, and then does it just the same way as you do. But me, I've never been able to put lipstick on.' I can't help thinking the topic of conversation rather trivial and decide to play on that feeling a bit,

the feeling that Anna and I have so often said is stronger

in me than in her,

that this or that is trivial,

not pointless but rather petty or inconsequential.

And she's right.

I can't imagine any subject more worthy of contempt than one smacking of inconsequence and this conversation smacks of inconsequence.

There's no point but I enjoy it none the less.

'We're both hooked on lipstick,' I say, and I ask whether we shouldn't kill time with a short lipstick story about my sister and me.

'I'll pop out while you're telling it,' says Valgeir, standing up.

'Don't go, I'll skip the story.'

'I'm going anyway, I have to go.'

'Where to?' I ask, slowly.

'I'm going to drive around town a bit. Who knows, I might find something out. I'm going crazy sitting here. It's enough if you two wait here, maybe I'll find her, maybe I'll come back with her. I'm going to drive round a bit. We don't need to sit here all three of us anyway, there's no point. I'll do more good by going out looking for her.'

'Do so then,' I say, and he leaves.

I feel how I'm beginning to be ashamed of myself.

I shouldn't be thinking what I'm thinking.

I must wean myself off this endless suspicion.

Gradually I calm down, I get up and make myself at home, go into the kitchen and have a glass of water, have a second glass of water and then throw myself on to the sofa, let out a sigh and smile at her.

I suppose she deserves kindness.

She can lump us together if she wants.

I know she's a decent person. She's surprised me.

Anna hasn't told me the whole truth about her either.

Anna knows how to play with truth.

She's not all she seems.

\*

'Valgeir's a good man,' she says as the door closes behind him. She stands there lost in thought in the middle of the living room.

'Yes, he is,' I reply and her comment doesn't surprise me, although I can't say it pleases me particularly at this moment.

'Anna was very fond of him at least,' she continues.

I'm not interested in her sharing these opinions with me so I move the conversation on to new ground without her realizing what I'm doing.

'Why do you always talk about Anna in the past tense?'

'Oh, did I use the past tense? I don't think much about what tense I'm using,' she says, blushing and looking embarrassed.

I'm sorry I've upset her and I want her to know.

'Oh, it doesn't matter. I'm sorry I'm so brusque and rude. I think it's the worry and uncertainty that's making me like this. Anna and I are very unlike in that respect, actually we are in almost every respect, except maybe the thing about lipstick. I was only being silly before when I talked about killing time by telling a story about lipstick. Of course there is no such story, but sometimes I don't know why I act like that, I'm just like that. I'm often unpleasant and short-tempered when I'm feeling bad.'

I feel I must do something about my behaviour and I manage to do so.

123

She doesn't deserve my bitchiness and coldness.

I'm pleased with myself now.

'You're OK, Arnthrúdur,' she says. 'People react to strain in different ways. I talk too much, whereas Anna doesn't say anything.' I can feel that she knows I'm trying to make amends once and for all.

She knows I want us to get on well in spite of how difficult I'm finding it.

'And I become disagreeable, is that what you mean?'

'That's not what I said.'

'In any event I want to tell you a story which shows how unalike we are. I want to talk and I want to think about Anna and me at the same time. Just Anna and me. It's hard for me to concentrate, of course it's right what you were saying about the strain. At least I'm finding it extremely difficult to fix my mind on any one thing, it's as if I need to keep an iron grip on it to make sure it stays on track. But I want to tell you this story so you're left in no doubt as to how different we are, "unfortunately" perhaps I should say.'

'Do so then, tell me the story,' she says, and I do.


*Once*


Anna and I decided to rent a cottage together at Laugarvatn as we had often done before. If we felt in the mood we sometimes rented a cottage from the Lawyers' Association in the summer. It was no problem for me and we normally didn't have any trouble getting one.

We always liked being alone together too.

We'd take a pile of books with us, twenty or thirty, and tons of food and wine, and lie in bed reading, and eating and drinking whenever we felt like it. I miss those trips, we stopped going on them when I met Valgeir and started devoting myself to him, as Anna termed it. Anyway, we set off one day in July seven years ago. I'll never forget that day, it was the most beautiful July day I can remember, the sky clear and the air clean and, like it says in some old Icelandic book, butter dripped from every branch or blade of grass. We went in my car, actually Anna didn't have a car at that time, you know she didn't have a car until she got one from the Social Security about the same time as she met you. Has she told you about this trip, by the way?

'No, I don't recall that she has.'
So I continue.

*We*

drive off, young and sure of ourselves. It was good to be alive and there were no obstacles in our way, never any difficulties, and certainly nothing special happened on the journey. I don't have a particularly good memory, at least not like yours, but I can remember word for word an interview that was on the radio while we were driving, or at least word for word the bit of the interview I heard. And I still don't understand today how it became etched in my brain.

There are lots of other things I'd prefer to have lodged in my brain rather than that interview.

Enough of that, the woman who was being interviewed was a member of an Icelandic band and the interviewer had wanted to talk to her because the band was on tour around the country and their concerts had been a sell-out. Strange that though I know the interview by heart and can't forget it, I can't remember who the singer was or what the interviewer's name was. But this singer's claim to fame was that she had been to see Roy Orbison and had got to go backstage after the concert and that was apparently a much sought-after achievement beyond the reach of the common herd.

But as I was saying I was engrossed in the interview and Anna was reading.

Anna's always reading.

So we were each in our own little world when the car suddenly lurched forward. I lost control of the wheel completely and we shot across the road and straight into a signpost which bent over and smashed down between the two of us through the windscreen and into the back seat. Bits of broken glass showered all over us and we were both half jammed in our seats. Me up against the steering wheel and Anna against the glove compartment, but, of course, our seatbelts saved our lives.

We were at the top of a hill and a German jeep freak had driven straight into the back of us because he'd been blinded by the sun.

The man put his head through the window and asked whether we were all right, and now I'm getting to the important part, the essence of this whole story, which will show you how different we are and might even prove that the only time we are alike is when we put lipstick on.

I blew my top, went completely crazy, didn't think I could possibly be like that, but I've got to know that side of myself better these last few years.

I screamed at the poor man,

that I was going to kill him,

beat the living daylights out of him,

cut him into little pieces,

chop him up, and I was going on and on endlessly and the man had started crying when Anna slapped me and I shut up.

She took his hand in hers, stroked it gently and said, 'There there, dear, it could happen to anyone.'

'It couldn't happen to anyone, it could only happen to an idiot!' I bellowed.

Then the police arrived and got us out of what was left of the car.

\*

'So do you think, Z, there are two sisters alive less alike?'

'Maybe not,' she says, smiling broadly at me.

'Why do you smile?'

'I scarcely dare tell you,' she says warmly.

'Do tell me, I know how to take things.'

'I thought you were alike when you were telling the story. It's not your voice, nor your gestures, but there's a something that is difficult to pinpoint but that is definitely there, and it's nice to see it.'

'Are you making fun of me?'

'No, of course not, I don't make fun of people, you don't need to worry about that. It's just what I feel.'

'Oh, it makes me feel uncomfortable, affected in a way,' I say. 'Why don't you recite another poem? Anna's poems calm me down, they make me relax,' and I lie back and look at her.

'Yes, I will, since they calm you down. Funny that, but they calm me down too.'

And she recites a poem and makes not a single slip of the tongue.

She's right.

It's as if Anna moves closer to us.

\*

*On Monday, 7 November 1994, I decided to write to my mother with some news about myself. I wanted to tell her that I had decided to do some supply teaching in Sauðárkrókur for three months to see how I liked putting my education to good use. It was so important to her that I made something of myself. When I was a child she had stressed it frequently and*

127

*then often in letters after she moved to Norway. I wanted to tell her that I had met a wonderful man and was expecting his baby, that she was going to be a grandmother soon and that if the baby was a girl I would name her after her. I never sent the letter. I phoned her instead and said that I had wanted to hear her voice, that I had no special news for her. Even though I'm good at saying the opposite of what I'm thinking, I couldn't.*

> *i hear your voice*
> *and measure in my mind the distance between us*
> *if i had a long enough plank*
> *i'd lay it over the ocean*
> *walk out on it one summer's night*
> *tiptoe to you*
> *and talk to you about happiness*
>
> *i'd take your hand that night*
> *and sing you a verse*
> *about the sisters who sat by their mother*
> *because she was so tired*
> *then i'd make a wreath of flowers*
> *put it around your hair*
> *and you'd be as radiant as a queen*
>
> *if i had a wide enough hook*
> *i'd pull the countries together*
> *lay my head in your lap*
> *and hear you whisper:*
> *'Come to me when tiredness knocks*
> *and your memory is clouded'*

*i hear your voice*
*but can say nothing more than*
*that the first snow fell today*
*it's so strangely late this year*

*i hear your voice*
*and put the receiver down*

*

'When did you say she wrote that?' I ask as the final words leave her lips, and getting to my feet I feel calmer.

'In November 1994.'

'That's just what I thought.'

'What do you mean?'

'I was always asking her to phone Mother and tell her about the illness. She always refused, wanted to put it off, didn't want to tell her until it was really draining her strength. She wanted to behave the same way as she did to you. She always loved her tremendously and would do anything for her but felt she couldn't do that. She lumped this illness together with what Mother disliked in her character. Mothers always find something to dislike, it's just part of their job, part of the mother–daughter fugue.'

'What do you mean?'

'You know, the mother–daughter syndrome. Mother was still pleased with her, and of course there was no reason not to be. Anna was a brilliant student but there was just the thing about work and what she was like when she stopped being interested in men.'

'Did she change then?'

'No, she never changed at all. Oh, I don't know whether I should be talking about this, didn't she ever discuss it with you?'

'Just that your mother wasn't happy about it but had never bothered her about it.'

'A funny sort of no-bother that was. Anna didn't want to be bothered about that any more than about anything else. But it was more of a bother than she expected. She regretted having told Mother about it in the first place and didn't really know why she had done. You could certainly say that it didn't give anyone any great pleasure. Mother is extremely conservative and wants us to be as well. In that respect I've done my duty to please her more than Anna, but it's cost me a lot of effort. But I stuck by Anna like I've always done, even though I didn't always agree with her about everything and especially about this. Like Mother, I felt that maybe she wasn't quite in her right mind when she came home one day when she was twenty-six and said she was in love with a woman.

'Mother was in Iceland then and was staying with us.

'And then there was how she went about telling us about it.'

'How did she do that?'

'She came dashing into the house one morning, beaming like the summer sun, threw off her coat and bounced in to where we were. We were relaxing, drinking coffee and telling fortunes. Mother's quite good at fortune-telling with cards. She hadn't seen this in the cards but then how can you possibly foresee this sort of thing? Anyway, Anna came bouncing in and crowed, "I'm in love!"

'"How nice," I said.

'"How nice," said Mother.

'"Tell us about it," I said.

'"Tell us about it," said Mother.

'We liked playing parrots, repeating what the other one said, chewing the cud as Anna used to say. She didn't like it, but she knew how to play. But, by the way, I'm sorry, is it uncomfortable for you if I talk about this?' I ask, recalling all of a sudden how uncomfortable it makes me if someone mentions Valgeir's former girlfriends.

I feel rather good about myself for thinking like this,

    for feeling this affinity,

    for feeling that it's genuine, not a façade or pretence.

I can see that it pleases her too.

'Go on,' she says in a low voice, and then adds, 'I'm not jealous of what's past. I may find it uncomfortable but that's OK, it's OK to feel uncomfortable.'

130

'I don't think I've ever been so much in love before,' Anna bleated, whirling round and round in circles in front of us.

'You always say that,' I said.

'You always say that,' said Mother.

'I'm saying it now,' said Anna.

'And what's the lucky person's name?' Mother asked.

'And what's the lucky person's name?' I asked.

'Her name's Elín,' she said, laughing.

'Elín?' Mother cried.

'Elín?' I cried.

'Don't you think it's a beautiful name?' she asked, and then out of the blue,

> the mimicking game was over,
>
> there was no aura of joy any more,
>
> no game,
>
> only Mother's heavy breathing and my light drumming on the table-top and neither of us answered when she told us to say something,
>
> she hadn't expected us to take it like this,
>
> what did it matter,
>
> why were we acting like that,
>
> were we planning to drown her in silence,
>
> send her mad with silence?

The worst thing that could happen to her was if people didn't answer her and there was no more effective punishment for her in the old days than silence, than not taking any notice of her,

> walking past her as if she didn't exist,
>
> looking through her,
>
> not replying to her,
>
> then she used to curl up in the nearest corner and start crying and lie there crying until she gave in.

That's what she did on that occasion,

> she went into her room and we heard her crying all day.

I looked at Mother and she looked at me. We didn't say

131

anything to each other all day, we just sat and smoked and drank coffee until I got up and, without saying a word, went into the kitchen and fetched a bottle of cognac. And we drank the whole bottle and waited in silence for her to come out and talk to us.

But she didn't.

And towards evening this pitiful crying ceased, she had a shower and was gone and didn't reappear in the house for ten days, and by that time Mother had left.

That was the bother.

They never spoke to each other again about that.

Mother never asked and neither was there anything to answer.

'It's dreadful to hear about that,' she says quietly, and then adds, 'but what about the illness, when did she tell her about the illness?'

'She never got herself together to tell her. I took the plunge and told her. Mother phoned her regularly of course to see how she was getting on, but Anna didn't go over to see her until last year. It seemed like she would never find the time to go, but fortunately she did. And Mother's coming over next year.'

'I'm sure she wrote something about that.'

'Let me hear it, I prefer it by far when I know what she's writing about, it all makes so much more sense, don't you think?'

'Maybe what Anna says is right, that it has a different meaning. I don't know, I need to think about it more.'

'OK, let's hear it.'

*

*On Monday, 23 June 1996, I returned from a trip to Norway. I went there to visit my mother, whom I hadn't seen for many years. I was afraid, when I said goodbye to her, that I would never see her again. I think it's a feeling most people are familiar with.*

*Perhaps i won't see the flowers in the river again*
*the bird on the branch by the house*
*the coffee pot on the table by the window*
*but you i'll always remember*

*and between us a fleeting moment*
*in which we say goodbye*

\*

'They'll see each other again, don't you think? She'll turn up, don't you think?' I ask her, becoming uneasy again.

Valgeir's been away for a long time, too.

'They'll see each other again,' she says, with the certainty and calmness in her voice that belongs only to one who is truly confident.

Relief floods over me and I'm grateful to her for making me feel confident.

'I believe you,' I say calmly.

'I think she wrote a poem about this Elín.'

'She must have done.'

'Why do you say that?'

'They were always messing about together. Always rushing about, always together, did everything together, went everywhere together, could never be apart from each other. Sometimes it was a bit pathetic, when it was impossible to get Anna on her own even for a moment, even for a confidential chat with her own sister. It was as if she couldn't be on her own, and if she was she became nervous, even jumpy, and was always making a beeline for the phone to see where Elín was. But still it wasn't as if she didn't trust her, it wasn't like that, she simply couldn't be without her. I never really gave it much serious thought, thought it was just a fad of hers and didn't take much notice of it. I remember I never thought of them as anything but friends, but that was then, that was when I thought she'd grow out of it. It's not the same now. I don't think that now. But they were rather idiotic, I thought so then and for some reason I still do.'

133

'What do you mean by that?'

'They rushed around like mad things and sometimes could hardly restrain themselves, they even slept out on the beach in sleeping-bags and buried cards in the sand and I don't know what. Oh, I felt almost ashamed that Anna should go on like that and I told her sometimes that she wasn't a teenager any more. She was an adult woman and had to think about her reputation.

'"I do," she said, and she kissed me. But she was always happy then, childishly happy. She still can be of course, but it's different now, the illness has changed her.'

'Arnthrúdur, do you want me to recite a poem?' she says.

I feel she doesn't want to know any more.

And I understand.

'Yes.'

*

*On Monday, 2 December 1994, I met an old friend of mine on Laugavegur.*

*I hadn't seen her for two years and when I looked at her I saw how I had aged myself. We went into a coffee shop and ordered coffee and rum, even though it was only two o'clock. Maybe it was because we were a bit shy of each other, or maybe it was because that was what we used to do in the old days.*

> *In our eyes lost nights*
> *when there was nothing but life ahead*
> *nothing but tomorrow's day*
> *nothing but this evening's evening*
> *and the moment*

*now we're bent over our memories*
*bent and crooked*
*like two old washerwomen on their way to the hot spring*

\*

'She was very fond of her,' I say, feeling that I must say something in spite of her possibly finding it uncomfortable.

But I'm not going to add anything more.

'I know.'

'How do you know?'

'She told me about her. We talked a lot about the past. She said there was nothing in her past that I couldn't know about and that if I asked her she would be the last person on earth to keep anything from me. Even so, there was obviously lots I didn't know. For example, I didn't know anything about that Gunnar. When I asked her once about him she said he was just an invention, cooked up to give the poem a little colour. But that wasn't so. She had some reason not to tell me about him, and of course she was trying to make sure I wouldn't be jealous. Only he doesn't matter to me any more, I'm not even curious about them. Still it's strange that for some reason I've always been more jealous of men than women, and I don't really know why. I find it harder to put up with men showing interest in her than women, maybe I'm afraid a man will be able to give her something I can't. Unless of course I'm devoid of all common sense, like she used to say.'

'What did she mean by that?'

'She just meant it seemed that common sense sometimes ran for cover when I was around, that in some matters common sense was afraid of me. That's how she put it.'

'I can imagine that Anna would have chosen to go out with men if they had given her what she needed. It certainly wasn't the case that she went out with women because she couldn't catch a man. All things considered I find it surprising that you should think like that.'

'I don't understand.'

135

'I just mean that a woman like you, a woman who's been married for a long time and lived a normal life, if you'll forgive the expression, and then falls in love with another woman, renounces everything in order to be with her, keeps all her options open, or whatever one says, how can she fear what you say you fear unless the reason is that there's something you yourself miss, something you feel Anna can't give you? I hope you're not offended but that's how it seems to me it might be, although of course I don't know the first thing about it. Have you ever thought about it in that way?'

'Yes, I have.'

'And what do you think?'

'I miss various things.'

'Like what?'

'Oh, I don't know whether I can be so prosaic as to say what I miss most often.'

'Go on, tell me.'

'Well, I have nothing to lose by telling you. I miss all the ordinary things, sitting and listening to the news together, cooking meals at normal times, washing up together and putting our feet up afterwards. I miss these ordinary moments in the evening, ordinary breakfasts, ordinary goodbyes when we were both dashing off to work and said goodbye as we flung our coats on. I miss the ordinary visits to my mother, I even miss my brothers' observations. Nowadays, on the few occasions that I meet them, they don't take the trouble to make any comments at all. I miss the ordinary peacefulness that I had. I miss the trips abroad with Hrafn. There's so much I miss but would rather do without because I can do without it. But I can't do without Anna, even though she won't see me more than once a week, even though she hasn't wanted to change anything. I can put up with that, although it's changed since she went into hospital. Now I go and see her every day.'

'So you're lonely.'

'Sometimes.'

'Do you think Anna misses the same things as you?'

'She hasn't had the same life as me.'

'And do you think there's anything in that sort of life which she sees as a challenge?'

'No, I don't think so.'

'So do you think you need to be worried about men?'

'No, but then there's so much else,' she says, and I know about so much else now too and when I look at her I feel sorry,

> not just for her,
>
> not just for Anna,
>
> but for all that they can't ever have together despite their
>> wanting it, despite their desire to live a normal life and
>> enjoy ordinary days with the ordinary stress of work,
>> quarrels and future plans.

I feel sorry for myself too for never having such thoughts about women like them. I was evidently intended to learn a lot in one night, unless this night and the waiting for my sister are supposed to confirm what I know and have always known,

> that in all truthfulness there's no difference deep down
>> between people, that at all times all ordinary people's
>> thoughts run along similar lines, with most of them
>> following the direction of the easiest path towards a
>> state of happiness.

And I don't know why an image of Anna comes into my mind, laughing as she leans back comfortably in the chair opposite me,

> sticks a toothpick between her front teeth,
>
> slaps her thigh and says, without anything being more
>> natural, the phrase that she so often used and that
>> she called her nervous tick, 'Necessity is the mother
>> of everything.'

# 7

*Anna: 'I will never tell how I put out the flames.'*

You wanted to have a baby.

To have a cute little baby boy with fair hair and brown eyes.

A little baby boy with your features and Hrafn's eyes, those deep, brown eyes you found it so hard to resist and so difficult to hurt. Then there was that priceless sparkle in his eyes when he lay next to you and went on at you.

You enjoyed so much lying next to each other, talking.

And you felt so fond of him when he pleaded with you.

'Let's have a baby,' he'd say.

'In a while, not now,' you'd say.

'Why wait?' he'd ask.

'I'm not sure I'd be a good enough mother.'

But you were sure.

You were surer than sure.

And you had so many stories about you and the baby you wanted. You had two favourite stories and they were about me too.

One was about a boy. The other about a girl.

Neither of them is in a letter.

I don't need to burn either of them.

I remember when you told me the stories and

how radiant you were,

how you glowed,

how you beamed and laughed and laughed.

You first told me the stories in January 1995, but you stopped a

138

year after I told you about my illness. You stopped talking to me about anything connected with the future then. But I saw those stories about children floating around you and you were happy then in a way that only the telling of those stories could make you. But as time went on you didn't want to talk to me about the children and I let you be on that subject.

Perhaps you were right anyway.

Perhaps I would have been hurt by your stories,

    I don't know.

But now I want you to be able to have that child.

You'll just have to be patient with your body and it'll respond as you wish and hope for.

And I'll be happy wherever I am.

I know you know that now despite my never having told you.

I don't need to burn these stories.

I don't need to see the fire consume them.

They'll be silenced along with me but will live on in you.

When I look into the fire your stories make me happy.

I'm no longer cold.

I feel well.

I'll change nothing now.

Perhaps your future really is linked to stories and emotions you kept quiet about to everyone except me and Hrafn, except that your dream with him was different from ours. After you fell silent I tried sometimes to make you talk to me about the children, although I wasn't sure about myself nor what I felt about our dream, the dream that was never going to come true,

    whether I had just become as jealous as you or whether

        I had turned into what I didn't wish on anyone and

        didn't want anyone to be,

    egoistic and self-obsessed,

    I didn't know for certain then but I still knew that if I was

        like that it was in a silent and secret way,

    and without wanting to be,

    of course it was because of thoughts like these that

I eventually stopped pestering you to talk about the
children because you thought it was best for both of us.
But before that there was a game we used to play together,
for a long time we used to play the game together,
it was fun,
childish and unaffected.

We'd be lying in bed – we used to spend an awfully long time in bed – if I had more time I'd buy a new mattress, it sags so in the middle. We'd be lying in bed, looking up at the ceiling and the game would always begin in the same way.

I'd lean up on one elbow,
look into your eyes,
deep and long,
that was how it began and you knew what would happen
next.
And it happened.
In this game we never cheated.

*

Me: Tell me about the boy.
You: What boy?
Me: Tell me about your boy.
You: The boy who has two mothers?
Me: No, not him, that boy would have one eye in the middle of his forehead!
You: What boy then?
Me: The boy who has two mothers and one father.
You: Oh yes, him.
Me: Yes, tell me about him.
You: I will.
Me: I'll be quiet while you're talking.
You: Be quiet then.
Me: I'll stroke your stomach while you're talking.
You: Do that.

Me: Begin.
You: Listen.


He

is born one day when the sun is just coming up over the
blue mountain in a little town in the northern seas. The
boats are moored in the harbour and the sea laps around
them as if it has never done anything other than stroke
them gently like this. The people are sleeping peacefully
in their beds, dreaming dreams about the white flags that
have been hoisted all over the town, and of which there
are so many it's as if there is one attached to every lamp-
post.

It must be that festivities are about to begin.

The houses lining the streets, big and little and wide
and narrow, are all painted in different colours. Some of
them are even striped and some checked. These houses
are incredibly beautiful, just like the people's thoughts
when they wake up and remember their dreams about the
white flags. They open their windows and, as they shoo
their dreams out into the fresh air, they feel how the
morning coolness clings to their cheeks and gladdens them.

They feel it must be that festivities are about to begin.

They feel it by the butterflies in their stomachs.

And they go round and round in circles on the floor
then stop suddenly and ask in great amazement, not
knowing why they're whispering:

'What was that sound? What was that sound? What
was that sound?'

And because they get no answer they get dressed quickly.

Everyone runs outside at the same time and they
stream towards the sound.

People stream on, looking like sheep on their way up

141

the mountain, except that there's no shepherd driving them on.

Then the crowd stops outside a large, white house in the middle of the town. In that house there's only one window open and the sound's emanating from it, the strangest sound the people have ever heard and yet so strangely familiar, like a mixture of laughter and crying.

It's the sound of a baby.

'It was the sound of a baby,' the people say to one another.

The people are standing below the window not saying a word and looking up they see two hands, two beautiful hands appearing from the window holding a little baby, a little baby boy who's howling, and finally a woman's face appears and her broad mouth calls over the crowd.

'Today a baby boy has been born who has two mothers and one father.'

And the people whisper to each other that that's why the baby was making such a curious sound, and as the whispering is heard the woman holding the baby disappears inside again and two women and a man appear at the window.

'Those are the mothers and the father,' says the same voice.

And the whole crowd starts to murmur and whisper and when they finally stop they start clapping and clapping and the two women and the man disappear and the woman with the baby appears in the window again and says, 'A fine, healthy boy, 8 pounds and 21 inches.'

And the crowd's shouts resound around the little town in the northern seas, 'A fine, healthy boy, 8 pounds and 21 inches.'

And then the people walk away and stream down the streets like a flock of sheep except that there's no shepherd driving them on.

And the boy stops crying and is put to his mother's breast, which is warm and heavy with milk, and she smiles at a woman sitting on her left and at a man sitting on the right.

And the boy begins to suckle like boys in the country in the northern seas always suckle.

That was the beginning.
But before the story could continue,
the beginning had to be repeated.
So we repeated it,
I looked into your eyes again,
deep and long and you knew what was coming.
And it came.


Me: Tell me about the girl.

You: What girl?

Me: Tell me about your girl.

You: The girl with two mothers?

Me: No, not her, she would have one eye in the middle of her forehead.

You: What girl then?

Me: The girl with two mothers and one father.

You: I'll do that. Take a hair from my head and lay it on my forehead, but make sure it doesn't stick, make sure it's free and loose on my forehead, otherwise nothing will happen.

Me: Done that.

You: Look at the hair.

Me: I am.

You: Now look into my head through the hair.

Me: I'm doing so.

You: And what do you see?

Me: I see, I see, I see the story about the boy happening.

But wait, good gracious, it's happening and happening and happening and it's just the same as before and there's the hand, but this hand, this hand is holding a baby girl and then everything happens the same as before.

You: That's how it will be too.
    Me: And now it's time for the story about the boy to continue.
    You: How does it continue?
    Me: With the words: 'The little boy comes home . . .'
    You: I remember now.


The little baby boy

comes home to his little blue house right down by the harbour in the town in the little country in the northern seas. And the people in the street have gathered in the windows of the lovely houses as the mothers step out of the car with the boy wrapped in a warm, soft blanket. And one face disappears from the window and the mothers watch as the woman from the next house comes leaping along laughing and goes up to the flagpole in the garden by the path running up to the little blue house and hoists a white flag.

    And the flag is flying as the mothers walk into the house with the baby and, looking back, they smile and laugh as they see all the faces in the houses in the street opening their mouths and shouting in unison, 'Welcome home with your fine, healthy baby boy who weighs 8 pounds and is 21 inches long.'

    And they lay the baby in the brown cradle by the bedroom window, next to the bed they sleep in and they sit down on the edge of the bed and watch him sleeping and sleeping and listen to the little contented sounds he makes.

    'He's sleeping peacefully,' says one.

'He's sleeping peacefully,' says the other.

And then they go to sleep and during the night they wake up twice to feed him and wait until he falls asleep again and watch him breathing.

The first months pass like this and the father sometimes visits them, chats to the mothers, picks up the baby, feels his gums for his first tooth, takes him out in his car, gives him waterproof trousers and a jacket, takes him to nursery school and, later, to school, and occasionally the little boy stays the night at his house.

And so life goes on in the little blue house with the white flag flying in the good old town on the island in the northern seas. They're always having fun there and singing and humming and time passes and passes and the boy gets taller and taller and the mothers grow older and older until one day the boy picks up his hat and stick and goes out into the wide world. And the mothers are alone and sometimes they miss him and sometimes they don't. But they never miss each other because they don't need to. And there are trees and flowers in their garden and one day when they're looking at the garden they see a rabbit running between the bushes.

Me: Tell me about the girl now.

You: Take a hair from my head, lay it on my forehead, look at the hair and see what you can see.

Me: I see, I see, I see . . .

\*

We haven't played that game for ages.

You wanted to.

I agreed.

And we needed to,

I know that now.

I know that now as I throw my poem of self-pity on to the fire ahead of letters and an egg. I watch as it goes up and I put my hand before my eyes. It's burning faster than many of the others and it blinds me with the same feeling I had when I jotted it down.

Here indoors by the fire everything is alive.

And everything dies.

*

*On Monday, 29 April 1996, I took the ferry to Akranes. The sea was rough and I went out on to the deck to feel the spray from the waves and from the rain bearing the spring to me. It was raining slightly. I was sitting on a bench with my head in my hands when a little girl sat down next to me and asked if I was cold and whether I wanted to borrow her mittens.*

*I got to my feet and thanked her.*

> i'll never see the brown cradle
> touch small hands and cold feet
> lay a baby to my breast and hush it at night
> rock a baby on my shoulder and sing to it at night
> but in the spring i'll give our dream a silken flower
> which will bloom next winter

*

So much changed after I told you about the illness.

'I have to tell you something else,' I said, and was so, so scared. 'Not just that about being restless, there's something else too. I should have told you already but I couldn't. I didn't want things to change, you see, I didn't want you to think about me differently from how I am. I wanted everything about us to be beautiful, at least I didn't want to destroy anything. That's why I've kept quiet.'

'Why don't you get to the point?' you asked somewhat brusquely.

'It sounds like you're going to tell me that you've been lying all along,' you added, 'that you've been having a relationship with someone else at the same time. Have you? Is there something I'm supposed to understand now that my circumstances have changed completely, now that I've changed my life and want to be with you? Is there something like that I have to come to terms with? That would be just typical.'

'It's nothing like that,' I said.

'What the hell is it then? It doesn't sound like good news, I can't imagine I'm going to jump up on the table and shout hurray, hurray. Maybe this restlessness thing of yours is enough for me, without anything else on top of it. Maybe it's quite enough for me to have to swallow in one go that you don't want to change anything, that you only want to see me once a week, only on Thursdays and now and then at the cottage, that you don't have time for me in your life. I've been a fool, in fact I'm ashamed of myself. I've always hoped that it was your dream too, not just mine and . . .'

'Calm down, please calm down.'

'I am calm! Come on then, out with it!'

'Perhaps I ought to tell you sometime later since you're making such a fuss. This isn't about pulling other women.'

'I'm sorry I got so upset.'

'Oh, Z, I'm ill.'

And then I told you everything,
    kept nothing back,
    described it all in detail for you and realized that this was
        perhaps the first time I was fully aware I didn't have
        much time left.
And my fear was unfounded.
I needn't have been afraid to tell you,
    I should have known you better,
    should have known your love better.
You didn't say anything,
    your expression didn't change,
    you put your arms around me and kissed me,
    touched me,

all over,

everywhere,

made love to me,

all over everywhere,

your tongue on me,

all over,

everywhere,

and I closed my eyes and saw those old-fashioned stars

that people so often see in books and films.

I saw them everywhere budding and blossoming into flowers and then you said, 'I love you, for ever.'

And I felt hope creeping over to us and spreading itself over us,

that ever youthful hope that life is actually a deceit,

that yes means no and white means black.

And then I asked you a question that I've never asked before nor since and that I'll never ask again.

'Tell me, Z, do you think God exists?'

You didn't answer,

you were speechless,

but I heard your breathing as I fell asleep.

And I hear it now, hear how it winds itself around me, actually I'm rather cold now again, it winds itself around me like your words used to do and it's no lie to say that I can almost hear your voice, I can hear it here inside me as I read your letter.

*

*1 February 1996*

*My love,*

*It's taken me a long time to write this letter. I began it the day after I left you and I've written a little every day since. Still it's not as long as some of my letters. I've always been adding little bits, until today when I decided to put it through your letterbox. I know you'll be in touch when you can and I want you to know that I've accepted that we go on seeing each*

148

*other as we have been doing, even though I had a different dream.*

*But I respect your wishes.*

*Nevertheless sometime you're going to have to tell me about this wandering about of yours, where you go and maybe a bit more than you say in your half-finished verses and the odd poem or so, because of course I never know what you really mean.*

*But that's not what I want to talk about.*

*I want to say so much, but I don't know how to.*

*I can't talk about it.*

*So I'll write it down and then you'll know more or less what I'm thinking.*

*I know you've said that words often don't mean anything, that silence can be just as important, that it can say more if one listens to it and that body language sometimes even expresses people's feelings better than what they say. You're able to say that despite the fact that it's you who deals in words and meanings, and you've also said that sometimes your days are nothing but a vain struggle with words that won't be controlled. Perhaps that's also true, but I've never thought about expression in that way. I'm used to expressing myself in words but I don't usually think about them to any extent. But when you told me you were ill I knew that no spoken words could express how I felt.*

*And I may not be able to write it down either.*

*But I'm going to try.*

*I have to try.*

*I felt as if I had been pushed out to sea on a raft and the waves were crazy and I was standing there in torn clothes on the raft holding a stick, and you had fallen overboard. It was very real and naturally I felt dreadful watching you being swept further and further away and not being able to do anything.*

*And yet I want to call to you now, sorry but 'call' isn't*

149

*right because in fact I want to scream a few sentences at you which deep down I believe may explain how I feel, maybe a little bit, just a tiny bit.*

*But I know all too well how powerless they are.*

*And in comparison to the orbit of the moon, the paths of the stars, the stars themselves and the laws of the earth they resemble the cry of a lonely man in the firmament, a meaningless, ineffective shout which alters nothing. I know that. But I still want you to hear them because I know that hearing them will make you understand, make you realize how I felt when you told me about the illness and how I feel now.*

*This is what I want to scream, what I wanted to scream when you told me the facts, what I will always want to scream whatever happens and whenever it happens:*

*To hell with it.*

*To bloody hell with it.*

*Fuck life.*

*I'll miss you, you bastard.*

*I'll kill you, you idiot.*

*I'll beat the daylights out of life.*

*I'll show life where to get off.*

*I'll get my own back on life.*

*I'll kill someone.*

*I hate injustice.*

*I hate the past.*

*I hate the present.*

*I hate the future.*

*I hate dreams.*

*I hate hopes.*

*I feel guilty.*

*About my selfishness,*

> *because of everything I've made you suffer,*
> *because of the time I've made you wait,*
> *because of what I've confided in you,*
> *because of what I've made you partake in,*

because of what I've made you responsible for,
because of the hopes I've forced on you,
because of my fits of jealousy,
because of the insolence,
because of the love,
because of everything.
I feel guilty,
guilty,
guilty.
I want to take life into my own hands.
I want to control your days.
I want to protect you.
I want to stop working.
I want to look after everything for you.
I want to wake up by your side.
I want to stay awake by your side.
I want to be by you and all around.
I want to look after you,
look after you,
look after you,
look after you.
I want my dreams to come true,
I want your dreams to come true,
I want us to take part in tomorrow,
I demand that we take part in life,
I demand that we take part in love,
I demand to be near you,
I demand to be allowed to love you,
love you,
love you,
love you,
I demand to get to love you always,
always,
always,
always.

*Perhaps you don't understand this drivel at all,*
  *some things can't be said,*
  *some things can be written because they have no voice,*
    *no sound, words like hell don't say what the letters*
    *actually spell out, no explanation is sufficient to open*
    *the word and show you inside its world, the world that*
    *I know, for that you'd need words too, just as useless*
    *and worn out as the word itself, you could say the*
    *same about all the other words and about that good*
    *old phrase,*
  *I love you,*
  *love you.*

I'll never be able to show you or tell you what that really means. Of course I've never been able to get across what my feelings are either.

'Don't try to describe it, just do it,' you said once, and at the time I thought that was neat and actually I thought it was strangely risible at the time, I found your comment funny only because I'm used to explaining and assessing things and weighing them up, it's part of my job, part of my upbringing, aren't people always saying it's so important?

'It's no good crying,' our mother used to say if we fell over and hurt ourselves when we were children. 'You have to try and tell me what the matter is.'

'Try to put your thoughts into words,' our father would say when I was having trouble explaining some mathematical formula to my brothers. I was good at maths, but they were useless so I helped them.

I can't be bothered to give you any more examples, there are lots of them and perhaps they don't matter.

And do you remember when I said, 'I usually put things into words and then carry them out, don't you think that's better?'

'Usually, yes, of course, but the other way round is OK for me,' you replied.

152

'You're weird,' I said, laughing.

'If you want us to make love, for example, don't talk about it, do it. I'm lying here waiting for you, that's all I mean.'

'That's what you mean.'

'And, Z, I don't think one should always be obsessed with childhood. You drown if you stay underwater for too long. I've been young. It had its ups and downs, sometimes it was bad but generally speaking it was good, and I think that in that respect my life hasn't changed much. Sometimes it's bad but most of the time it's good and I don't want to waste time or energy understanding and defining why. I take the bad out, try to lie down and let it pass when things are going well. And I enjoy the good. I try not to punish myself with life. It may sound childish, stupid and extraordinary, but I love life.'

'Well, goodness gracious me,' I said (strange how well I remember that conversation). 'You don't have to be so pompous about it.'

Now I know, now I understand why I found your attitude so strange. Evidently I can't imagine what it's like to view each day in terms of the end of time. And you must do that indirectly, even though you say you don't.

But how often I must have hurt your feelings,
        pained you,
        pushed you,
        trampled on you and how often, knowing what you did,
            you must have found me laughable, extraordinary,
            stupid, idiotic.

If I had had my choice you would have told me straight away, but I do understand you and respect you, our time together might have been better, might have been worse, but it would without doubt have been different:
    more bruised,
    more maimed,
    more injured,
    more loving,

*more understanding,*
*more tender,*
*more beautiful,*
*and yet,*
*I don't know what I would want to lose,*
*I know what I wouldn't have done,*
*I don't know what I would have done.*

*I only know I've never been so savagely angry as when you told me about it. My blood clotted in my veins and fought against flowing. You've often seen me angry, I've often had attacks of jealousy, I know that and I'm sorry about it but all that anger was child's play compared to this. It felt like the whole of me disappeared inside myself and laid waste my vital organs with a sword and spear. I think I managed to run every organ right through and my heart I managed to overcome in a few seconds*

*and then I was dead.*

*Two minutes of anger like that are the equivalent of years of life,*
*they pass so slowly,*
*but afterwards I seemed to come alive again,*
*all thought of death slipped completely from me,*
*I was young, passionate and strong and I loved you.*
*I know you want us to pretend that nothing has happened,*
*I'll try my utmost, forgive me if I go wrong.*
*I'll try to do and not to talk.*
*But of course I'll go on writing to you about God knows what,*
*you won't get out of that, my dearest,*
*you won't get out of me,*
*you won't get away from me,*
*you won't get free of me,*
*there's been no change there,*
*there'll be no change there.*
*We'll try to enjoy life however things turn out and however long things go on for.*

154

*We'll do our best.*
*I love you,*

Z.

\*

I smile.

You always knew how to talk yourself round.

And I didn't regret having spared you, because of course I was sparing you, or it might be truer to say that I was sparing us both.

At least that's what I thought then.

I only know now that if I hadn't done it then I wouldn't have received those two travel- and baby-dream letters in October and November 1994.

And then I wouldn't have experienced those strange emotions I experienced when I read them,

    I wouldn't have agreed to go to Vopnafjördur and

      Akureyri in November either,

    I would have been busy with other things, that's for sure.

I throw the eggs on to the fire.

I throw the poems on top of the eggs.

I pass my fingers through the flames.

I walk around the room a few times and then read those letters of yours which, when I got them, made me run around the room like a madwoman and fall about with laughter, until all of a sudden I was sitting there with my hands crossed on my knees,

    then I put the Moonlight Sonata on,

    blended in with the music,

    became the music,

    and rocked myself backwards and forwards,

    backwards and forwards.

It's good to rock oneself.

I'm rocking myself now while I'm reading.

Z, Z, you certainly knew how to light candles.

You really knew how to pretend nothing was wrong.

155

But I shall never tell you how I put the flames out.

*

*My dear Anna,*

*I'm writing this from Copenhagen. I came here with Hrafn, he's making a feasibility study or something of the company over here. You ought to know that trying to get hold of you was nearly the death of me and I never did. Where are you always rushing off to, woman, anyway, can't you ever stay quietly at home? Do you think the world'll come to an end if you stay at home for a whole day?*

*No, it's all right, I'm just joking. Of course it's none of my business, of course you can go anywhere you want without reporting to me. But somehow it's just so annoying not being able to get in touch when one has to zoom off, but what the hell, one zooms off anyway.*

*Still it's not as much fun now as when I went to New York with Hrafn a while ago. Remember I wrote you a letter then as well. Maybe I just wasn't as tied up thinking about you a few months ago as I am now. It certainly wasn't the place itself that occupied my thoughts. Naturally you feel much safer here than in a city where you're always thinking about crime and how dangerous it is and how it isn't safe to be wandering around alone. To my mind Copenhagen isn't much bigger than Reykjavík in that respect, even though I suppose it is really. I can walk about the gardens and squares here without having to worry and go wherever I like without always looking over my shoulder. But, like I said, I still felt freer in New York, freer with Hrafn. I was able to have fun and enjoy myself with him because even though I did think about you it was in a completely different sort of context. Maybe it was more romantic, maybe there was more excitement in it, you know, the fact of sharing a secret with someone that nobody knows about. That nobody will ever find out about, but especially a secret that you don't want anyone to discover, that you don't want to be brought out into the open.*

*Actually there may be something about that last bit that's changing. I don't know.*

*Or like you say yourself sometimes: 'The more time you spend with people the closer you become and the more time you want to spend in their company.'*

*That's probably right.*

*But never mind that, I'm trying to get rid of all these thoughts, which disorientate me. I know how to orientate myself, as they say, and as you know.*

*Hrafn is talking more and more about us having a child, making an extension of ourselves, something real which will outlive us. Maybe he's rather old-fashioned, but he's hardly the only one. At least I fully understand this desire of his. I'll tell you what he does. I think it'll amuse you, and I'm sure you'll understand him. You understand people so well.*

*So perhaps we're out for a walk.*

*It's a bit cold and we're wrapped up warm. It can be cold in Copenhagen in the autumn, calm and cold, but always lovely. And he wants to hold my hand. I always like holding hands when I'm abroad, though I have a strange feeling when I'm holding someone's hand, it's like you can't walk without support. And then there's the fact that by holding hands you're making a sort of statement of unity, that the two of you are one and that you belong to each other. That's the feeling I find so uncomfortable and don't want to have.*

*One doesn't own people, one never can and should never want to. It's a threat to other people's independence and to that freedom that everyone needs.*

*I don't ever want to end up with the knowledge in my body and my soul that I can't live without some other person. It might be natural for children to think like that, I remember thinking when I was little, 'I'll die if Mummy dies, I'll die if*

*Daddy dies,' but that was then. Then you get older, and then it seems to me that your thinking should be, 'I can be without, I need to be able to live without.'*

*Maybe, but that was just a red herring.*

*So Hrafn wants to hold my hand here in the autumn chill and he wants to walk along past shops selling baby clothes, snowsuits, hats and so on, and then he looks at me while we're looking in the shop windows and says, 'Don't you think they're pretty? Don't you want to dress a little boy in a snowsuit like that, or a little girl in one of those dresses? Don't you want to see a little boy in that shirt running round a Christmas tree, or a little girl in that skirt?'*

*And, though my feelings have begun to change, I reply like I always do, 'In a while, Hrafn.'*

*And then I start thinking about you.*

*Whether you were joking when you said you'd want to look after a child of mine. Whether you'd mind my having a baby if I wanted to. And when I think about what you said, I somehow feel my spirits lift and I say to him, 'Maybe soon.'*

*'Maybe tonight,' he says.*

*'Are you joking?' I say.*

*'Shall we make a baby boy tonight?' he asks.*

*'Not yet. Maybe soon,' I repeat. And then we go back to the hotel and have dinner, because it's getting dark. We eat slowly and I look at him and think about where you are. He doesn't turn into you and I don't see you at the table like I did in New York and I'm not as happy and don't feel as well as I did there and it's not with a particularly light step that I set off when we decide to walk up the stairs to the eighth floor rather than take the lift.*

*We always have the same room when we're here and we always walk up the stairs so that we'll work up a sweat and it'll be fun to have a bath together.*

*But on the way up (I think it's as we reach the fourth floor) I want to run down again, but I don't, I can't, I'm not used to giving in to feelings on the spur of the moment, perhaps the feeling isn't strong enough anyway.*

*And so we have a bath together and wash each other's hair and it feels good when he rubs me. It feels good when he clasps my breasts and says he could eat me, says he could stay inside me for ever, and I feel better than good and don't have time to think about how odd I am as I say, 'Let's make a baby boy.'*

*And we jump out of the bath and don't get any further than the floor in the passage and we try to make a baby boy or a baby girl. And it's incredibly good, incredibly passionate and incredibly full of promises and it's only afterwards when we're lying there together holding hands that I fall to thinking about you and what you're doing.*

*And it annoys me to be thinking about you at this moment, it takes away the pleasure, it alters me.*

*I feel I'm becoming different.*

*I've finished reading the letter through.*

*I've decided to send it. I'm not sure I should, but I want you to know the real me.*

*I'm looking forward terribly to seeing you next Thursday. Perhaps we can get over to the cottage at the weekend.*

*Hrafn has to work a lot, I hope we can be together. Be at home so I can phone you when I get back.*

*Warmest regards!*

*Z*

*

I can feel the same weight on my chest as I did then.

I'm red and hot and angry like then.

But I don't wish that you hadn't sent me those letters.

Because then I wouldn't have known you like you wanted.

But now I don't wish for anything, even though my mind is in turmoil like then.

# 8

*Arnthrúdur: 'I'm unluckier than you because I'm jealous of everything and everyone.'*

And as Anna's voice disappears I look at this woman for a long time, this woman who has confided in me what she misses but prefers to do without because she can't do without my sister, even though she knows there's no future in a life with her.

And the longer I look at her the closer she becomes to me.

She becomes more akin to the me who a while ago had trouble saying her name either to myself or to her, as if both she herself and being close to her disgusted me. That, of course, was the problem, although I had trouble coming to terms with it.

I am not the sort of person who feels disgusted by other people.

I make a point of not being so banal.

I like people and that point's been proved tonight.

And Z has confided in me what she feels is despicable about her own character and I feel that there's more than just the affinity that jealous people share. I feel a real fondness for her and for the second time tonight I want to embrace her and offer her the same security that her words and her sincerity gave me.

But I can't,

there's still something that holds me back and I can sense
that she knows how I feel.

I can see it by how she smiles silently at me.

And then it begins, the silence,

not that soothing silence which, like Anna says so often,

it's good to float around in but that oppressing silence
which makes you withdrawn and embarrassed.

And I look at her and feel how reserved I am but I pull myself
together there in the chair because I don't want her to think that her
putting her trust in me makes me so pitiful.

I want her to know that I'm a person who is worthy of trust, so I
say, 'Z, you said you weren't jealous of what is past.'

'I'm not, but I can't change what's past. I've never tried to. I have
enough trouble with the present and the future.'

'I envy you, you know,' I say, quietly, and, having voiced this
thought, I want to have her confidence for always.

I always want to have her to turn to.

And I want her to have me to turn to.

'But what about you?' she asks, unhesitatingly, although she knows
perfectly well that I know she knows everything. Anna was comparing
us once and told me that she had talked to her about me and my
jealousy.

'I'm luckier than you because I'm jealous of everything and everybody, jealous of everything that breathes is what Anna said and then of
everything that doesn't move as well. She's told you about it, I know
she has.'

'She talked to me about you but only in general terms, just to make
it easier for me, I think.'

Anna never told me things that she knew she was supposed to keep
to herself.

'I've often made a fool of myself,' I said.

'She never said that.'

'I've still often made a big fool of myself.'

'I'm not sure she looked on you like that.'

'But I did it even so, not just in my eyes and Valgeir's, but also in
other people's eyes. Maybe that's what I find worst, maybe it's always
other people's eyes that are worst, the judgement people around you
make, that merciless judgement that spares no one, those merciless
eyes that are watching you everywhere.'

I'm going to be candid with her.

I'm going to be frank and not leave anything out.

I know that no one understands me better than she does.

'You mean the worst thing is to make a fool of yourself in other people's eyes?' she asked, with a smile.

I pretend not to see the smile.

I'm not going to contemplate whether that smile conceals sarcasm.

Unwaveringly, I continue.

'Yes, to make a perfect and hopeless fool of yourself. It's possible, in fact it happens when it's least deserved, when you're hoping above all to do your best, hoping above all to restrain yourself. It happened to me once, but then you can only make a perfect fool of yourself once. Once and for all.'

'Do you want to tell me about it?'

'I've never spoken about this incident but it's often hung over me like a shadow and turned me against people, made me terribly scared and frightened. I'm always waiting for someone who saw what happened to pop round the corner suddenly when I'm standing there or doing my shopping or something. That's why I prefer wearing sunglasses. It's not because I don't like the brightness, which is what I always say if someone asks. I have a whole collection of sunglasses and whenever I put them on I feel safe and protected. But it's only people who have written themselves off by being idiots and fools who know that feeling.'

'Tell me about it.'

I can sense that she's interested.

But I'm also aware that she has no idea what I'm like.

My openness makes me feel good.

'You mustn't ever tell anyone about it, not even Anna. I haven't even told her the whole truth about this. I just told her that there'd been some terrible trouble, but I didn't say what. I just couldn't. But I had to tell her that there'd been some trouble, because of what happened later. There were some slight repercussions, though nothing too bad. It could have been much worse.'

'I'll keep quiet about it. Trust me, I trusted you.'

She's said the words that matter.

We've understood each other.
And wagered right.
I tell her about it.

*

It happened just over a year after Valgeir moved in.

We had our ups and downs but we were happy.

Things have generally been up and down as far as I'm concerned recently.

I've really changed a lot. I used to be a peaceable person in every respect, violent emotions were unknown to me and jealousy was something I had only heard of.

In that respect I was like Anna.

But you mustn't think that I'm some sort of trouble-maker intent on disturbing the peace. I'm just an ordinary woman who prefers staying at home. I feel safe there and of course Anna's right when she says that I'm not only a home-body but I like to have my own way too.

I love ordinary days and an ordinary, secure life just like you do. I know exactly what it is that you miss, so I understand you, because I'm just an ordinary woman who enjoys watching television, reading and chatting with friends and my husband, doing simple, everyday things, and working, of course.

I want there to be peace and quiet around me,
 everything that a normal home-life provides,
 but I have this tendency, and it's rather an excessive
  tendency,
 I have this tendency to become a terrorist at the drop
  of a hat.

Things had been OK between Valgeir and me for at least a week. He hadn't done anything that had displeased me, he'd come straight home from school every day and had stayed in every evening with me. That's how I wanted it to be and I think he liked it too. At least he said he did.

I'm always trying to believe what he says.

I've got better at that too the past few months.

Anyway,

it was the school's annual ball.

It was the first time I was going with him to any social event connected with work and I was particularly concerned about making a good impression and making him feel proud of me. I'm rather a vain person, maybe because deep down I'm unsure of myself, I don't know, but my greatest wish that evening was that his colleagues would put their heads together and say:

'Look at Valgeir's new girlfriend!'

'Isn't she attractive!'

'She's much more attractive than his ex-wife.'

'Much, much more elegant.'

'And she's fun, too.'

'It's quite understandable.'

'In his shoes we would have done the same thing.'

It was of such paramount importance to me that his colleagues should like me that my knees were shaking as we walked up the stairs at the Perlan. The restaurant is up at the top, I can't remember what it's called but it revolves and you can look down and see Reykjavík like a village of stars in some alien firmament. The restaurant turns faster and makes everything like a moving adventure, especially if you've had a drink or two.

And of course we'd had some schnapps before we left, so I was quite flushed by the time I'd finished my cocktail up there. And some woman mentioned it to me and I felt happier about myself than I had done for a long time.

I felt I was beautiful.

I smiled at everyone.

And then we sat down.

Everyone had been allocated a seat so that couples didn't sit together. I was next to the headmaster, who, according to Valgeir, is very nice but gives an impression of coldness to preserve his dignity. Valgeir was sitting opposite me, next to a woman about the same age as me. They seemed to know each other pretty well, but maybe not.

Valgeir is the sort of person who can talk to anyone and puts everyone at their ease. I could see that this woman was enjoying talking to him and, unusually for me, it didn't bother me, but then Valgeir was in my direct line of vision and me in his.

But I wasn't keeping tabs on what he was doing,

    not at all,

    just winking and fluttering my eyes at him

    so he wouldn't forget how much I loved him.

It was a three-course meal and there was wine with every course. Our glasses were kept well topped up and before I had finished the prawn cocktail I knew I was tipsy, not drunk but just a bit tipsy, somewhere in between, you know. And as soon as I realized that I realized as well, much to my annoyance, that I was watching what Valgeir was doing,

    noting how he ate,

    how many glasses of wine he had,

    how his waved his hands about or shifted in his seat,

    how he smiled,

    whether he looked over in my direction often enough,

    whether he was too interested in the woman.

I felt worse and worse and I drank more to make myself feel better, but of course that only made me feel worse still.

So, the main course arrived.

There was a choice between fillet of beef or pork.

I chose the beef,

    so did the headmaster.

I saw that Valgeir was having pork and the woman next to him beef.

And when everyone had been served somebody proposed a toast for the teachers and the students and we gave the school a round of applause. It was some sort of custom. Actually Valgeir had warned me in advance and told me what would happen. And then we all started eating, slowly and quietly, politely like well-behaved people do. Then I suddenly got this unpleasant feeling that one minute everything was happening too slowly and the next it was happening too fast. People were either shovelling the food into their mouths or could barely force

165

it down. It started about the same time as the headmaster turned to me to say something.

I could feel he was a likeable person.

Headmaster: How's the meal, Arnthrúdur?

It was kind of him to have found out my name.

Me: Very nice.

I couldn't remember his name but I knew it was of no importance.

Headmaster: The meat's very good, if anything maybe a little over-done, but apart from that very good.

Me: Yes, I agree, and the gravy's excellent.

And as I said 'excellent' I noticed that Valgeir had turned towards the woman and was saying something.

I leaned across the table to hear what they were saying.

Valgeir: This is nice.

The woman: So's mine, very good.

Valgeir: You've got the beef, haven't you?

The woman: And you the pork?

Valgeir: I usually find beef tough.

The woman: This isn't tough at all, it's nice and tender.

I didn't catch what Valgeir said then because the headmaster nudged me and asked very enthusiastically, 'So you're a solicitor?'

Me: Yes.

For some reason I couldn't reply with a full sentence.

He was distracting me.

I was concentrating on Valgeir and the woman.

But Valgeir didn't look at me, didn't even look in my direction and I gripped the edge of the table when I saw him offer her a forkful of his pork for her to taste,

    as if nothing was more natural than to sit next to some

      woman,

    right opposite one's wife, or more or less,

    and give her a forkful of meat.

And I half choked on my wine when I saw her getting ready to give him a taste of her meat. But I had to look at the headmaster. He was quite obviously extremely interested in me because he was well

166

mannered even if I wasn't. So I counted up to a hundred, took a deep breath, looked him in the face and tried to forget about them.

I truly did my best to forget about them.

I tried as hard as I could.

Headmaster: And you have your own office?

Me: I specialize in matrimonial law.

Headmaster: And you can choose the hours you work?

Me: Of course, but the office is open at certain fixed times.

I felt I was being rather brusque but I didn't think he had noticed and in any case it suddenly didn't make any difference to me,

I really wasn't an actress,

I definitely couldn't act

and so I started stretching across the table again.

I pretended I was reaching for the salad,

pulled it over towards me and caught these words as I did so:

Valgeir: I'm the PE teacher. One of them, that is, because of course there's a woman to teach the girls.

The woman: Do you have to split them up?

Valgeir: Yes, I think so, at least to begin with, you know what kids are like. Then in their final year they get put together so we don't teach them separately in their fourth year.

The woman: I see.

Valgeir: What do you do?

So it wasn't one of his colleagues.

It wasn't another teacher and yet it was as if he had never done anything else in his life but talk to her.

Valgeir the free and easy,

Valgeir the sociable,

Valgeir the lovable,

I thought, and felt my heart beginning to beat faster and

once again things alternated between happening fast

and slow,

slow and fast

and refraction in the dark.

I took another breath and heard dimly:

167

Headmaster: I've been on the look out for someone to teach two courses in law next year, in methodology.

Me: Oh yes.

What was the man trying to say?

Couldn't he understand that I had other fish to fry?

Headmaster: Perhaps you'll think about it?

Me: I have enough work.

Headmaster: How silly of me, people are always getting divorced.

Me: What do you mean?

What was he insinuating?

What did the man mean?

Headmaster: I mean I understand that you have enough work.

Me: Yes, exactly.

Headmaster: I hope I haven't said anything to offend you or upset you. That certainly wasn't my intention.

Me: No, what a thought!

Headmaster: My intention was just to offer you these courses.

Me: There's no need to offer me anything. There's never been any need to offer me anything, any need to offer me anything.

And I repeated these words over and over again and didn't hear what he was saying, and started helping myself to more wine.

I didn't need any more help.

I saw Valgeir leaning towards the woman,

    I took a mouthful of wine,

    I saw the woman laugh,

    I took another and saw him laugh,

    took a third and a fourth and a fifth and then I started
        gulping it down.

And I vaguely remember bending down and peering underneath the table to see whether I could kick Valgeir's shin, or whether the table was too wide,

    and perhaps all the blood went to my head

    and the wine of course

    because the next thing I remember I was being carried
        downstairs

and I couldn't for the life of me understand why.

I was calling for Valgeir, crying and howling but I couldn't hear anything.

And then I woke up at home the next morning.

He was sitting on a chair by the bed with a flannel in his hand. His eyes were sad when I looked into them and I knew straight away that something had happened.

He wiped my forehead.

Me: I can't remember anything about what happened at the end.

Valgeir: Try to go back to sleep.

Me: I don't feel well.

Valgeir: You'll get better.

Me: Did something happen?

Valgeir: Please go back to sleep. It's only eight o'clock and you've been very restless.

Me: Restless, what sort of restless?

Valgeir: You just haven't been well at all.

He wiped my face gently with the flannel.

I had an awful headache.

I couldn't think straight.

I decided to go to the lavatory.

On the way there I realized my nose was hurting.

I touched my nose.

When I made it to the lavatory I saw that it was terribly swollen.

And I had a scratch on my cheek.

I remembered everything only hazily and nothing at all after I saw Valgeir's feet under the table and thought I saw him nudge her feet with his.

I called out from the bathroom:

Me: My face is all swollen.

Valgeir: I know.

Me: And my cheeks are scratched.

Valgeir: I know.

I knew I had drunk too much.

I didn't usually, although it did happen occasionally.

But it had never happened unless I wanted it to.

And I had intended not to drink much that evening.

That plan had gone down the drain.

I went back to bed.

Me: Lie down with me.

Valgeir: I'd rather sit here next to you.

Me: What actually happened?

Valgeir: Do you really want to hear that now?

Me: I want to hear it now.

I'm not the sort of woman who puts things off.

I'm not the sort of woman who paints things over.

I'm not the sort of woman who lets herself be fooled.

I'm the sort of woman who wants to hear the truth as it really is.

I'm the sort of woman who wants the whole truth.

I'm not the sort of woman who shies away from unpleasantness.

Me: I want you to tell me what really happened.

Valgeir: You just went crazy all of a sudden.

Me: I went crazy?

I was calm.

I was resigned.

I was going to listen without cracking up.

I knew he was telling the truth.

Valgeir: He said you were acting a bit strange.

Me: Who said that?

Valgeir: The headmaster.

Me: I see, go on.

Valgeir: And then your behaviour suddenly changed and you almost disappeared under the table. He wouldn't have taken any notice, he knew you were a bit drunk and was familiar with how women act. And then you suddenly appeared from under the table, you face bright red, and demanded what he thought he was doing harassing you, which he said he hadn't been doing at all. You were talking very loud of course and I could see you were spoiling for a fight. I got up and was going to come round to your side of the table but before I could get to you you'd taken off one of your shoes and you

170

were hitting the headmaster with it, first about the shoulders and then on his head, and you were pulling his hair and saying it was all his fault. Some of the other teachers got hold of you. I just stood there rooted to the spot, totally unable to move a muscle. You were shouting and screaming and when they dragged you past the bar you were fighting so hard that you managed to smash your face on the counter. So that's why your face is like that now. You've been almost delirious all night and I've been on the point several times of phoning the doctor, just to be sure.

It felt like he'd slapped me round the face with the flannel.

It felt like he'd punched me in the face.

It felt like all the blood had drained from my body.

I didn't want to face the day.

I didn't want to face him.

I was scared he'd leave me.

I was scared he'd never be able to forgive me.

I couldn't imagine myself being in that condition.

I couldn't imagine myself being like an animal.

Me: Lie down with me.

Valgeir: I'd rather sit here.

Me: Lie down with me, please.

Valgeir: This isn't on.

Me: What?

Valgeir: You know perfectly well.

Me: I must have got alcohol poisoning.

Valgeir: That was no bloody alcohol poisoning.

Me: I'm not usually like that.

Valgeir: You know perfectly well that it's jealousy. You don't have to keep up any front, we don't have to make out it's anything else. There's the truth you want. And the truth is you're not only a danger to yourself, like you were last night, but you could be a danger to other people too. By the way, we've got to pay some enormous bill for the glasses you managed to sweep off the bar when they were carrying you out. But that's the least important part of it, we can cope with a bill, but what's worse and what could be more frightening than you can even imagine is that this jealousy of yours could easily make you kill someone one day. And then it'll be too late to get your act together, Arnthrúdur.

Me: I promise it won't happen again.

Valgeir: Of course you promise.

Me: Lie down with me.

And he gave up and lay down.

He lay down next to me and kissed me and my body was shaking.

I don't know whether you know that feeling. It's the feeling of oblivion, oblivion and intensity, when you feel you have to disappear into a man, when you feel you cease being as he comes into you,

and there's nothing but that and the warmth,

you were married so maybe you know what it's like,

to fuse together at the chest,

fuse together at the hips,

and the feeling is strong and overpowering,

overwhelming and tremendous,

if you're afraid of losing it,

if you're scared that this is the last time,

and, God knows, I was more scared then than I've ever been.

*

'So how did it all end?' she asks, and warmth flows from her.

'As well as it could do. I went and settled the bill and the waiters were friendly and rather amused when they saw me. They must have died laughing when I'd gone but of course I just had to accept the humiliation. Then I phoned everyone who was there that evening to apologize. Everyone was very understanding, I didn't meet with any unpleasantness. Some people even seemed to think there was nothing more natural, but of course they didn't talk about anything else in the staff room. People must have looked at Valgeir and felt sorry for him. Though he said he wasn't aware of anything, that nobody looked pityingly at him or joked about it.'

'People aren't as bad as you sometimes think.'

'You've never been that far gone, have you, Z?'

'I don't know what to say. Hasn't Anna ever talked to you about it?'

'She says you sometimes have rather a sharp tongue, but I'm sure I'm worse.'

'I don't know about that. Hasn't she ever told you about when we went to a karaoke?'

'She mentioned once that you'd been to a karaoke and that you'd thrown a glass of wine in some man's face, but that's all, and I didn't ask her any more. Is that the evening you're talking about?'

'Yes, that's it. I didn't want to go actually because Anna had been ill all day. But she insisted on going, she gets a kick out of listening to people sing and she often sings herself, says it gives her an incredible surge of energy. So I gave in.

'I think I was watching Anna particularly closely that evening, both because I was sitting by myself, she was engrossed in conversation with some woman, and also because Anna was feeling worse than usual. I was quite worried about her. But anyway there were lots of people there who saw me throw the glass of wine in that man's face, and I wasn't even so lucky as to be able to blame the alcohol, since I was perfectly sober. I don't know what would have happened if I'd been drunk and whether things would have gone further. I rarely get drunk so I don't need alcohol to make me jealous and unable to control myself.'

'People say that jealousy is more common in relationships like yours.'

'What people say isn't always true.'

'But it's what people think.'

'That may be,' she said. 'It may be that it's more obvious, though I don't know, I don't know it well enough. I don't have much to do with these people, but of course I've heard stories,' and she stands up and winks at me.

She winks at the me who could possibly think of asking her about this after telling her about myself.

It's like I always feel the need to make amends for myself, to apologize for myself in some way,

    if not directly,

then indirectly, by passing the ball into someone else's
   court,
showing that others can be as bad as me,
   if not worse.

That's why I often pry into other people's affairs, to be able to justify myself. I who don't usually poke about into other people's business.

'You're a past master at changing the subject,' Anna said.

'What do you mean?'

'A past master at switching to another topic of conversation if you don't like what you see.'

'I don't understand what you mean.'

'No, that's OK.'

'Explain what you mean for me. You owe it to me. I always tell you exactly what I think, I always have time to talk to you.'

'Well, I can't think of any exact examples on the spur of the moment,' she said, 'but it often comes out when you've given something of yourself, confided in me about something, then it's like you regret it, take it back, and want to cover it up. And you often do that by asking me about something similar or about something completely different. But, Arnthrúdur, it's OK to do that, there's nothing wrong with you.' And she meant what she said.

Z winks at me again and goes out of the living room.

She's in the kitchen for a while pottering about and then she comes back out with a bottle of white wine and two glasses.

She fills the glasses and hands one to me.

My hands are shaking.

I feel her concern and calm down.

'Is this appropriate now?' I ask.

'It'll make us feel better while we wait,' she replies, then adds, 'and then I thought I'd show you the glasses I have which are still in one piece. I used to have twelve, in fact I got all the glasses when Hrafn and I got divorced. I had twelve of every kind. These are the only two wine glasses left. But there are a few more of the others. That's

174

life.' She fills my glass and doesn't seem to care a jot for what's appropriate and what's not.

'So you break glasses?' I say.

'I do.'

'Why?'

'When I feel bad.'

'When you argue?'

'Nobody argues with Anna. You must know that.'

'So when do you break glasses?'

'When I'm going crazy.'

'And when she's here?'

'No, I break glasses when I'm alone, and I break them because she isn't here with me. Some people shout and scream when they feel bad, others argue and bicker and some people fall apart into misery and wretchedness. I know all about that, but I also hurl glasses around. It's like it melts my anger away. I stand here in the middle of the room and hurl glasses around and nobody sees me. It doesn't disturb anyone at all but I feel better while I'm doing it and afterwards as well. I feel that I've got revenge on myself and on life. But Anna knows about it, of course. She's seen that there are always fewer and fewer glasses.'

'Try to look after your glasses better,' she says, teasingly.

'I look after them as well as I want to,' I reply, tetchily.

'But why did you throw a glass of wine into the man's face at the karaoke, like you were saying?'

'Because I wanted to.'

'You wanted to and you just gave in to that?'

'I'd been thinking of doing it all evening.'

'Why?'

'He had been pestering her and annoying her. He was all over her, staring at her and nudging her, stroking her hair, touching her thighs, and trying to get her to kiss him and finally I saw red.'

'And then you just stood up, cool as a cucumber, and threw a glass of wine in his face?'

'No, I didn't actually do that. I stood up slowly, walked over to him, leaned over to where he was sitting staring at her and said I wanted to

175

have a word with him. He was quite agreeable to that, turned towards me with this incredible sneer on his face and asked what he could do for me, obviously knowing full well why I had come over to their table. He had that goading look on his face, that unbearably sarcastic look that only the person it's intended for is aware of. It's the look that you adopt if you want a fight, if you want trouble, but I pretended I didn't see it because I didn't want either. I just wanted him to stop this ogling, so I asked him to leave her alone. She didn't like him at all. Nobody liked behaviour like his. He knew exactly what I was talking about. Then he asked sarcastically whether it was me or her who didn't like him and if she had anything to complain about why she didn't do so herself. He said he saw exactly what was going on, it was as plain as a pikestaff. It was so obvious from everything that I was gay that nobody could miss it. And I said curtly that that was just how I was and that it was no business of his. And he said that him and his doings were no business of mine either, and that I should just piss off and take my lezzy arse with me.

'Then I punched him in the face. His lip started bleeding and then I threw my glass of wine in his face. He gasped for breath and I just walked away laughing and told him not to forget the evening when a woman hit him.'

She stopped and took a deep breath.

But I could see that it was a relief to her to have got this off her chest.

Just as it was a relief to me to listen to it.

'So what happened then?' I ask.

'Well, it would be fun to make you guess.'

'He must have hit you back or something.'

'No, he didn't have to put himself to such trouble. All he had to do was to shake the wine off his face and put his hands up to his face. People crowded around him to wipe his face for him and the bar girl even called the police. Perhaps that's the difference, some people don't get the chance to account for their behaviour, let alone apologize if something they see offends them, which I wouldn't actually have done.

176

'But, to cut the story short, I was arrested because there were witnesses to the fact that I had been disorderly and offensive and hurt the poor man.

'So I was locked up for the night.

'I really didn't care, that wasn't the problem. I thought it was OK, except for Anna's sake. I felt bad because of her. She's so restrained and couldn't do anything about what was happening.'

She speaks quietly and we sit there for a while in silence, drinking our wine, maybe I should say sipping it, but we both leap up when the doorbell rings,

> rush out to the hall
>
> open the door on to the veranda
>
> and wait impatiently by the lift.

Valgeir's alone.

She's not with him.

Our wishes haven't been granted.

He looks disappointed too and his eyes look tired.

'I could do with a glass of wine,' he says, as he sits down.

And we continue to sit in silence,

> me and her,
>
> and he takes part in the silence,
>
> it's not oppressive,
>
> it demands nothing from us,
>
> it doesn't make us feel uncomfortable, actually neither
>
>> awkward nor good.

It's an empty silence which implies fatigue and may be the seed of some kind of resignation or hopelessness.

'So you haven't found out anything?' she asks.

'I've found out lots but nothing about her,' he says, closing his eyes. He opens them again, glances at her and continues, 'Something may have happened that we have no inkling of, at the moment I haven't found out anything. I think we'll just have to go on waiting. I feel so ill at ease, annoyed I suppose. A poem might make me feel better. Will you recite another poem, Z?'

She does as he requests.

She stands up with her glass in her hand and recites a poem, but in
her voice there's an emptiness,

>no warmth,
>no eagerness,
>no beauty,
>only an emptiness that unavoidably transmits itself to us
>although that's surely not her intention.

*

*Monday, 19 December 1995, was a cold day and I met an elderly lady in a
shoe shop in Hafnarfjördur. Suddenly it started snowing so hard you could
scarcely see anything. The woman was fussing about by the door so I
offered to drive her home and she accepted. When we got to her house she
invited me in and the first thing that caught my attention was a picture of
two women on the wall in the hall. The woman looked at me and said
quickly that she had loved one of the women in the picture but had been
ashamed of it.*

*'Times were so hard when I was young,' she said.*
*And I wondered how much they had changed.*

>*Of course it'll come*
>*day bringing daylight*
>*and broad smiles*
>*when everyone runs along*
>*the streets and square laughing*
>
>*everyone*
>
>*and then*
>*then you come to me and say*
>*that now it's the right weather to love*
>*and screw old ways and customs*
>*why am i always*
>*struggling along anyway*

*with mouldy hay and bags of turf*
*so young and promising*
*i'm just like a*
*16 mm*
*sad comedy*
*only the accompanist*
*is missing*

*but now the time has come*
*to study the weather*
*i'll just have to*
*trust you to play*
*magic notes*

*i look at you*
*and know there must be something*
*that i'm forgetting*
*it's just i don't know what it is*

*but i know*
*that now it's calm*
*after a thousand years*
*and the sound of the violin*
*is heard across the square and the streets*
*where we dance*

*of course it'll come*
*the day bringing daylight*
*and then you'll come to me*

\*

She's passed her emptiness on to us and enriched us.

But it's not emptiness that we need now.

'For some reason I have the feeling that Anna is somewhere so obvious that we just don't see it, can't see it,' I say slowly and firmly.

I have to try to know better than these people.

'Where could that be?' she asks. I can feel that she accepts my determination. She stands up, thumps her chest and tries as hard as she can to appear calm. But she isn't calm and she is scared.

'Valgeir, where did you go?' I ask.

'There's no point telling you. I've told you I didn't learn anything,' he says, still visibly annoyed.

'Tell us anyway,' she says. 'Perhaps it'll give us some clue. There's no harm at least in listening to a travel story, perhaps something you say will give one of us an idea.' Her tone of voice resembles mine now.

I repeat her request to Valgeir.

And Valgeir gives in.

As he begins to speak the fatigue clears from his face and we listen.

# 9

*Anna: 'I believed in the power of reason and determination.'*

Your two baby letters from 1994 really upset me.

It's certainly not an exaggeration to say so.

I lost all my sense of reason when I read them. It was like I had never had any reason, and I became completely disorientated, I who never lost track of time and place.

But it never dawned on me to throw the letters away, let alone tear them up.

I didn't know the reason why I acted as I did.

I didn't want the churning, painful feelings that I was feeling. I wasn't used to them and didn't know how to react. But I felt them and that seemed inescapable.

I, Anna Gudmundsdóttir, who was shaken by nothing, not even the knowledge that death was at my heels, couldn't bear your letters, couldn't bear the tone of them, that inflatedly happy tone I termed it to myself.

But naturally I didn't mention this to anyone, not even to Arnthrúdur, who would, of course, have been the only person who would have understood.

She knew how to talk to me and make everything better. But I couldn't come face to face with her and say that I was no better than she was,

      say that the position now was that we both shared the
        same agitation,
      that jealous agitation which I was always advising her to

181

rid herself of because it could destroy her life. And I
advised her at the same time to tread the narrow path
of calmness and coolness so she could obtain the
happiness to be found there.
I thought I knew that path.
I respected that path and wanted to associate myself with it. That's
why I decided to keep quiet and pretend nothing was wrong,
condemn anger to eternal rest,
pack it off to my heart,
not pander to it,
not nourish it,
never to water the foul flower it bore.
You had the right to live life as you chose.
It had never been a matter of debate that I wanted to do the same.
So there were no differences of opinion about that.
And I believed in the power of reason and determination.

*

I'm doing the same now as the first time I read the letters.

The effect of the second letter was greater but they echoed each
other.

And yet I knew then, when I held the letters in my hand, just as I
know now, that reason alone would not suffice to dismiss the anger
and the fear and that's the reason, even though I didn't know how to
go about it and even though you would never know about it, I decided
to get revenge on you.

I had to do something to annihilate the load on me.

I was aware I was being childish.

I was aware I was being cheap.

But I decided to get revenge on you.

I decided to do it in a way that I knew you would have understood
and that would have hurt you if you had found out about it.

I decided to disappear after the second letter.

Disappear and not let anyone know where I had gone.

Somewhere in the middle of nowhere and that would extinguish the effect of the letter.

I'm doing the same now as I did then.

I'm rocking myself back and forth.

That's how I still quieten my thoughts.

That's how I calm my body.

The drugs alone aren't strong enough any more.

I'll read the letter aloud before throwing them both into the flames.

*

*27 November 1994*

*My own Anna,*

*My ideas have begun to change.*

*Somehow they're moving in a different direction from what I expected. Not that I don't think I can cope with them, not that I think that will-power isn't all one needs. You know I believe in will-power and I still know what I want, but even so it seems like my ideas are making fun of me, scorning and mocking me. It's like some unbridled force somewhere in my head is popping its head up again and again and it's so unlike the will that I know and that I'm used to keeping in check that I don't know how to deal with it. Sometimes I call it the goblin, the goblin in the church rafters, sitting there on a broad beam in my head. Most of the time he's asleep or dozing but from time to time he wakes up and says something unpleasant or plain nasty. He doesn't beat about the bush.*

*Do you have a goblin like that, a destructive little creature like that, inside you?*

*I'll explain this better to help you understand what I mean, since this goblin power is focused almost entirely on you and us and the sort of future it thinks it sees.*

*You know I'm always trying to make a baby, a baby boy or girl for Hrafn and me, trying to form this extension of the two of us that he so wants to have and to hold, and that to a*

183

*certain extent I also want. It's not true what you were hinting at the other day, that it would just be convenient for me to have a baby now so no one would suspect us of anything. I understood exactly what you were trying to say, I just pretended not to. I know I don't want anyone to find out anything but I'm not so stupid or so cruel as to use a baby as some sort of shield to conceal my sins.*

*It's just that I don't want to have to answer any accusations and I shouldn't have to. I want to have this baby whether you believe me or not and I feel that I owe it to Hrafn to make this dream of his come true. So we lie there together at night after making love and talk about the baby that we must have just made, that must be embedded there now. And he's so romantic and kind and I try to be too, like I used to be once, but my mind obeys me less and less often and the creature pops up more and more often, clapping its hands together, shaking its head, sticking its tongue out at me, laughing out loud, spitting and shouting, 'Where is Anna, anna, anna, panna, nanna, ranna, anna, panna, where does she, she, she fit in, hee, hee, hee!'*

*And I start to think that I won't be able to make a baby with Hrafn, won't be able to make his dream come true, that my relationship with you has begun to get in the way and has drop by drop made me infertile. I know this sounds half crazy and I may be demented when the goblin takes the reins but isn't everyone round the bend and in my shoes wouldn't you be?*

*No, what nonsense, you would never do the same as me. You could never live a double life.*

*But it's me who has to make a choice and then maybe suffer for it and the bugger sits there firmly and mocks, offends and scorns my desire for an ordinary life. He whispers unbelievably disgusting things to me:*

*Z, don't you want to bloom?*

*If you do want to, why don't you have them both at the same time?*

184

*Why don't you get her into bed with the two of you?*
*Why don't you roll off her and over on to him?*
*That's what you're doing anyway.*
*Go on, be open about it.*

*But however that may be, my ideas have begun to change and your part in them is constantly becoming larger and larger and it's getting harder and harder to be me.*

*To begin with I only thought about the excitement and the thrill of it. Once exciting, always exciting. But now I feel more and more, think more and more about Thursdays, try more and more often to find a way to get away with you and be with you.*

*But I still love him, Anna, I love him a lot, often passionately.*

*And maybe one day I'll get my wish, maybe I'll be able to give him what he desires most of all, maybe, maybe, maybe. I'm going to do everything within my power at least to suppress that goblin who's always popping his head up and making fun of me and my life.*

*I suppose that's enough for now.*

*Be good to yourself.*

*You're often so pale these days, it's like you're always tired.*

*Perhaps you should take some vitamins and ginseng to perk yourself up. And apparently royal jelly is wonderful. And the name is just right for you.*

*With love,*

Z

*

I throw these letters into the fire.

I set fire to the memories attached to them.

I laugh out loud as I watch the flames lick them.

And then I hurl two eggs into the flames.

185

And permit myself to be angry like I was then.
The colour runs as the eggs land in the fire.
And the eggs turn ugly and black.
Perhaps this is the way I'll face death.

*

I never told you what went through my mind.

I never spoke to you about the contents of these letters and I never mentioned the goblin you had inside you. I knew you must have had it to contend with, knew that it was nothing but the combination of your conscience and guilt. But of course you knew that too. Because I didn't want to add my suffering to yours, I never told you what went through my mind when I read those letters.

I'm thinking the same now.

I'm thinking about you and Hrafn.

I have the starting point for doing so, you hid nothing from me.

I think about how you wrap yourselves around each other,
    how you embrace,
    how he bites your ears,
    kisses your neck,
    licks your breasts,
    sucks your nipples,
    how your whole body tenses,
    how it moves underneath him,
    how your hips start to plead and plead and plead and
    how he knows that in a moment he'll satisfy all your desire,
        how he teases you, how he tortures you by not coming
        straight away, drags it out until you're begging him and
        saying now, now, and how he comes inside you then
        and I hear you calling out,
    I hear it even though I don't want to,
    I know what you're like together.
And it hurts.
It hurts more and more all the time.

I can picture you more and more clearly all the time.
I'm becoming fonder and fonder of you.
So I'm more and more scared of being without you.
But I never tell you.
I'll never add to your suffering even though you made it mine.

*

I'll never tell you what I'm thinking.
I won't tell you how much these two letters hurt me, wound me.
I don't feel I have any right to because I'm ill,
because it's my job to go and yours to stay behind and
carry on,
that's why I read your letters and listen to everything you
tell me about you and Hrafn, saying only that it's fun
to lie next to you and hear you talk,
fun to share life and words with you,
saying that I feel no jealousy,
I'm unfamiliar with such emotions,
and at the start that was the truth.
But when our first year together was coming to an end,
autumn was creeping up on us,
and I would have liked the chance of a different life with
you,
life with you,
with you,
you.
Perhaps I'm the one who's to blame.
I'm the one who decided not to tell you straight away.
I'm the one who denies being familiar with feelings she is familiar
with.
I think about you sitting together at the table at dinner.
You've related this to me so often.
Yet again he's cooked the meal,
because Hrafn is so dreadfully good at cooking,

187

because Hrafn so enjoys domesticity,
because Hrafn wants so much to be of service, notwith-
    standing that he's very manly,
but naturally he serves only a few,
perhaps none but you,
because he knows what you like,
because he knows how to make you feel like a queen, he
    knows you like to purr and be stroked at the end of a
    hard day's work, he knows which of your back muscles
    are sore when you've been sitting at the computer in
    the office all day, he has the trick of creeping up behind
    you in the evenings with massage cream on his hands
    and massaging you in the right places,
Hrafn, he's such a good masseur,
he has such firm, lovely hands too,
so trustworthy and dependable,
and Hrafn, he's so strong that when you've finished eating
    he picks you up,
you like it so much when he holds you and carries you
    into the bedroom and shakes your pillow for you,
Hrafn, he knows what you want,
so you doze while he washes up,
Hrafn, he so enjoys working in the kitchen that it's no
    surprise you'll do anything you can to have his baby,
Hrafn, he's so manly,
and it's so nice to be with him,
any woman would feel good in Hrafn's arms.

*

And I think about how much you have in common and how much
there is that brings you together,
    not only your hobbies,
    trips abroad,
    outdoor life,

skiing trips,
walks,
films about animals,
theatre,
concerts,
furniture,
passion for collecting crystal,
money,
bank balances,
and politics,
but also your whole outlook on life.

You can sit and discuss politics for ages and he always reads your articles and acts as such a good sounding board because even though you're leftwing your views mustn't come across in your articles so you're really lucky to have him at your side, knowing as much as he does about politics and being so clever that he can always point out inconsistencies and debate points with you if you lose your sense of objectivity.

And your origins, of course that's the best bit, how similar your origins are, both of you from that middle class which forms the backbone of society, which pays taxes and keeps everything going no matter what, that middle class which people like me can thank for working as hard as they do, who don't just work part-time and live off grants so they can produce culture, as you term the two volumes of poetry I've written which you say you don't understand, even though you claim people like me should write books.

I'll never tell you that I read all your articles too and debate them with myself, because it's so obvious that you don't think I know anything about politics, at least you never attempt to discuss your articles with me. And I can't remember you ever asking me whether I read them.

I never tell you either.

Yet I often want to.

I often want to tell you that I think you write well and that writing seems to come naturally to you.

But I don't.

It should be enough for me to know that you and Hrafn talk about it.

That you share it just like you share everything else.

I'm only the woman you sleep with.

I'm only the woman you share a secret with.

I'm only the woman you don't recognize on the street.

Yet I can't help smiling as I pick up your short letters from the summer of 1995. I liked them then, and I still do. But I have no trouble throwing them on to the fire, thinking as I do at the same time about time and how you slowly changed. I'll never tell you how happy it made me, and yet perhaps you know anyway that it cheered my little heart when you were jealous and angry, even though I always claimed the opposite and begged you incessantly not to wreck our time with jealousy.

You ought to know how strange it is for me to sit here and confront all of that as it really was

and not as I told you it was,

not as I wanted it to be,

I played my imaginary flute for you,

and you heard the tune,

but you didn't hear how my heart was pounding,

you'll never hear how it pounded.

I read your summer letters now and smile.

They counterbalance the other two which are crackling in the fire.

You know I'm a woman of equanimity.

I'll always be a woman of equanimity.

\*

*26 July 1995*

*Dearest,*

*I may not really know what it is that I want.*

*But you won't find that very surprising.*

*You who are so lively, cheerful and always mean well.*

*I just had to get a few lines off to you to let you know that*

190

*of course I saw you yesterday, and maybe I saw you better than ever before.*

*And it was uncomfortable.*

*It was uncomfortable to have gone out for an ordinary evening walk, and to be miles away in my own thoughts, thinking about you of course like I usually do when Hrafn and I go for a walk in the evening, and then to see you all of a sudden arm in arm with that girl. Do you imagine I don't know that she's like you, that girl? One of your lot and all that. I don't need to ask, it's so obvious, just like a boy and pleased as punch with herself. Still, of course, it's none of my business who you go around with.*

*But it was uncomfortable when you waved to me as if we didn't know each other, as if I was just some acquaintance, and it wasn't nice to pretend I hadn't seen you and to have that conversation with Hrafn in the evening sunshine.*

*'I think that girl on the other side of the road was waving to you.'*

*'What girl, I didn't see any girl, but I was miles away.'*

*'Didn't you see her? It looked like she knew you, at least. Didn't you notice those two girls who walked past us laughing? You're really in a world of your own, have you stopped noticing where you're going?' he asked, teasingly.*

*Naturally you have to lead your own life.*

*But why do you have to be outside laughing and giggling right in front of me? Couldn't you have stopped and looked in a shop window or something? Don't you give a damn how it affects me, or how I'm going to feel afterwards when you've turned the corner?*

*Next time it happens you could at least bend down and do up your shoelace or something so I don't look like a complete idiot. On the other hand it seemed to me that I wasn't of any great significance to you, like you're always saying. I couldn't see there was anything about you to say that it's only a week since we were together in the cottage, only a week since I*

191

*heard you say you loved me, only a week since you put your arms around me and told me not to be sad, that time would sort things out if I was feeling so awful.*

*It seemed to me on the street there that you were feeling just as happy with that girl, and naturally you'll never see any reason to tell me about her. In any event, you needn't pretend there's nothing going on there, that she's just a friend of yours. I know there's something between you, I know you share something more than just going clubbing together. You say I should trust you but how can I when I see that glint in your eyes that I know so well.*

*Well, I'm still looking forward to seeing you on Thursday. Maybe we'll talk about this then, maybe we won't, but you ought to know that I'll want to, you ought to know that it'll hurt me if you don't but that I won't broach the subject.*

Z

*

*29 August 1995*

*Anna,*

*How can you do this to me again?*

*I know you decided not to tell me about that girl. Decided not to go into how you know each other. Even though I almost begged you to talk to me. But how can you play the same game again?*

*Why couldn't you do what I asked you to do? Crossed over the road or looked away?*

*How could you bring yourself to play that game again? What do you think I am anyway? Do you think I'm made of stone? Fortunately it's only two nights until we meet and you won't escape this time. This isn't just jealousy, Anna, it's a question of trust. You must be able to understand that, I shouldn't have to suffer like this. I know you don't like spending the time we have together talking. You'd rather go to*

192

*bed, make love and not say anything, and of course I want that too. But this time I can't.*

*I can't make it out to the cottage until the second week in September and that's too long for me to wait. I have to talk to you about this. I'm not going to take the risk of meeting you again with the same person. I just can't.*

Z

\*

I like those two letters.

I liked it when you came striding in the door two days later, without even ringing the doorbell like you usually do,

> perhaps it pleased me most that I didn't show any surprise,
> that I didn't tell you the truth,
> although I didn't lie about anything,
> I had promised you that,
> but I didn't tell you the truth,
> and I felt good after we had talked,
> one Thursday morning that we had spent together
> > without making love, without annihilating time and
> > place, and that's the morning which confirms for me
> > that I did the right thing, in spite of everything, in
> > never telling you how much my feelings troubled me.

I liked you more and more.

And I told you so.

I'll tell you again now.

I know you can hear me.

And I know that you know.

\*

You storm in the door.

> Amazing how you can storm.
> I'm lying in bed waiting for you.

193

I've been a bit under the weather recently,
    I'm looking forward to going up to the cottage with you,
    charming energy out of the countryside,
    strengthening my skin with the autumn mud,
    sitting up late by the fire and sleeping in the attic where
        the walls slope to the roof and the wind breathes
        through the wood, breathes over us and blows the
        breath of life into my nostrils, cleanses the wretched-
        ness from my soul and sends me to sleep,
    it's so good to fall asleep by your side and wake up by your
        side and watch you sleep and remember nothing but
        the good we've given each other.
And I look at you standing on the floor in front of me.

I know you're angry even though you feel you don't have the right to be.

I know you're upset but didn't intend to be.

I know what you're going to say.

I'll answer you as gently as I can.

You: Who is that girl, Anna?

Me: A friend of mine.

You: What friend?

Me: I've known her for ages.

You: And do you spend a lot of time with her?

Me: I wouldn't say that.

You: Do you sleep with her?

Me: No, Z, I don't sleep with her.

You: So why do you spend so much time with her?

Me: Do I do that?

You: Is it just chance then?

Me: What?

You: Bumping into you two twice.

Me: Can't I just as well say that I bumped into you two?

You: You haven't complained about that.

Me: No, but isn't it just as possible to describe this putative bumping into from that point of view?

You: Oh, stop it.

Me: But I don't quite understand what you mean.

You: What don't you understand?

Me: It's you who wants to lay down the law.

You: But that doesn't mean you have to hurt me.

Me: Are you asking me not to go out?

You: Why won't you answer the question?

Me: It's not my fault if we bump into each other.

You: That's not the point.

Me: What is the point then?

You: What matters to me is who this person is.

Me: I've told you who she is.

You: I don't like it when you won't answer the question.

Me: I've known her for ages, we went to Vopnafjördur and Akureyri together once. It was ages ago.

You: I didn't know you'd been there.

Me: I've been to lots of places.

You: And were you working there?

Me: You could say that.

You: For my sake, please consider my feelings.

Me: I do that as far as I can, you know that.

You: And can I trust you?

Me: I've told you, you can trust me just as much as I can trust you.

You: There's no chance at all that I'll cheat on you.

Me: How do I know that?

You: How do you suppose I could do?

Me: Stop thinking like that, we're not talking about cheating.

You: Sometimes I don't think I can go on with this.

Me: You'll have to have a good think about it if that's how you feel.

You: I'm so full of insecurity and unhappiness.

Me: I've told you so often that there's no need for that.

You: Sometimes I wish I'd never met you.

Me: There's no need to regret anything that we've had together.

You: I've changed.

Me: You don't have to regret that.

You: It's not the excitement I need any more.

Me: I know.

You: I look forward more and more to seeing you.

Me: That can't do you anything but good.

You: I don't always feel so happy with Hrafn.

Me: Love him when you're with him and me when you're with me, that's the best thing for you and for me and it's best for him too, lie down next to me and tell me about the babies, or we can just be quiet, or we can make love, let's at least be friends and if you can't do that any more, then leave and don't think of me with regret, never think of me with anything but happiness. But if you decide to go on meeting me like it's been up until now, learn to value what we give each other.

You: And what's the greatest thing we've given each other?

Me: Love.

And then you start crying,

> you cry a lot,
> I try to comfort you but I can't,
> you won't be comforted,
> you just cry and you can't speak, I know how you're
>> feeling and I stroke your hair, I love your long hair, I
>> stroke your cheeks and draw around your mouth with
>> my finger, I kiss your mouth, I love your mouth and
>> your cheeks,
> I'm also crying within myself,
> but not in front of you,
> I never tell you why I cry,
> I never tell you that I know the feelings that hurt you,
> I've tried them all myself,
> I'm crying because for us there's no future,
> I'm crying because I have no right to wound you,
>> crying because I can't speak plainly even though I say I do.

I can't tell you for example how I got revenge on you for your horrible baby letters.

I'm crying because you still don't feel that I'm a person like you.

You're crying because you're desperate.

You're crying because your life's taken a turn you don't like,
   because you don't like yourself,
   because you still don't understand love,
   how can you understand something you despise?
I comfort you,
   I put my arms around you and comfort you, knowing that
      it's beyond my power.
But despite all the crying I'm happy,
   happy to have you,
   happy to feel that you're changing,
   to know that we're becoming closer
   and for a moment I forget reality.

*

I sit here and recall everything just as it was.
   Everything just as it is and always will be until the end.
   And suddenly I burst out laughing.
   What an extremely tragic and sad person I am.
   I'm sitting here alone tossing letters and poems on to the fire.
   Like a character in a romantic novelette.
   Like a character in an old-fashioned film.
   But this is my life.
   Every word of mine is true, every feeling real.
   And my march will end here.
   Not because no better places exist.
   Not because I think it's best to die alone and with lots of clothes on
in front of a crackling fire in an old cottage in the Svínadalur valley,
      but because I've had some good times here,
      I've loved best here,
      I've chosen this place
      and I've chosen well.
   I throw your letters on to the fire.
   And my poems follow.
   And I'm beginning to feel tired, I stretch out and look at the beams

in the ceiling, the nails that we nailed into them last year and the dried roses hanging there, the ones you gave me in the autumn, our last autumn together, the autumn that we both knew would be our last but dared not name as such. Neither of us wanted to say it.

'Here are some roses for the beams,' you said, handing them to me, red and yellow ones.

'The most beautiful colours, of course.'

'The best of everything for you and the most beautiful colours for you,' you said, kissing me.

I recall I didn't want you to do that.

I recall that was the first time I thought I might be a strain and an encumbrance to you.

'Isn't it difficult for you?' I asked.

'What?'

'Dragging me here when I'm so ill and stupid.'

'Be thankful while we can get here,' you said, in a teasing tone.

'And who am I supposed to thank for that?'

'Me and you, we're so bloody energetic.'

'I asked you whether I was a burden to you.'

'You mustn't talk like that.'

'I want you to answer.'

'You could never be a burden to me.'

'Tell me the truth.'

'I love being with you.'

'Have you seen Hrafn recently?'

'A couple of days ago.'

'And how is he?'

'Just fine, doing well at work and travelling all over the place as usual.'

'Does he know how far gone I am?'

'Yes.'

'Will you go back to him?'

'No.'

'Why are you so definite about that?'

'I know what I'm doing.'

'You know it wouldn't matter to me if you did. You know it would only give me pleasure if that could make you happy. You do know that, don't you?'

'I know as well as I possibly can that I won't ever go back to him.'

'But doesn't he want you to?'

'Yes, he does want me to.'

'So why don't you?'

'I can't. I've met you and I won't go back to him. You must understand that.'

'You can be happy again together.'

'I'll be with you and we won't talk any more about that, it's you I love, you silly thing, and you that I want to be with and be near and all that, and now do try and behave yourself,' you said, and you brought me some cocoa,

    you liked fussing about me the last year we had together,

    liked doing everything you could for me and I enjoyed it.

How can I but smile as I recall that?

How can I but be grateful for those times?

Although I remember how I got my revenge on you.

How I enjoyed that.

I've forgiven myself now.

I've come to terms with the violence of my feelings and the anger,

    have realized that I could never be anything but the

        person I was however different I wanted to be.

I know it was nothing but jealousy that sent me off on that plane to Vopnafjördur and then to Akureyri.

And what's more, I am rather fond of her now.

I felt bad about it then.

I didn't want to acknowledge my feelings then.

I was ashamed of myself for your sake and for my sake.

Despite the fact that you would never find out anything about that trip of mine.

And you will never know anything about it.

I was full of the desire for revenge because of your trips.

I'm not seeking revenge any more.

You managed to go abroad.

I managed to get away from you.

And I made myself vanish, knowing that you would do everything within your power to find me, search every nook and cranny for me.

That made me feel better, if anything it made me happy though I didn't show it, I just looked up an old friend, the girl you saw me out walking with, and asked her to go away with me.

She couldn't have been keener and so

I just disappeared from you,

and from everyone,

told no one I was going,

went away, knowing full well it could be a costly exercise,

and went on one hell of a bender and made a name for

myself both in Akureyri and Vopnafjördur.

I woke up in bed with both men and women, unable to remember how I had got there. All I could remember was that you were somewhere bent on making a baby and thought that it was all the same to me and that you were supposed to think that. And I couldn't think of anything but how your letters upset me and made me increasingly angry. And yet I never showed it,

I just reached for the glass of wine on the breakfast table

or the bedside table and slugged and slugged

and went on drinking anything in liquid form, even when

I didn't want any more.

I made the people in the hotel in the east look at me with amazement in their eyes,

this freak from Reykjavík who didn't know to control

herself, who on the contrary was wild and crazy was

what I heard people say.

And I stood up and told them to bugger off, hadn't they ever seen a woman like me before?

Puked up, sick as a dog, in the doorway,

was thrown out of the church in Akureyri for disturbing

the peace and behaving disrespectfully

and ended my stay in the capital of the north by falling

asleep on the library steps,

maybe symbolic for me, although no one there was aware
of it,
I who have such a passion for books.
And she tagged along behind me all the time, the girl you saw me
walking down the road with, faithful as an old dog like best friends
usually are and astounded by how the placid Anna was acting.
She didn't get to know anything either.

*

Without a doubt I showed my worst side.
Without a doubt I wasn't myself.
But I understand now why I was like that.
And now I am like myself.
I'm calm and collected and I'm not making a fuss.
But I am extremely tired.
And my time is running out as the poet said.

*

Strange how, faced with death, the whole of life is like a poem,
pours and rushes forth in clear, transparent pictures,
flows on like clear mountain water and every stone can
be seen.
And strange how words and their meaning don't matter much.
But of course I am extremely tired.
Of course all of me is awfully near to death.
But maybe that's why I can say that I have been happy.
And maybe why I didn't want to move,
chose my night's resting place myself.

# 10

*Arnthrúdur: 'Now I know we'll always be together.'*

I contemplate Valgeir as he sits opposite me holding a glass of white wine. He's agreed to tell us about where he's been but would prefer to sit quietly or doze off,
> I know he would without him having to say so,
> unless there's some other underlying reason.

And as soon as that thought pops into my head it comes as a shock to me how often he surprises me,
> how often I just can't make him out,
> yet he's not the sort of man to shock society,
> he's a nature-lover,
> not given to excesses,
> trustworthy in matters of finance,
> a friend in need,
> slow to anger,
> even-tempered,
> hard-working,
> popular with his students,
> in all respects a reliable type,
> all that and much more I've heard people say about him,
> and I've never known anyone speak badly of him, not even
>> his ex-wife and she probably had good reason to,
>> she would certainly have been within her rights to get
>> angry with him when he told her about me
> but she didn't,

202

she said she couldn't,

    if he had to come to me for something that she couldn't
        give him then she didn't want to stand in his way.

Even she couldn't get angry with him and accuse him of being dishonourable but instead preferred to say that it could happen to anyone,

    she understood him even though she was hurt and was
        having trouble getting over it,

    she didn't want a bitter divorce,

    they'd shared too much that was wonderful for her to
        want that.

But despite her understanding him and forgiving him as he says, and despite nobody harbouring any doubts about him,

    there's still something I don't understand,

    something about his manner I can't quite put my finger on.

I've wondered so hard what it is and now and then I look deep into his eyes and ask him what he's thinking,

    often he doesn't answer

    and says he can't be bothered to get involved in "female
        curinonsity",

    sometimes he simply longs for peace and quiet.

'And what is this "female curinonsity"?' I asked in amazement, because he had never said that to me before.

He only ever said it once.

I remember it was almost a year after he moved in with me.

Valgeir is not one for repeating himself.

He says that he can't bear saying the same thing more than once.

That he doesn't expect other people to do so and doesn't want them to expect him to do so, because if people are interested in what is said they'll take note of it, if not then the words and even deeds are of no importance.

But, like I say, he'd never mentioned the thing about "curinonsity" before.

So I asked him.

'It's these eternal questions about how I'm feeling and what I'm thinking,' he said, 'whether I'm thinking this or that or perhaps something else, whether I think this about something or that, eternal never-ending discussions about everything under the sun, never-ending post-mortems about everything, important things and unimportant things. You know what, Arnthrúdur, sometimes it is possible to sit in a comfortable chair and not think about anything in particular, to be simply tired and to try to relax, has that ever occurrred to you?' He laughed quietly so the absence of feeling in his voice wouldn't shock me.

'And is this "curinonsity" something that all women have in common?'

'Oh, I don't know. I don't know what all women have in common and if you're secretly trying to find out whether you resemble the other women who've featured in my short history then you can reassure yourself that you don't. You are definitely very special, the most special of all, the best and the most beautiful and there you are and that's exactly what I call "curinonsity", this bizarre inquisitiveness.'

Valgeir always surprises me,
    I don't know how I manage to forget that,
    but I know he's annoyed now,
    because he's tired.

I can see that by the way he's sipping his wine and breathing deeply.

'Are you tired?' she asks, her voice still empty though she's waiting just like me for him to start talking.

'Not exactly tired but I don't feel at ease, I've got some blasted premonition that things aren't all right, that something we just aren't expecting has happened. I don't know why I feel like that. I don't usually. But I feel that I've done all the searching I can and now I have to come to face the fact that I haven't a clue what's happened, if anything at all has happened.'

'And that's not for certain,' I say, remembering all of a sudden that Anna told me, only a few months earlier, one of those times when she went into hospital to recover from treatment, that she didn't want me to worry about her.

She: Don't get upset if you don't know where I am.

Me: What's that supposed to mean?

She: I mean if you don't hear anything from me for a while you know that time will come to an end and you will hear from me again.

Me: I manage to keep track of you.

She: You don't need to keep track of me.

Me: What do you mean?

She: I'm not a child. I won't get into trouble.

Me: I'm not concerned about that.

She: I just want you to remember that you don't need to be scared if you don't hear from me or don't know where I am. I'll always turn up.

Me: I suppose I know that already.

She: Don't forget it.

Me: Don't you mean you'll be with her?

She: Not necessarily.

Me: What are you talking about, for heaven's sake?

She: I'm asking you never to be afraid for me.

And I recall that as I looked at this extraordinary sister of mine I had seldom thought her more extraordinary than at that moment. There she lay, sick as a dog, in bed and told me not to be afraid for her. At that time I didn't understand what she meant, in fact I thought she must be half delirious or at least confused, but I can see now that she was only reminding me that despite her illness she was an independent person who didn't need to be looked after like a child,

> she had all her faculties and was capable of making
> decisions,
> I need no more be worried about her than she about me,
> her words were the security.

I decide to tell them about this.

It will surely lessen their anxiety, just as it did mine.

'Every month makes a difference now, she's become much weaker recently,' says Valgeir.

'But I think we can believe this. What do you think, Z?' And, asking her, I notice that the empty look in her face has given way to a redness in her cheeks and that she keeps on blinking her eyes.

She gets to her feet and goes out into the hall, saying, as she closes the lavatory door behind her, 'There's nothing more we can do.'

'That's odd,' I say, looking at him.

'It's hardly surprising, the woman's terrified.' As he speaks we hear a noise coming from the lavatory,

    quiet at first then louder,

    we hear the sound of water running into the sink and her

        retching and retching.

'Poor thing,' Valgeir says.

'Yes,' I agree, and add, 'You ought to tell us where you went when she comes back. It might make her feel better. She's got to believe that everything's all right. She's got to, just the same as us, there's no point giving up hope. I don't think we have to be any more worried about Anna now than before anyway. We have to respect what she says. She is an independent person even though she's ill.'

'You're being strong now,' he says.

'I'm not being strong,' I reply, 'I'm just being realistic,' and to her, when she comes back into the room, I tell her

    that she must stay calm,

    she's given me strength,

    now the time has come to use that strength herself,

    now she must show self-control,

    and reason,

    and be as strong as she has been up until now.

She turns her head away and I know there are tears in her eyes.

I know that she's worried in the same way as I would be if I were in her shoes.

I know that she loves in the same way as I do.

'Valgeir's going to tell us where he went. It may help us in some way, maybe we'll see something new, who knows, try to calm down.'

'I'll calm down, but before you tell us where you went I'd like to let you hear a few poems Anna wrote in 1996. They're short poems but the time is right for them now, at least I suddenly had the feeling that she wanted me to recite them and that they contained a message for us here, almost as if she's talking to us. I seem to hear her now, she seems so incredibly close to me. I'm tired of course but that's not why I can feel her closeness. It feels like she's here with me.'

I don't say anything. I just listen good-naturedly.

I don't want to hear her recite poems now.

I'm too restless to listen but I'll have to put up with it.

'Recite the poems, then,' I say, and Valgeir asks her to as well.

And fortunately it's not emptiness that flows to us from her this time, but rather a sort of happiness, equanimity and acceptance, which may be an unusual threesome in the atmosphere that's prevailed tonight, in the fear that has actually coloured all our dealings but that we've tried to avoid mentioning.

Fear can't be measured in words, it lurks under the surface.

'Don't always talk about what's under the surface,' Anna said to me once. We were sitting in a café drinking coffee and cognac, which was going to our heads that Friday afternoon at the end of November two years ago.

I was killing time until Valgeir had finished teaching.

Anna was wandering about as was her wont.

She was in a good mood as usual,

happy with life,

despite what was hanging over her or maybe because of it.

'Who's going to talk to you about it if I don't?' I asked.

'Do I in particular have to be talked to about what lies under the surface?'

'Don't you have to confront death?'

'I'm not scared.'

'I just think you don't know.'

'Believe me, I'm not scared, I'm not scared of death, there's no deeper meaning to those words, they don't say anything other than what they mean literally. I'm not scared of death even though I can't say that I'm looking forward to greeting it. I'm really not sure that I want to have it coming to visit straight away but that's not the same as being scared of it. You aren't always scared of an unwelcome guest, are you?' she said, with a laugh.

207

My cheerful sister.

What do I have compared to her?

Nothing but love for her.

Nothing but hope for her.

'Recite the poems, Z, I can feel her too,' I say and I know that makes her feel better.

I want to listen now.

Patience has come to stay.

\*

*On Monday, 11 March 1996, my brother-in-law gave me a present. It was a large brown wicker basket filled with dried flowers.*

*Flowers are, and will always be, a symbol of life and joy.*

*Sometimes one sees a hidden meaning in everything.*

> *Why are you giving me dried flowers, my friend*
> *shall i sit down by the dried-up spring and drink the water*
> *shall i warm myself by the burnt-out fire*
>
> *don't you see the spring in my eyes?*

\*

*On Monday, 12 August 1996, I was admitted to hospital for a week. The woman in the bed next to mine was on her deathbed and nobody visited her. If I had been more than semi-conscious myself I would have sat with her and pretended to be a visitor.*

*I was happiest the day I made my escape into real life again.*

*Illness is a nuisance.*

*Don't grieve for life, my dear*
*instead follow it while it passes*
*and enjoy the birds singing outside the window*

\*

*On Monday, 14 October 1996, my sister came to visit me and told me what she was most afraid of was the day she would be alone if she would be alone. She said she was afraid of old age and harboured the wish to flee it like a mad dog running away.*
*I understood what she meant.*

*The lines on your face tell me how passionately life loves you*
*enjoy love and cultivate the tree in your garden*

\*

*On Monday, 30 December 1996, I slept all day and the night passed without me noticing. It's best when everything happens as normal, a bright day following a dark night.*
*I don't want to miss anything.*

*When i woke up*
*you brought me*
*water and ice cubes*

*i found love in every drop*

\*

My patience was rewarded.
I enjoyed the poems and managed to concentrate.
I must say that pleases me more than I can say.

209

'I didn't know she wrote a poem to me,' says Valgeir thoughtfully.

'Nor did I,' I add.

'She's had something to say to all of us,' she says, turning away. I sense that she's still crying though I can't see her tears.

She's still scared about what is to come.

'I've never given her a basket filled with flowers,' says Valgeir, 'but I've often spoken to her about the transience of things, how everything falls apart and disappears, fades and becomes nothing, except maybe a replica of itself. I like that poem and would like to write it down, but naturally you can't let me do that. We'll have to wait for her and get her permission. What did you say the last line was? Yes, "don't you see the spring in my eyes?" Of course I've always seen the spring in her eyes. I've met few people who look to the future as positively as she does, and I mean that literally. I truly hope you'll tell her that you recited these poems for us here so that I can tell her I've never thought of her as something faded and lifeless.' She replies that she's never had any secrets from Anna and won't ever have.

'I think I understand these poems better than the other ones I've heard and certainly better than the ones I've read myself. There's something simplistic and clean-cut about them and what she writes about me is definitely no interpretation of something I nearly said. It's exactly how it was and so often has been. I've complained to Anna so often and I've even let myself do so when I should have held my tongue. But at the same time I've always tried to be the real me, tried not to change even though it's been hanging over us. I know I've been nasty, demanding, whingeing if it's been necessary. She wants people to turn to her and she wants to be a support to them, but she doesn't want to upset others with her worries. That's what she's like and always has been, if she wasn't she wouldn't have tried to keep her illness a secret, for example. It's true, though, that she finds being ill a nuisance, isn't that one of the things she said?'

'Who doesn't find illness a nuisance?' asks Z, rather stiffly, it seems to me. She glances at Valgeir but for a moment it looks like she's looking at something else. At least she's miles away as she asks him to tell us where he went earlier that night. She had only wanted to recite

210

these poems because they'd been in the forefront of her mind. Now she thinks (and she reminds me of myself as she says this) that it'll do us all good to hear what he has to say, at any rate she wants to lie down and listen. The police may phone in a while, they may know something more, and if not, well, in any event we'll have to have another think, go out again and search more thoroughly.

She's filled with energy now.

She's got her second wind.

Her strength infects us too.

*

It's not as if I had anything remarkable to relate. Just because I tell you where I went doesn't mean I'm likely to come up with an entertaining story, but since you insist, I'll tell you.

I think it was about half past four when I left you and went off. Naturally there was nobody about here in this part of town, even though it was Saturday night, and it was really only to get my bearings and make a plan that I drove over to the library in Sólheimar. I stopped in front of it, lit a cigarette and debated with myself where to go. I sat there for a while and was half hoping there'd be a miracle, that Anna would pop up in front of the car and grin one of her famous mocking grins.

But that didn't happen, of course.

I must admit I was rather irritated at not being able to find out where she was hiding and I was probably scared too. It's awful to say it but I felt annoyed with Anna too, annoyed that she should drag herself out of bed, sedated as she was, and wander off somewhere without telling a soul. Even though, of course, she must have known that the nurses would notice she wasn't there and would notify us at once. Anna's a wonderful person. She's a great person, she's kind, and all that, but she can be, and often has been, extraordinarily inconsiderate, especially since she became ill, and she's getting worse. Simply taking off for two days, even three, and not caring that people are scared, not wanting to face up to reality. It takes less than that to scare people. But

211

she's just like that. It's her declaration of independence, but it's intolerable and of course we've had to put up with it. It's not as if this is the first time Arnthrúdur and I have stayed awake all night worried out of our minds, let alone you. But of course it's her right. And I tried to shame myself out of being annoyed with her on the grounds that there are few people I'm more fond of and few who have been truer friends than she has. I was also scared that she'd thought to hell with everything and gone off on a major binge, or just another ordinary binge. They've become rather frequent over the last few years and aren't good for her because she can't always tolerate much alcohol on top of the drugs she's taking.

But you know all of this and it's not much fun listening to me moaning on about it. But it was also because of her binges that I racked my brains trying to think where she might have gone to get hold of some alcohol at that time of the night. We'd phoned everywhere we could think of but then it struck me that I could pop round to the house opposite her, be bold and just ring doorbells to check whether she was with one of the three friends of hers who live there.

So I drove there and on the way over I felt so optimistic that I was probably on the right track. Anna's spent the evening drinking with the old man on several occasions and they've sat rocking backwards and forwards long into the night. She's told me about lots of amusing adventures she's got up to with him. He's an extremely strange character.

So there you are, that's what I decided to do and I set off.

I parked the car outside her house and saw two things that gave me hope.

All the lights were on in the first-floor flat.

And the top flat wasn't in total darkness.

I get out of the car quickly and, half running up the steps, ring the bell for the first-floor flat. The old man comes to the door in trousers and a vest, dishevelled and scruffy, with a frown on his face.

I can tell straightaway that he's the worse for drink.

'I've seen you a few times,' he says, with a suspicious grin on his lips, making no attempt to invite me in.

212

'I'm looking for Anna. I thought she might be with you,' I reply, hoping he'll ask me in, because it's bitterly cold outside as you know.

'I've often seen you coming out of her house,' he continues, kneading his right eyebrow with one finger.

'I'm her brother-in-law,' I say drily. He's either insinuating something or making fun of me, which annoys me.

I don't really care which it is he's doing.

'Brother-in-law, eh?' he says, weighing me up with his eyes.

'I'm looking for her, is she here?' I ask, unable to control the irritation in my voice.

'If she were here, do you think I'd tell you?' he asks. 'Don't you think she'd want some peace and quiet, don't you think we'd want some peace and quiet? She doesn't come here very often now, not since she became so very ill.'

'That's why I'm looking for her, because she's ill,' I say. 'I'm not ringing strangers' doorbells in the middle of the night just for my own amusement. Tell me if she's here. We're all worried about her. We've even notified the police.' I manage to control my annoyance, but I'm sure I can hear a noise, someone moving about, inside the flat.

'She's not here, I'm sorry, you'll have to look somewhere else. She goes her own way and you won't find her because she doesn't want you to,' says the old man with a mournful look, as he pulls the hall door closed so I can't see into the flat.

'Can't I come and have a look for myself?' I say, pushing the old man aside to get past him into the hall.

'Don't you believe an old man? Do you think I don't know how serious Anna's situation is?' he asks quietly, but he doesn't try to stop me going in to the living room.

There's nobody there.

On the table there's a copper glass and a half-empty bottle of aquavit, a small transistor radio playing accordion music, and at one end of it a plateful of milk which two cats are lapping up.

'That's all the company I've had tonight,' he says. 'They were miaowing outside in the cold so I let them in. You can believe what old

213

men say. She's not here, why don't you look around the flat and make sure yourself on your way out?'

I do just that and Anna isn't there, nor is there any sign of her, except her first volume of poetry open and upside-down on the old man's bedside table.

'She gave it to me, I'm trying to get through it,' he says, and I take my leave and give him your telephone number, Z, in case he's any the wiser as to where she is. I ask him whether she could be visiting upstairs or whether he has any clue where she might have gone.

'There's nobody upstairs except the lady there, I'm sure of that. I knocked on her door just a little while ago and invited her in for a drink but she said she was tired. She said I must have heard that her son had been to see her and they'd had a fight which ended with him rushing out yelling that he would never come to see her again, because she was always so awful when they'd had dinner together. She was exhausted and had been sitting reading the Bible and intended to do that until she fell asleep. No, Anna's not upstairs, that's for sure, and I can't imagine where she is. Have you tried her friend in Sólheimar? Yes, of course you have, you're all there – the phone number, I'd forgotten. And she's not in any bar at this time of night. But have you driven out to the cottage? She might have gone there, to warm herself by the fire. She loves that cottage and the fire. I've actually been there with her, not so long ago, and we sat there and warmed ourselves by the fire and swapped stories. It's a lovely cottage, have you tried there?'

'The snow's too deep, you can't get there now by car,' I say.

'Is that so? Then I can't help you much, but I would have thought she was there, keeping warm, Anna's such a one for keeping warm. She often wrapped herself up in a duvet when she sat here with me.'

'Thanks for your help,' I say.

'Not at all, not at all, but is it all right if I phone even if I don't see her? I want to know if anything happens, I'm fond of her, we're friends, you know. Are you sure the road out to the cottage is blocked?'

'Yes, I'm sure,' I reply, jumping down the steps, pleased with myself for having called in on the old man and being able to cross him off the list of possible places. I start the car and go on thinking things

214

over. A few seconds later the old man comes out of the house, with an anorak and a balaclava on and the cats following him. They jump in the back and he calls to me as he closes the car door, 'I'm going to drive around for a while, I usually do around this time.'

And so he drives off but I sit there in my car thinking.

I think about Anna and all we've been through together since I first met her at your place, Arnthrúdur. I think about all the conversations we've had, the walks, the drives and the holidays, the Christmases and the Easters and all that you've told me about the two of you. And I'm lost deep in thought when suddenly I come to, feeling ashamed of myself when I realize I've been thinking of her as if she were dead. Recalling her as if we won't ever meet again, and that's not like me and not how I want to think. I drive off, down Raudalækur, out on to Laugarnesvegur, I drive slowly and scour the streets, down Borgartún, on to Laugavegur. I cruise down the road slowly but there's nobody about, a town dead at nighttime with the exception of the occasional tramp wandering around, hearing and seeing nothing. There's no one in the square, nor by the lake, and Anna is of course nowhere to be seen. But as I'm driving past the Free Church it's like I hear someone whispering to me to drive over to her friend Thórdur's mother. And I realize that's the last place she could possibly be, it seems like a very long shot. But I know I have to try there because the idea of it came to me. I had driven her there when she used to visit her in the old days and remembered where she lived.

It's nearly six o'clock when I ring her doorbell and Anna isn't there. And hasn't been there for a month, which is a long time because after they made it up she used to go and see her every week. She had tried to phone but Anna hadn't answered so she thought she must have gone off somewhere. Anna had said something about going on a long journey in the near future. But she found it strange that Anna hadn't come to say goodbye, but never mind, Anna was special, not like other people, and she might have gone off without saying goodbye.

'And hasn't she been seen for a long time?' the lady asks in a worried tone.

'Not tonight,' I reply.

'It's not so extraordinary if you don't hear from someone for one night,' she says, surprised now.

'She discharged herself from hospital. She'd been ill for a few days, she had a very high temperature, and we're all worried about her.'

'The hospital? Ill?' she asks in amazement.

'Didn't you know?'

'She's never mentioned any illness to me, not once, but I told her occasionally that she looked pale and out of sorts, and then she's always getting thinner. But, no, she's never told me about any illness. Is it serious?'

'Yes,' I say, and explain briefly about her illness. The lady offers me a cup of coffee, which I accept because she's so upset, poor thing, about finding out like this.

'That's awful,' she says again and again. I don't say anything, I just drink my coffee, knowing I can't get up and leave until she's got her composure back. Then I decide to intrude on her thoughts and enquire about this long journey Anna said she was going on.

'Did she tell you anything about that journey you mentioned before?' I ask while I'm looking at the photographs on the sideboard. All of her son, at different ages. Ten or so pictures and a rose in a glass vase in front of the largest one.

'That's Thórdur,' she says cheerfully.

'I know.'

'Anna was fond of him, she was always fond of him.'

'I know.'

'No, she didn't tell me where she was going, in fact I don't think she had made a final decision. She said something along the lines of wanting to go south, somewhere where it would have to be hot and calm all day. But she gave me a short story about that trip that I found very pretty, although I somehow felt that it was intended for me and was about Thórdur's journey rather than about hers, that it was something she wanted to comfort me with. She's a nice girl, an extremely nice girl, and she took it very hard, that business about Thórdur. Would you like to see the piece she gave me?' she asks, getting up and fetching a sheet of paper, which she hands to me. I run my eyes over the text and feel sad, in spite of how beautiful the piece is, and feel that I must show it to you, even though it'll scarcely be of any practical use to us.

'She gave that to me in August,' she says.

'May I borrow it?' I ask and she agrees, asking me to return it to her later. She says she's very attached to it and often reads it in the evening. I promise I will, get to my feet and take my leave, assuring her that I'll let her know what happens. I'm pleased I went to see her even though I haven't got anywhere and I've had to tell her about the illness Anna herself chose to keep secret from her. I've also managed to get her mind off her own troubles and as I'm leaving she tells me she feels better.

'I get in my car and now I can't see any reason for driving around town any more and decide to come back to you and go on waiting,' says Valgeir as he fingers the piece of paper he's holding,

> with a somewhat strange look on his face,
> a somewhat empty look in his eyes,
> but the irritation that filled him when he began talking
> > has vanished.

I feel odd.

There's so much Anna and I haven't talked about.

There's so much I've let pass me by.

There's so much she hasn't been able to share with me.

*

'She never mentioned to me that she visited this woman,' I say quietly, and Z says the same and adds that there's so much they haven't talked about, so much she's let pass her by.

She feels the same way as I do.

There's the same sense of loss in her voice as there is within me.

'But aren't you going to let us read that story or read it for us yourself?' she says. I can tell from her voice that she's annoyed that Valgeir hasn't produced the sheet of paper yet.

'I'm sorry,' he says apologetically. 'I've been a bit flustered since I got back. I borrowed it from her so I could let you hear it, of course I should have done so straight away, but I must be more upset than I realize.'

'I'm sorry too,' she says, looking down. 'It's not my business to tell you what to do.'

'Read it out, dear,' I say.

I'm being firm now.

I'm not going to let anything put me off course.

I'm not going to let my emotions make me do anything silly.

I'm responsible for the circumstances here.

They're tireder than me, they're paler than me.

It's me who's strong.

He reads slowly.

His voice is calm and deep.

And everything around him seems to become crystal clear.

*

*In the country i'm looking for*
*the sun shines down all day long*
*and warms the ground the trees and the lakes*
*toes become warm in the grass*
*and fingers soft as they wave*
*through the air*

*a guest is expected there*

*the sky is blue and clear*
*and the birds sing a song of praise to the silence*

*people walk along the warm pavements*
*with baskets of fruit*

during the day they tread wine from grapes
and sunlight plays over their bodies

children run around laughing
collecting the flowers which spring up as fast
as they vanish from the earth

and when the guest walks straight across the land
they throw flowers over his naked body
and cover his face with kisses

he doesn't need to ask
he needs to enjoy

in the evening the sun turns a yellowy-orange
and gilds the countryside and the sky
the people become hot and red-faced
drinking wine and telling stories
to the accompaniment of wooden instruments

and the guest smiles and tells the story
of his long journey and the long way he's been
and he scorches his shoes on the fire

then he's back home

and as night falls the sun becomes
a huge red ball throwing dusk
at every waking eye which falls asleep
by the burnt-out fire

tomorrow another guest is expected

*and in the early morning i'm the first to wake up*
*i walk merrily towards the sun*
*i know you're on your way*

*and when i see you coming over the hill*
*the sun all around you*

*i know the waiting is a dream*

*in the country i'm looking for*
*i'll find you there*

*

'I know that land, we've had a dream about it,' says Z. 'We've been
there together, and stayed there for a long time. She wanted to give the
woman part of some sort of beauty she thought was missing in her life.
I hope she was able to.' She's looking hard at Valgeir, just as she did all
the time he was reading.

'It's only another poem,' I say, adding that I'm not criticizing it
even if it is, but I feel it's time we contacted the police. They might
have heard something or devised some plan of action or done something we ought to know about. It's past seven o'clock, it's OK to ring
now, we're just letting them know that we're still waiting and that
we're still worried that something unforeseen has happened.

'Is it seven o'clock already?' she says, and I can hear the anxiety in
her voice.

'It's ten past,' says Valgeir.

'Phone them,' she says, disappearing into the lavatory again.

He phones while she's out of the room
    and the only information he obtains is that we can go
        along to the station at ten o'clock to discuss plans with
        them, everyone will be there then and they'll be able to
        organize a search if she hasn't turned up by that time,
    we hear a quiet groan,

she's still crying,

she's still throwing up,

and all at once I seem to hear Anna's voice.

I hear an old conversation we had once when we were little and shared a bedroom. It was nighttime but we couldn't sleep, or didn't want to go to sleep, I can't remember which, it was always one or the other.

We often stayed awake together.

We were always great ones for staying awake.

'I don't understand how life can go on after you're dead,' she said.

'What do you mean?'

'I mean it just goes on as if you hadn't ever existed and the buses go on running just like you've never used them and school is just the same, and Mummy and you and everything is the same even though you're not there.'

'But you're not dying.'

'But how can life just go on and you don't know anything?'

'It has to be like that.'

'But where are you then?'

'In some beautiful land, I think.'

'Aren't you just lying dead in a coffin not knowing anything about anyone you care about, not about you or Mummy or your friends or anyone?'

'No, no, you don't stay there for long, your soul doesn't want to be all shut up, it always escapes and goes off where it wants to be,' I said. I can remember I didn't like hearing her talking like this.

I didn't want to talk about death.

I didn't like one bit talking about something I didn't understand, something I found strange, so I told her to stop, that I wanted to talk about something else.

I was afraid I wouldn't be able to look after her.

I'm afraid now I won't be able to find her.

I don't want to think about death.

'So it's seven o'clock,' she says, as she sits down.

'Twenty past, and there's no news,' says Valgeir.

221

'Shall we drive up there?' she says. 'It won't make any difference, there'll be as much snow as there was yesterday. But I think it'll make me feel better, it'll make me feel calmer if we go. It's not far. I'm going to go anyway. I have to. Perhaps you should wait here, you can have a lie down while you wait. Perhaps it's better if someone is at home in case there's any news.'

'I'll come with you,' I say. 'Valgeir can have a rest. You look like you need one, dear. Lie down for a while.'

He agrees to do so.

And we set out.

But have only got as far as the car
    when he comes running after us
    and says he can't get to sleep
    says he can't be without us
    nothing is likely to happen while we're gone
    but he's put the answering-machine on with a suitable
        message in case she phones.

It's nice to hear him say he can't be without me.

It's nice to drive off and hold his hand.

I feel secure in a way I haven't done before.

Now I know we'll always be together.

# 11

*Anna: 'There's nothing in fact that I can't see now.'*

My time is running out,
    I see it coming slowly round the corner,
        bent over and broken,
        an old man with a battered hat and a stick,
        but that's my man,
        look, he's straightened himself up, he's standing upright
           and straight just once more,
        he puts his hat on the shelf, his stick in the corner and he
           sits down next to me,
        strokes my cheeks and my legs and asks for something to
           drink,
        'give an old man something to drink before he sets off into
           the storm or the gale, the wind or the breeze, the
           darkness or the light, the heat or the cold,
        'give an old man something to drink before he sets off on
           his journey, before he takes your hand and you walk
           together over the frozen snow to the white mountains.'
My time is running out,
    but he doesn't leave straight away,
    not until I'm ready to take his hand,
    it's still me who makes the decision and I want to eke out
        my existence a bit longer by the fire, reading your
        letters and throwing them into it with the poems and
        the eggs,

it's of no consequence to me how bizarre I am,
how tragic I seem,
how poetical my thoughts appear,
everything flows on towards one thing,
and I'm here alone,
all alone, by myself, without you,
but I'm not lonely,
nothing else matters.
How often have I sat here and enjoyed the flames,
stretched out my hands in the cold and felt them
warming up,
felt the heat flow into my body, taken my hat and my coat
off and let the heat attack my body, how often with you
and with others who have also been cold, but most
often with you and looked into your eyes which are
reddish gold in the firelight and your golden skin and
stroked your face and heard you say something
improving and beautiful:
'It's so nice to sit here together like this.'
'Mmm.'
'And it does you so much good.'
'Mmm.'
'That's a rather limited vocabulary.'
'Mmm.'
'Have you been feeling unwell recently?'
'Mmm.'
How often I've waited for this day too, the day that has finally
arrived,
this night,
this morning which is reaching in through the window,
which is changing the flames from red to white,
the darkness to light and the memories to a story or a film,
there's nothing in fact that I can't see in this final daylight,
everything flows over the fire and circles over our words,
which, like pieces of blackness, lie next to the burnt

logs, everything I remember is here and seems
worthless in comparison with time,
that old man who's still drinking,
and yet everything matters.

*

Everything matters.


It matters to have been a kid growing up in Laugarnes,
waking up in the morning next to my sister, stretching out
a hand and feeling the warmth from her body, leaning
over on one elbow and watching her eyes swimming
beneath her eyelids, seeing her breath streaming from her
lips and changing into a cloud above her duvet, giving her
a shove and then another shove and saying, 'Arnthrúdur,
it's time to wake Mummy.'

And watching her wake up and stretch, grab the clock
and say, 'Let me sleep for another ten minutes, you go and
wake Mummy.'


*And*

going into the passage,
with cold feet, creeping down the passage, standing by
Mummy's bed, lifting the duvet ever so carefully, sliding
one hand under it, then sitting down on the bed, lifting
the duvet a tiny bit more and slipping underneath and
sometimes bumping my toes against a bare leg by mistake
and stroking her shoulder and saying, 'Mummy, it's time
to wake up.'

*And*

getting out of bed again,
putting the coffee-machine on and switching on the radio,
pouring soured milk into bowls and carrying them
through into the living room, having everything ready for
when they come out with their combs in their hands and
begin to brush their hair


*or*
*or*

having
that long, thick ponytail the boys used to pull, saying,
'You're a horse, Anna,' and coming home and asking
Arnthrúdur whether I am like a horse and if not why the
boys say so and hearing her laugh, saying that everyone
knew why boys said things like that to girls, it was because
they fancied them, because they wanted to kiss them and I
should be careful with my mouth. And the next time a
boy pulled my ponytail I was quick to reply, 'I'm being
very careful with my mouth, you!'

And it didn't matter that they started laughing, they
only did that because they were shy and because they
were embarrassed that I had seen through them


*or*

being
on my way out to the shop and seeing a man with long hair, a
beard and beautiful blue eyes, running after him, stepping in
his footsteps, from one to the next until he turned round and
asked what I was doing and I wasn't slow to answer, 'Chasing.'

'Why are you chasing me?'

And then I started laughing because his voice was so hoarse, he had obviously forgotten to clear his throat and I went on laughing and didn't reply straight away. Instead perhaps I started pulling his grey jacket gently and there was something strange about him when he sat down on his haunches, put his arm around my shoulders and asked, 'What's the matter with you, little girl?'

And I laughed and laughed because I wasn't ill at all.

'Nothing.'

'So why are you pulling at me?'

'Perhaps you're my daddy.'

And then I made a face and ran away and darted round the corner of the yellow house and hid there and watched the man stumble in the street and then carry on walking down the street, maybe to the bookshop, maybe to the sweetshop, maybe to the grocer's and then he came back holding a little boy's hand; he was seven, like me. And then I knew that he had only been going to meet him from school.

*or*

being

at school all day, then coming home, being so strangely tired, going to bed and sleeping and sleeping and sleeping and then waking up when Mummy came home from the office and called out, 'Are you asleep, Anna?'

And leaping out of bed and saying I didn't understand at all why I needed to sleep so much, because I slept so well at night and never went anywhere that tired me out, but I was always so terribly tired and hearing the same words, 'Teenagers have to rest, they grow up so fast.'

It was so good to hear her say that.

*or*
*or*
*or*

It matters
to have loved, felt those different hands on my body, each
with its own peculiarities, each with its own breathing,
watched those faces asleep on the pillow and remember
each one's eyes, remember the breathing, the tossing and
turning, the groping, the mouths, the cheeks, the feet, the
toes, the nails, the chins, the tongues, the chests, the
stomachs, the thighs, the hair,
   remember everything and love it,
   the caresses,
   passionate and always true,
   to have loved all those faces
   all the mouths that said:
   'I love you too'
   the eyes that laughed:
   'I'll miss you too'
   the hands that whispered:
   'I'll never forget you'
   to have loved
   but never as wildly as you,
   never as much as you,
   never as often as you,
   never as long as you,
   never as lovely as you,
   as soft as you,
   as madly as you,
   as gently as you,
   as fervently as you,
   as uncontrollably as you,
   you who said:
   'I'll always love you.'

You who didn't know that years later it would come
about that I would hold you responsible for the word
'always', would take you to court, pronounce another
sentence, a sentence that included the paradox, included
the 'never' that you had to face just like me. You who were
able to say 'always' had to be able to say 'never' again as
well, I never said 'always' and never 'never', but I asked
you to help me face lives which have to obey the rules of
both words, both worlds.

I did it for me.
I did it for you.
I did it for my sake and for your sake.
That's how the book of our life had to close.


Everything matters.

*


You were standing by my bedside with the blue flannel in your hand,
you'd wiped my forehead, dampened the flannel again and washed
under my arms and over my breasts.
It was a Sunday in July four months ago,
the sun was shining in through the window directly on
to my bed, the sheet was wet with sweat and on the
bedside table lay the rye bread and cheese, the bowl
of curds, a bag of chocolates from Valgeir,
the yellow rose Arnthrúdur brought,
the red one you brought
and *Candide* which my old friend had brought me, saying
he had done so because that fellow hadn't let things get
on top of him,
not thousands of lashes,
friends dying,
scorn,

love or praise,
he always went his own way, and eventually found the
person he was searching for, just like I should do.

And there next to *Candide* were the gloves from my mother, gloves made of Norwegian leather, and the ring Gunnar gave me when I left and which I was never parted from, it lay there and waited for the swelling to go down so I could put it back in its rightful place.

And, looking at all these things and at you as you stood bent over the washbasin, squeezing out the flannel, then came back to the bed and plumped up the pillow, I knew
that I had to talk to you,
that I had to speak to you about something I hardly dared
mention, not because I was afraid of you, not because
I feared that which I longed for, but because I was
scared for you and feared you might refuse me. There
was nothing I could bear less that July day than you
refusing my request,
the only request that really mattered to me:
'Z, I need to talk to you,' I said.
'When you're feeling better.'
'I feel well enough now.'
'You're too weak.'
'I'm strong enough, it isn't that.'
'I'll sit here as long as you like. Talk to me when you're feeling better, it'll be soon enough.'
'I need to talk to you now.'
'OK, talk then, Miss Stubborn.'
'I scarcely dare.'
'Don't, then.'
'Have you stopped being curious about what I have to say?'
'Why do you say that?'
'You're not interested, you're miles away.'
'Maybe I'm just tired.'
'Why are you tired?'
'I was awake last night.'

'Couldn't you sleep?'

'I sat up with you here.'

'I didn't know that.'

'You were delirious.'

'Did I say anything in particular?'

'Nothing that made sense.'

'What a pity.'

'Hardly.'

'I still need to talk to you now.'

'Stop beating about the bush, then.'

'I can't keep this up for much longer, you know.'

'Of course you can keep it up for longer.'

'I don't want to for much longer.'

'What do you mean?'

'You know as well as I do that there's no point.'

'Are you going to give up?'

'It's not a question of giving up.'

'Then what do you mean?'

'I want to leave here on my feet.'

'You will, Anna my dearest.'

'Don't evade the issue, you know what I mean.'

'No, I don't know.'

'I don't want to waste away, not more than I have done already.'

'You're not wasting away, you always feel like this when the course of treatment is coming to an end. It's nearly finished, just wait and see, and then you'll feel better. You'll be up and then you'll be about.'

'Maybe once more.'

'Don't start feeling sorry for yourself.'

'That's exactly what I'm not doing.'

'What are you doing then?'

'I want you to help me.'

'Help you? I'm doing everything I can.'

'I don't mean like that.'

'Then what do you mean?'

'I want you to help me to come to terms with the decision I've made.'

'I've always done everything I can to help.'

'I want to leave here before I'm helpless.'

'Are you asking me to help you do that?'

'Yes.'

'What are you actually saying?'

'I want you to help me be at peace with myself when I die. I want you to know when I go, I want you to think of me at that time, I want you to remember me like I was when I was well, I don't want your last memories to be like now, or worse, much worse.'

'My dear Anna.'

'Do it for me.'

'I can't.'

'You can if you want.'

'I can't.'

'This is the last time I come here. Next time I'll get out of here, I won't lie still, I'll go away, whenever it is. I won't take any more of this because I don't want to. I'll go out to the cottage and I'll go from there. I want you to know. I want you to stick by me too, I want you to keep quiet about it. I've kept quiet for you, I've kept quiet when I've wanted to speak out. I've kept quiet about your life, I did what you asked me to do, and I did it for you. I want you to do this for me.'

And then you were quiet, you didn't say anything, you stared in front of you and your eyes were dry, perhaps you were angry with me,

I didn't know then,

I don't know now.

But this evening when you came and sat by me I touched your hand lightly, watched you laugh and tell me that I'd be home again soon, perhaps I could go to your place tomorrow evening, 2 November, you were going to have a party, a really extravagant party, and invite lots of people to your birthday, you had never celebrated your birthday properly, it was about time you did.

'I'll be there in spirit,' I said, and you smiled.

And I think you were calmer when you phoned at eleven, two hours before I left. You may have accepted what you knew I was going to do, you may not have, but you will. You may have thought I would

never go through with what I said I was going to do, you may have
hoped that I wouldn't,
> that I'll never know
> and when I said goodbye to you and asked you to tell me
>> the story of the children for the last time you
>>> whispered it to me over the phone, you didn't say 'no'
>>> like you usually did,
>> like you had done all year,
>> you whispered it to me over the phone and it was more
>>> beautiful than ever
>> and then when it was over and I said I was tired,
>> you said more beautifully than ever before, 'I'll always
>>> love you.'
> And for the first time I repeated your words.

I knew we could both take the word 'always' that once and I knew
it had a deep significance that would always be with us wherever
we went.

And then we said goodbye.

*

The fire within me is hiding away,
> but I know it's there
> it can't conceal itself for long,
> not from me,
> I know it'll be back until it finally stifles me,
> but it won't manage to,
> I'll take it by surprise,
> I'll overpower it,
> take one more tablet,
> it'll give me strength until seven o'clock.
> I still have one hour left.
> I still have time.

I see you in my mind's eye sitting there, alone maybe, or maybe
Arnthrúdur and Valgeir have phoned and come round, maybe you're

all sitting there together. I know if you're all there you'll be struggling
to keep quiet, but I also know that you won't say anything, I know you
won't let me down,

> you can't,
>
> but I want you to know that I sympathize with you,
>
> you're scared and covered in sweat on account of me just
>> as you have been so often during the past year,
>
> now it's coming to an end,
>
> now you'll stop suffering and a new period in your life
>> will begin,
>
> I won't be there but I'll try to keep track,
>
> I'll always try to keep track of you.

I pass the letters you wrote last year from one hand to the other, the
letters you wrote after that long letter full of self-pity, the letters you
sent me after Hrafn had moved out and nothing had changed between
us. Perhaps I forced you to live with me and yet not with me but it was
also because I didn't want things to change too much when I went
away

> went away
>
> wonderful and strange words
>
> arouse, at the same time,
>
> curiosity, fear, fatigue.

To go away,

> I can accept that
>
> but not to know where
>
> that I can't accept.

I can't accept what I don't know

> unconquered territory
>
> in an undefined distant land
>
> if it exists
>
> I'm scared to conquer it.

And then there's the doubt,

> that unbearable endless word of uncertainty,
>
> that's the worst thing.

But it wasn't words of uncertainty that embellished last year's letters from you. You knew what you were doing eventually, when you got down to it.

I'll read last year's letters.

I'll read them slowly and in silence.

Then I'll get up and go to bed.

I'll read your letters and then I'll go to sleep.

*

*11 March 1996*

*My beloved Anna,*

*I'm getting accustomed to my life now as it is and as I chose it to be. You've told me so often that being free to choose means being free to suffer and I've been thinking recently that there's a lot of truth in that. I haven't been able to talk to you much about my divorce but you must know that getting divorced after such a long time is tough. There are a lot of things you miss even though you've taken the decision to leave. I've sometimes wondered whether people really understand what it's like to be the one who leaves. No one sympathizes with you if you're the one who leaves, you wander off and the most people do is try to make you change your mind, which fortunately doesn't usually happen. If you're the one who leaves you end up feeling guilty and bitter, you're the traitor, you're the dishonourable one, you're the one who's wronged your neighbour, forgotten all the vows and the promises, and all the decisions that were taken jointly.*

*My brothers have even gone so far as to say that I've humiliated Hrafn, themselves, my mother and father, and everyone close to me and disgraced the family. My brothers and all my family, even our friends, have chosen to keep up with him and not with me. In my opinion they've made themselves guilty of choosing between two people who never asked them to make a choice.*

*'We can't be on good terms with you both,' my brothers say.*

235

'Don't then.'

'It's Hrafn who's hurt, not you.'

'Are you sure about that?'

'It's him who's taking it badly.'

'Has he asked you not to talk to me?'

'No, you know what sort of a person he is.'

'Yes, I do know.'

'Why don't you go back to him? He'd take you back, he's told us.'

'I don't love him any more like I used to.'

'Oh yes, are you trying to tell us that your love for this girl is in any way comparable to how you used to love Hrafn? We know exactly what you two were like, you couldn't bear to be apart from each other.'

'It's her I love now.'

'And you don't feel ashamed of yourself?'

'Not any more.'

'Have you thought about how Mother feels?'

'Is she upset?'

'She's not upset, she's in pieces.'

'There's no need for that.'

'She never stops asking what she did wrong.'

'She didn't do anything wrong.'

'Have you tried to talk to her?'

'I don't feel I have to.'

'You're a selfish person, Z,' they say as they leave, and then they come to visit less and less often and only seem to be able to talk about that one thing.

'You go on as if I'm a sinful woman.'

'Maybe you are.'

And then I start laughing.

What is it that people think, Anna? Why is it so disgusting if one's love is directed a different way from where it should be? What's so awful about loving someone of the same sex? I've never asked my brothers why they go on like this but I *think that they sympathize with Hrafn just as a pretext. Of course they're fond of him, they get on well with him and all that, but first and foremost they're prejudiced, even though they won't admit it.*

*'Have you known us to be prejudiced?'*

*'Not until now.'*

*'Don't you think we have a sense of decency?'*

*'Oh yes, definitely.'*

*That's the scenario and I'd be lying if I said it didn't upset me. It upsets me too when Hrafn phones and asks me to go back to him, asks me to let him come home, says everything can go back to normal, he knows me. I'm not a lesbian, I'm a woman, he's proved that. It upsets me to hear him talking like that, so I invite him in for coffee or a glass of wine and we sit and thrash it out. Sometimes I think I shouldn't invite him in, but I'm lonely, Anna. I'm always wanting to meet you and it's not enough for me to see so little of you, and I don't know many people. Hrafn and I have always been good friends and there are lots of things we can talk about without talking about our relationship, which, as I've told you, he doesn't want to do at all.*

*Sometimes I've even wanted him to sleep here with me. He's a good, kind man and there are times when I feel sorry for myself for being so lonely and sometimes I feel half crazy inside. So I try to get hold of you, but I can hear straight away on the phone, if I do get on to you, that you're not going to give way on your Thursdays plan.*

*Then I want to ask him to stay the night and put his arms around me but I don't because I don't want him to be hurt when I say 'no', which I'll have to do when he wants more than just to lie next to me.*

*I know you'll say that you don't care whether I sleep with him like I always have done, as long as I don't tell you. But I don't want to, and I don't want you to go out with other people either. You know that. I want to ask you yet again to reconsider whether we can't meet more often. Please do so and I'm not asking because you're ill. I'm asking because it's what I crave. Spring is on its way, Anna, let's start a new game this spring, let's do something we've never done before, go on holiday together or something. Think about it for me.*

*If I don't get any answer from you I'll leave you alone, but don't make me suffer too much for choosing the path I know you recommended me not to take.*

*With love,*

*Z*

*

*My own Anna,*
*I know the summer is your time.*

*I know you feel best then and can feel at your happiest, feel at your most lively both in your body and your soul, and it's kind of you to let me share this with you. We've been out to the cottage twice now. Tell me, why do we have to cut down on our trips there, even if you are ill, why do you seem to need more and more to be alone, need more and more to play alone? At times you seem to me like an irresponsible child roaming about all over the place just like you've been let out of a cage.*

*I know you don't want anything to change, let alone compromise on anything I ask you for, everything is supposed to be as it always has been and illness mustn't be mentioned. But since you won't change anything, why are you distancing yourself more from me now than before and when I didn't know anything?*

*Don't come out with that old line about it being best for me, that I will have got used to the distance by the time you leave.*

*You know I can't bear you saying that.*

*Once you asked me whether I thought you were a person.*

*At the time I was surprised but later when I thought about why you had asked me I understood. I'm in that position now. I don't feel that you treat me like a person, but rather like something you have control over, that it's up to you to decide whether I'm happy or not. I read your poems over and over again in case I can find any answer in them, but they don't tell me anything.*

*Be nice to me, Anna. Don't take the time we ought to have together away from me.*

*Love me like you say you do.*

*With love,*

*Z*

*

*15 October 1996*

*My beloved,*
*This situation has become weird and truly awful. Don't throw this letter away, read all of it, I won't be nasty, but it's not normal, you know, to feel relieved deep down that you're ill, that you're getting worse.*

*You know I was so happy when you phoned on Friday and asked me to stay at your place over the weekend, that you were allowed to be at home if there was someone with you, otherwise you'd have to go into hospital. You know I jumped up and down and laughed and sang and did everything people do when they're over the moon with joy. But then I stopped all of a sudden and fell to wondering what on earth I was doing. There I was in the middle of the room singing and dancing because you were so ill you couldn't be alone. I felt wretched, I felt like a selfish fool but despite all the reasoning and going over things seriously in my mind I couldn't throw off that feeling all weekend.*

*It was so nice to wake up at your side even though you were burning hot and in pain. It was so nice to jump out of bed*

239

*and so nice to be able to fuss about you and nice to see that it made a difference and your temperature went down and that beautiful brightness came back into your eyes.*

*My dear Anna, don't do this, give me a share in your life, don't push me away, I can't live without you, I don't want to live without you.*

*Why can't you just say the same?*

*Why don't you tell me that you need me and that you want me to be near you?*

*You don't say it because you don't want it.*

*Because you're the most stubborn person north of the Alps.*

*But I still love you.*

*Remember I'm awake and waiting for you to phone.*

*Love,*

*Z*

\*

*30 December 1996*

*My beloved,*

*My letters are getting shorter, but then I have less and less to tell you. You probably know, of course, why I'm writing this letter.*

*You know, having to be alone at Christmas really hurt, it hurt more than anything has done since we've been together. You could easily have told Arnthrúdur and Valgeir that you wanted to be with me.*

*You could have told them that I was alone and wanted you to be with me. Since when are you so frightened of them that you daren't speak out to them? Unless deep down you've become like that and just say the opposite, maybe you can't stand being near me, can't stand the way I look at you, my movements, my smile, my words, can't stand me at all.*

*Why don't you say so instead of coming out with that old line, 'I do love you but it's best like this, it's best to keep it like this for the time being.'*

*Why is it that you always know what's best for both of us and why do you feel it's right that you take all the decisions about our lives? I almost hated you on Christmas Eve, and that's not the time for hating, it's the time for loving.*

*I rang Arnthrúdur three times and each time I put the phone down. Of course you know it was me, I was just hoping I'd hear your voice.*

*But you didn't phone back.*

*You didn't think about how I was feeling, yet you know me better than anyone. You know how I suffer, you know how much I want to be near you. I thought you were being cruel, evil and callous and I revelled in thinking like that about you. Illness doesn't give people the right to do that, they shouldn't do it and mustn't do it.*

*But I'm no angel either.*

*I phoned Hrafn and he came over and stayed the night with me and we made love and it was good and it was bad and I know you don't think I should be telling you this but I'm going to just the same.*

*I'm trying feebly to get you to reconsider your position. By everything I hold precious I'm trying to put pressure on you. Come back to me seeing as nothing is supposed to change, don't throw me off like this and postpone our life together, don't go off into the wings away from me.*

*Love you,*

Z

*

I throw the letters on to the fire and smile.

And, having done so, I fling my poems on too.

And the eggs.

The fire crackles and burns.

I did what you asked me to do.

And now I'm ready.

I empty the pill bottle into my mouth.
Drink the whole bottle of spirits.
Watch the fire die down.
Go upstairs and lie down under the sloping ceiling with your last
letter in one hand and my last poem in the other and two eggs, two
coloured eggs and when you get here,

> you'll know where I'm lying,
> you'll see the poem and even though you've never
>> understood my poems
> and even though they're no good you'll understand this one.

You'll take it from my hand and you'll understand it.

*

Now the mist is coming.
> It's heavy and warm and soft
>> and time touches my hand.
> We walk away.
> I think about us when we make love,
>> about your mouth and your tongue,
>> and how it winds itself around mine,
>> how it winds itself about me
>> how it slides down my throat
>> I think about your teeth as they
>> bite my nipple
>> and your hands as they touch my breasts
>> and your legs as they coil around mine
>> and your fingers as you enter me
>> and your tongue as you enter me ·
>> and your laughing eyes
>> and my laughing eyes
>> and I'm happy
>> and
>> round about me there are colours
>> and your body

white
and smooth
and clean
and the sun

I'm a guest
on my way to an unknown land

and I'll keep vigil there
and wait for you

# 12

*Arnthrúdur: 'My sister who understood me.'*

And we drove off, without saying a word to each other,
>   the way she had chosen even though she knew it was
>   impassable.

I take Valgeir's hand as he changes gear up the hill to Ártún and I can understand the woman who previously was as a closed book to me. I can sense how she's feeling in the back of the car, I can feel her breathing coming from the back seat where she's lying with the book over her head. I know she doesn't want to say anything but simply float onwards through the noise of the engine, know that she feels words will disturb her, which they may do, but I don't agree with her.

I don't think it's good for her so I squeeze Valgeir's hand and I know he agrees with me, he doesn't need to say a word for me to know,

>   not now, he squeezes my hand in reply.

'Shall I put some music on?' I ask, looking over my shoulder.

She doesn't move a muscle and I wonder whether she's fallen sleep, whether she's just sleeping and dreaming as I might have done in her shoes,

>   no, I wouldn't have done that,
>   I would have got up and said something,
>   tried to dredge up some topic of conversation,
>   asked questions,
>   got answers,
>   I would never have lain motionless in the back of a car if

I'd been feeling bad so when she doesn't reply I repeat
the question.

'Z, shall I put some music on?'

'Did you say something?' she asked in a quiet voice, then added, 'I think I fell asleep, goodness me, I think I nodded off.'

'Arnthrúdur was asking whether she should put some music on,' says Valgeir.

'Oh yes, of course, do put something on,' she says absent-mindedly, sitting up now and looking out of the window.

'Anything in particular?' he asks.

'No, nothing in particular, just something, I don't mind.'

'Don't you like music?' I ask.

'Yes, of course I like music.'

'Shall we just put the radio on?' he asks.

'That's fine,' she replies, so he tunes into a channel and there's some-body called Gedda singing 'Sunday of a Mountain Maid' and it's nice,

his quiet voice is soothing in the early morning
and there's no avoiding it, I'm feeling rather wary,
imagining various things about my sister,
hoping that the road to the cottage isn't blocked by snow
    and that she's sitting there waiting for us,
I can't stage any other scenario.
I can't stage the scenario in which she's dead,
in which the time has arrived,
in which she has stumbled on in the snow,
clambered over snowdrifts in order to die alone and
    abandoned in this cottage I have never seen, she had
    never invited me there with her even though she seems
    to have invited almost everyone else,
even the old man on the first floor.
I can't help feeling slightly angry with her about that,
    but it's only a mild anger,
    only a taste that vanishes as quickly as it appears.

*

245

'You fly off the handle so often, Arnthrúdur,' Anna said to me when we were living together on Hverfisgata.

'Do you think so?'

'Yes, it's obvious from your face when you're annoyed about something. Your colour changes and you blush, did you know that?'

'Somebody once mentioned it to me.'

'You ought to try to curb your temper.'

'Oh, it blows over straight away. It comes over me and then blows over at the slightest thing. You're not upset about it now, are you?'

'No, no, it just strikes me as funny now, but it was sometimes difficult to take when we were little.'

'Was it? I don't remember, but give me an example since you've brought it up. We don't have anything else much to do.'

She always took it well when I asked her to do something for me.

She didn't let me down on this occasion.

'Don't you remember the shambles, as you called it?'

'The shambles?'

'Yes, the shambles in our bedroom. You thought that my side was always in such a terrible shambles, magazines on the floor, lumps of chewing-gum on the wall above my bed, stacks of paper on the table of course with my compositions, just the worst sort of shambles.'


*and once*

you actually got yourself together and threw the whole lot away. So when I got home from school the room was all tidy and clean and I got a knot in my stomach because you usually only tidied up if you were angry and there you were, sitting on your bed looking very serious and tapping a pencil against your leg.

I didn't say hallo, I just sat down on the bed opposite you and said, 'What's the matter?'

'What d'you think's the matter, dopehead?' you

246

answered. You were always rather rude, even when you were having an angry scene.

'How do I know, but I can see you've tidied up very thoroughly.'

'It would've been amazing if you hadn't seen that. You really are so bloody messy, what d'you think it's like for an ordinary person like me to live with such a slob? How many times have I asked you to tidy up after you, is it such a big problem to put your magazines into a pile and keep them in the rack and keep the table in order and throw your gum into the bin? Or perhaps you just do it because you know I can't stand it?'

'Arnthrúdur, I'm sorry,'

'I don't forgive you at all. I couldn't take it any more, that's why I threw all the junk away, the papers, the magazines and all that.'

'I only hope you didn't throw my chewing-gum away,' I said, deciding to go out and have a look for my stuff in the dustbin.

And the culpable thoughtlessness and goading implied in that comment were obviously too much for you, because you stood up and roared like a lion and you went on roaring all the time I was fetching the bags from the dustbin, and then the roaring subsided when I came back into our room.

You had thrown the pencil on the floor and you were sitting on your bed, hiding your face in your hands.

'I'm sorry, Arnthrúdur, I'll put my things back,' I said, feeling truly remorseful. I felt that I'd encroached on your rights and I pitied you for having such a temper.

And then you put your arms around me.

All the anger had melted away.

*

247

The anger I harboured against her disappears as I recall that incident. Of course it was up to her who she invited to the cottage and who she didn't. Of course I didn't have to take offence and feel insulted just because I wasn't always the first to be chosen for everything.

It makes me smile to contemplate that.

I've certainly become critical of myself.

This night has brought me such composure.

I'm pleased with myself.

'Are you sure the road up to the cottage was impassable? Didn't you say you'd tried to drive out here a few days ago? The road's clear now.'

'There are often snowdrifts in the valley even though the road itself is clear,' she says.

'She can't be at the cottage, I don't think she's nearly strong enough to wade through snowdrifts. Her legs are so bad now,' I say.

'She didn't get over the drifts,' she says, then we speed on in silence, listening to the music.

I take Valgeir's hand again and she lies down and covers her face with the book.

If I could actually see into her mind I'd know more precisely how she's feeling.

But my imagination reaches her.

She's thinking about the time they had together,

    the time she wanted to spend in a different way,

    the opportunities that have been taken from them,

    and the future that belongs to her alone.

'Are you feeling very bad?' I ask, calmly.

'Yes,' is her reply, and I stroke her hand cautiously.

'It'll be OK, just you see, it's happened before, she'll turn up.'

'You can be sure of that,' says Valgeir.

She doesn't reply, just reminds Valgeir that we're nearly at the turning and as the car turns the corner it's like driving into a new world, white reigns supreme all around us and the road, although white, is still clear.

Suddenly hope kindles fiercely in my breast.

And that hope changes to certitude.

Anna is there, I can sense it.

'She is up there, I can feel it,' I say quietly, and at the same moment we drive past two cars.

'She's not by herself there,' she says, quietly.

'No, she's taken someone with her,' I say, trying to neutralize the accusatory tone I can hear in her voice.

'Do you think so?' she asks.

'And they've come out here in two cars,' Valgeir says, mentioning as well that he recognizes the other car, he's seen it before, maybe it was outside Anna's house, he's pretty sure it was.

'Come on,' she says, impatiently.

'Do you think we should disturb them?' I say, somehow unable to face barging in on my sister. 'I don't know whether Anna would want us to do that, she might be offended, you know how she hates people interfering.'

I feel it's scarcely right for me to go in, let alone the three of us, in frightened single file, it would look so much as if we didn't trust her.

'Never mind, let's just knock,' she says, without giving us the chance to discuss it any further.

She storms out of the car and along the path to the cottage. She really storms along.

'Hurry up,' says Valgeir, 'we can't let her go alone.'

'It's quite a long way,' she calls, 'but it's obvious that more than one person's been along here, you can see that from the footprints in the snow. Some of them are a man's, some of them were made by a man!'

We catch up with her and examine the footprints.

These snowy footprints are the only sign of life along the track, and they become closer and closer together as we approach the cottage until they merge together outside the closed door.

The windows are nailed up and there's no sound coming from the cottage, no sign of conversation, but I seem to hear someone moving around inside.

'We nail the windows shut for the winter. Some people broke in once, that was before we started coming here, before Anna and I started coming here, but after that the windows were always nailed up,' she says, as she knocks on the door.

249

And we hear noises inside, as if a table's being pushed away and then heavy footsteps, and then the door opens but there's nobody there. We go inside, into the small entrance hall and there's a smell of burning and coffee.

Z squeezes in first and we see a cat dash past us. We follow it and I prepare myself to meet my sister's gaze, amazed and annoyed, and feel nervous.

'You, here,' she says and we all look at the old man sitting by the fireside raking the embers.

There's a cup of coffee on the table in front of him and two cats lapping milk from a bowl.

'You came here, the drive around town ended here,' says Valgeir, and I can hear how quizzical his voice is.

'I'm here,' he says slowly, without even looking in our direction.

'And where's Anna?' asks Z in a quiet voice.

'Upstairs,' he says, reaching for a bottle from underneath the table and pouring himself a drink.

He passes the bottle to Z and tells her to have a slug, which she does. She gulps it down.

'I thought I'd check up on her. It occurred to me that she was here after all seeing as she wasn't anywhere else, she always felt comfortable here. We've had some good times here together, by the fire, not necessarily talking much, sometimes just sitting quietly, sitting in silence with Anna is great, you don't always have to be talking when you're with her. One shouldn't always have to talk to people.'

'Is she asleep?' I ask.

'I don't know whether she's asleep,' the old man says, staring straight ahead.

'Did you talk to her when you arrived?' she asks. I notice that her hands are shaking in a way I haven't seen before, a slight trembling which she can't hide as she puts her hands to her face.

*

'I can always tell whether you're feeling well or not, you don't need to tell me,' Anna said.

'What do you mean?'

She'd come over to see me and to talk things over yet again. I wasn't feeling particularly happy, I hadn't seen Valgeir for a week and he hadn't been in touch. It wasn't that I didn't dare phone, I was just going to put the receiver down if his wife answered and deny having phoned at all if he asked me later, but I never did. I had promised never to phone him at home. But I didn't have to put the receiver down, the answering-machine was on and his wife's voice said that they would be away all weekend.

So I drove past their house and saw that the car wasn't there and assumed they had gone off into the country. They sometimes spent the weekend at a farm in Biskupstungur where Valgeir used to go in the summer when he was a boy.

'I'm so transparent, so pathetic, always crying.'

'It's not that. You're not always crying and there's nothing particularly pathetic about crying. No, you start trembling slightly and put your hands up to your face more than usual, that's why you can't ever keep how you're feeling secret from me.'

Z's like me.

I know how she's feeling.

*

'No, I didn't talk to Anna,' the old man says. 'I didn't need to and neither did she. Go on up to her, dear, she's almost certainly got something for you.' As he speaks a look passes between them the like of which I've never seen before. A sort of mixture of warmth, concern, love and fear and the slight trembling in her hands becomes more pronounced.

'Go on up to her, you needn't be afraid.'

'Do you really want to wake her up if she's asleep?' I say. 'She would have come down if she was awake. It'll do her good to sleep while she can, and we can sit down here for a while.'

251

I feel I'm in the right,
>I feel she ought to rest and yet I feel a certain uneasiness,
>a certain strange fear which I don't fully understand,
>I feel it hanging over me like a bad dream,
>I feel a heaviness in my legs and a sickness in my stomach,
>I must try to get my bearings and understand why,
>perhaps she's not asleep,
>perhaps . . .

\*

'Do you have to try to understand everything?' Anna asked.

'What'll happen to me if I stop trying?'

'Nobody can understand everything, nobody can find an explanation for everything or a reason for everything. That's just how it is.'

'I try to understand, otherwise I feel worse and worse. I try to understand why Valgeir keeps putting off leaving his wife and moving in with me, the person he says he loves. I try to make myself believe it's for her sake, because she's such a good person and that's why it's so difficult for him to tell her about me, that they made this pact years ago not to cheat on each other, that it's so difficult for him to face her and say that he's broken his promise, so difficult to face up to his own cheating, that he needs time to build up his strength and then when he finds the right moment he'll tell her the whole truth and come to me. I try to understand that time will help him do this but I know I don't understand and so I feel worse and worse the longer it drags on. I even start wondering about the fact that he doesn't have any children and what he would do if he did, whether in that case he wouldn't tell me to get lost, whether he would ever leave them and her. And then the very worst thing. I'm so scared the woman'll get pregnant. That he'll come to see me and say that he's in trouble, what they've always wanted to happen has happened at last and he has to choose her now. I know he says he doesn't want to sleep with her and that he hardly ever does and then only because he has to, but that doesn't help the pain. I can't understand that a man of such vigour as Valgeir can just lie in bed next to a woman he loves in a way, though not in the way he once did, without touching her unless he has to. I don't understand it and I don't understand it because I don't know whether I could do it myself, I don't know whether I would want to myself. I don't understand it, I try to understand it for my sake but I still say, 'What happens if she gets pregnant?'

'She won't.'

'How do you know?'

'I'm careful.'

'Are you always careful?'

'There's no "always" about it.'

'But is it often?'

'I've told you over and over again that it happens, you must be able to understand that.'

'And is it nice?'

'Stop it.'

'You must be able to tell me whether you find it nice.'

And then we start arguing.

'You must stop digging around for a meaning,' said Anna. 'If you can't see it straight away perhaps it'll come to you in a while and then you'll understand too. Stop scraping and scratching around, Arnthrúdur, it does you terrible damage.' Anna was sure she was in the right. Sometimes she was and then there was a decisive tone in her voice which told me she was unshakeable and convinced in her belief.

We didn't always agree.

But we never argued.

We never gave way to each other either.

'I don't think I'll ever agree with you about that,' I said, and had the last word.

I had the last word more often than she did.

*

253

'Have you been up to her yourself?' I ask, trying to understand the fear lodged within me.

'Yes,' replied the old man, taking a sip from the bottle and passing it to Z, who has another drink, her cheeks now red. 'Of course I've been up to her.'

'And was she asleep?'

'She was peaceful, she looked extremely peaceful as usual, peaceful and beautiful. Anna's such a peaceful person, and so beautiful. But go upstairs now, go on upstairs and see her. We'll sit here and chat, sit here and chat or keep quiet. We'll wait while you go.'

'Go up to her,' I say as well and she looks at Valgeir, who in turn tells her to go upstairs.

'We'll wait here and then we'll come up,' he says.

She stands up and walks over to the stairs.

She walks with a heavy step.

She steps to one side as the cats rush past her on the stairs.

She closes the door.

'It wasn't difficult getting here,' says Valgeir.

'We expected the road to be blocked by snow, it was a few days ago when they tried to come out here,' I say.

'The road up here is often blocked, it might be blocked tomorrow. You never know about the roads, which ones are blocked and which ones aren't, you can never be sure about the weather, it can take as long to figure the weather out as it does to figure people out, perhaps you never figure people out. But I figured Anna out and she figured me out but we never knew anything about the roads, she didn't know anything either. We often talked about the weather, she liked talking about the weather. Do you like talking about the weather? Perhaps you're not interested in the weather. Did it surprise you how clear the roads were?'

'I just said it for something to say,' says Valgeir calmly, glancing constantly up the stairs.

'It's best if they can be alone together,' the old man says.

'Yes,' I say.

'It's best for good friends to be alone when they need to be.'

'I agree with you about that, at least,' says Valgeir.

'Good friends are never alone for too long and those two haven't had much time together, life's been hard on them.'

'Did Anna tell you?' I ask, unable to disguise my amazement.

'She told me, she told me a lot, even though she never talked much. She told me about you two and she told me about her mother and she told me about her girlfriend who I've met a few times actually. She's a good-natured soul and she deserved to have had more time with Anna. They should have had longer together.'

'You knew each other better than I realized,' Valgeir says, smiling at him and accepting a drink and then another and a third, and then hunching himself over the table,

> he doesn't want to appear impatient,
>
> he doesn't want to look up the stairs,
>
> doesn't want to be indiscreet.

But I know he wants to leap to his feet and run upstairs, push the door open and ask how it's going,

> whether everything is OK,
>
> whether he can help in any way,
>
> how Anna's feeling,
>
> whether she's worse than she was this evening.

But he leans across the table to calm himself down,

> he has three drinks to calm himself down,
>
> he rocks backwards and forwards to calm himself down,
>
> he doesn't want me to see that he's frightened
>
> and I don't want him to think that I know he is.

He's as frightened as I am,

> he's in the power of that fear just like me and the old man,
>
> everything he says is tinged by fear,
>
> suspicion,
>
> a strange feeling we can't confirm
>
> and don't want to confirm.

There are things one knows without wanting to.

There are things one has to be told in order for them to stick in one's mind.

'One never knows what it is to know people,' the old man says.

'Perhaps one never knows,' says Valgeir, without looking up.

'Perhaps one never knows anything. For example, I've never known when I've done the right thing or the wrong thing. I've never known when I'm annoying people and when I'm not and when you turned up tonight I didn't know what I should do. And I couldn't ask anyone, so I let the cats decide for me. I locked them in the toilet and put their bowl of milk under the kitchen table, and then I said to myself, 'If they find the bowl as soon as I let them out, that means I have to drive out to the cottage and have a look around for my little Anna.'

Then I let the cats out. It didn't take them a moment to rush out, straight into the kitchen and straight to their bowl, and then I knew what I had to do. I often play games like that with myself to find the answer to whatever problem happens to be bothering me. That's what I do because I don't know anything. Anna thought it was really clever of me. She said she wanted to take up doing that later if she had time, perhaps she will have time, I don't know.' He gets up as he's speaking and throws some bits of paper on to the fire. They burst into flame and throw a yellow glow over the table and brightness surrounds us for a moment.

I get to my feet and go over to him.

I notice an egg or an egg-shaped stone in the fire and I know and remember.

*

'I want to give her something every time I see her.'

'And what sort of thing?'

'Something unusual.'

'How romantic it sounds.'

'But then I am romantic.'

'Why don't you give her eggs?'

'Eggs?'

'Yes, they're such a beautiful shape.'

'Do you mean ordinary hen's eggs?'

256

'Don't be silly, Anna, I mean those eggs made of stone that you can buy or stones the shape of eggs that you could paint.'

'And what makes you think of eggs?'

'Eggs, eggs of life, you know.'

'That's what I'll do,' she said.

*

'There are loads of stones like eggs here,' I say.

Valgeir gets up and walks slowly and calmly over to us, and his breathing is heavy as he asks, 'Are the eggs here? I didn't see them on the shelf.'

'She's thrown them into the fire,' the old man says. At the same moment we hear Z saying in a quiet voice that it's all right for us to come up now.

And she comes down the stairs, with the cats following her, sits down calmly next to the old man and takes his hand. In the other hand she's holding a piece of paper and, as we mount the stairs, I hear him saying something to her about a letter she had written and that the best and the most proper thing to do is to throw it on to the fire.

She lays the piece of paper on the table,
> throws the letter on to the fire and puts her head on his
> > shoulder.

And then I know that Anna's dead.

I know my sister's dead.

I don't need to open the door
> and look at her and imagine to myself that she's asleep,
> she won't sleep any more,
> won't be awake any more,
> she's gone on the journey whose end she so feared.

My sister with her dolls,
> my sister who spilt food down her clothes,
> my sister who was never going to be able to say 's' and 'th',
> my sister who hid herself in silence,
> my sister who was afraid of the dark,

257

my calm and kind sister,
my sister who understood me,
my sister whom I miss,
my sister whom I love,
and I open the door
and step inside the room and see that my fear is not
    groundless.
I stroke her hair,
    I stroke Valgeir's hair,
    make the sign of the cross on my forehead and go
        downstairs again, with Valgeir behind me.
And we sit down next to them and I say, 'Were you talking about a letter?'

'She left a poem for me, she was holding it in her hand. I'll read it for you, I'm going to learn it later,' she says.

*

*On Monday, 2 November, I decided to embark on a journey I both look forward to going on and am nervous about. I'm looking forward to it because I've always loved the unknown and I'm nervous about it because I don't know where I'll end up. The thing I hate the most is saying goodbye and thank you, especially if I'm going on a long journey which is what I'm doing now and I'm finding it easy.*

*This poem is for Z, my last thoughts are for her.*
*And then it's time to set off.*

my love was
like the autumn rain
and the pavement outside your house
covered in red leaves

i won't walk there any more
there's no way from there

and yet the sky was never
tinged with anything except the spring
there were no clouds shooting across the sun
or building up behind the mountain
only the colours of spring and silence
neither sun nor mountain

then your eyes kissed mine
and the baby in my breast
sang about the first of the world's paradoxes
winter and summer
black and white

now i know that nothing is permanent
yet there's no cause to feel the loss

but i look over my shoulder
like a woman in a lost poem
and recall you

over my hair
birds swoop
joy in my breast

\*

i recall you
when you're silent

and i feel how
the words around me
take on a new meaning

the verb to long
now signifies
both desire and want

and i know
that i long
to lay mayweed
and poppies
at the head of the bed
where we slept
so they can fade
and i can scatter them
on the grass in the garden
so it'll grow better

\*

i recall you
as you look at me
and ask for peace
some stillness
which can hide your body
like water hides fish
or love friendship

though i was never uneasy
and between us no war

*

if i had a present
i would give you a washing-line
to hang between poles
so your washing
would flap white

in the breeze behind the house
and would be perfumed by summer

our all has been perfumed
our all has been perfumed by autumn
the time of colours
when summer melts
under red and brown
and winter spreads
its desire
into white

in our season
lies the basis
for a new spring

*

*i recall you*
*as you touch my hand*
*run your fingers along the veins*
*and ask whether you can stay*
*saying you're tired*
*saying and saying*
*that you're tireder than tired*

*during the night i walk*
*through the gate in the back garden*
*the cats don't prowl around by the dustbin*
*and i forget to gaze at*
*the rose by the wall*

\*

*i recall you*
*as i ask you to go home*
*he's lonely and misses you*
*and i'm leaving*

\*

*did you know that my love*
*is warm and soft*
*like the autumn rain*
*never leaves*
*always stays*

\*

*and remember*
*that tomorrow it'll rain*
*red leaves on the pavement outside your house*

\*

She looks at the poem for a long time, contemplates each word, strokes the piece of paper, puts it on the fire, then turns to us and says, 'I suppose it's time to douse the fire.'

# MARE'S NEST

Mare's Nest brings the best in international contemporary fiction to an English-language readership, together with associated non-fiction works. As yet, it has concentrated on the flourishing literature of Iceland, which appears under the Shad Thames imprint. The list includes the three Icelandic Nordic Prize-winning novels.

The poetic tradition in Iceland reaches back over a thousand years. The relatively unchanging language allows the great Sagas to be read and enjoyed by all Icelandic speakers. Contemporary writing in Iceland, while vivid and highly idiosyncratic, is coloured and liberated by this Saga background. Closely observed social nuance can exist comfortably within the most exuberant and inventive magic realism.

# Brushstrokes of Blue
## The Young Poets of Iceland

Edited with an introduction by
Pál Valsson

112 pp. £6.95 pbk

'Exciting stuff: eight leading northern lights constellated here'
Simon Armitage

Sigfús Bjartmarsson   Gyrdir Elíasson   Einar Már Gudmundsson
Elísabet Jökulsdóttir   Bragi Ólafsson
Kristín Ómarsdóttir   Sjón   Linda Vilhjálmsdóttir

A representative introduction to contemporary poetry in Iceland,
*Brushstrokes of Blue* is full of surprises, from startling surrealist
juxtapositions and irresistible story-spinning to gentle *aperçus* and
the everyday world turned wild side out.

# Epilogue of the Raindrops

Einar Már Gudmundsson

Translated by Bernard Scudder

160 pp.   £7.95   pbk

'A fascinating and distinctive new voice from an unexpected quarter'
Ian McEwan

Magic realism in Iceland is as old as the Sagas. Described by its
translator as 'about the creatures in Iceland who don't show up
in population surveys', *Epilogue of the Raindrops* recounts the
construction (and deconstruction) of a suburb, the spiritual quest of
a mouth-organ-playing minister, the havoc wreaked by long-drowned
sailors, and an ale-oiled tale told beneath a whale skeleton, while the
rain falls and falls and falls.

# Justice Undone

Thor Vilhjálmsson

Translated by Bernard Scudder

232 pp.   £8.95   pbk

'Thor Vilhjálmsson's hallucinatory imagination creates an eerily
beautiful vision of things, Icelandic in far-seeing clarity, precision,
strangeness. Unique and unforgettable.'
Ted Hughes

Based on a true story of incest and infanticide and set in the remote
hinterland of nineteenth-century Iceland, *Justice Undone* is a
compelling novel of obsession and aversion. An idealistic young
magistrate undertakes a geographical and emotional journey into
bleak, unknown territory, where dream mingles sensuously with the
world of the Sagas.

# Angels of the Universe

Einar Már Gudmundsson

Translated by Bernard Scudder

176 pp.   £7.95   pbk

'Einar Már Gudmundsson, perhaps the most distinguished writer of
his generation, is generally credited with liberating serious writing in
his country from an overawed involvement in its own past, and with
turning for inspiration to the icon-makers of the contemporary world.'
Paul Binding, *The Times Literary Supplement*

With humane and imaginative insight, Gudmundsson charts Paul's
mental disintegration. The novel's tragic undertow is illuminated
by the writer's characteristic humour and the quirkiness of his
exuberant array of characters whose inner worlds are
gloriously at odds with conventional reality.

# Night Watch

Frída Á. Sigurdardóttir

Translated by Katjana Edwardsen

176 pp.   £7.95   pbk

'She has written a book that has no equal in recent Icelandic literature.
It is remarkably well written and tells several stories
that all merge into one . . .'
Susanna Svavasdóttir, *Morgunbladid*

Who is Nina? The capable, self-possessed, independent,
advertising executive, the thoroughly modern Reykjavík woman?
Or is she the sum total of the lives of the women of her family,
whose stories of yearning, loss, challenge and chance absorb her
as she watches by the bed of her dying mother?

# Trolls' Cathedral

Ólafur Gunnarsson

Translated by David McDuff and Jill Burrows

304 pp.   £8.95   pbk

'It is a vagrant, morally unsettled form of story-telling on the same
wavelength . . . as Dostoevsky.'
Jasper Rees, *The Times*

'*Trolls' Cathedral* is a formidable work, mesmerically readable.'
Paul Binding, *The Times Literary Supplement*

The architect yearns to create a cathedral echoing the arc of a
seabird's wing, the hollows of a cliff-face cave. His struggles with debt
and self-doubt appear to be over when a seemingly random act, an
assault on his young son, destroys him and his family. Obsessions,
dreams and memories lead, inevitably, to violence.

Nominated for the 1998 International IMPAC Dublin Literary Award

ICELANDIC
LITERARY
PRIZE
1991

# The Swan

Gudbergur Bergsson

Translated by Bernard Scudder

160 pp.   £8.95   pbk

'For many days after reading *The Swan* I remained preoccupied and enchanted with it. No one should take this as a novel of Icelandic exoticism. Here is a great European writer who has, with extraordinary subtlety and in a unique way, captured the existential straits of an adolescent girl.'
*Milan Kundera*

A nine-year-old girl is sent to a country farm to serve her probation for shoplifting – a characteristic Icelandic sentence. This is no idyll: she confronts new and painful feelings and has to face the unknown within herself and in her alien surroundings. Gradually, by submitting to the inevitable restraints and suffering of remote rural life, she finds freedom.

'The hallucinatory qualities of the south Icelandic landscape, with its marshland, cloudy glacial rivers and endless sweep across to the mountains, is wonderfully realized . . . Odd, rather than horrifying or mysterious, *The Swan* succeeds as an exploration of a rare type of consciousness – that of the no longer quite innocent, yet still unknowing, child.'
CL, *The Times Literary Supplement*

'It is a haunting, bleakly complicated book, but one that settles in your mind and refuses to leave, with the image of a melancholy child ultimately liberated by her immersion in a rich landscape suffused with history and folklore.'
Dominic Bradbury, *The Times*

'*The Swan* is a novel of exceptional originality and distinction, informed by *duende*, or poetic apprehension of death . . .'
Paul Binding, *Independent on Sunday*